Curse of the Mourning Ring

A Dark Ghost Paranormal Romance

M.A. Cobb

Copyright © 2023 by M.A. Cobb

Cover Design: Lorissa Padilla

Illustrator: Bunny Smith

All rights reserved.

No portion of this book may be reproduced in any form without written permission from the publisher or author, except as permitted by U.S. copyright law.

Formatting by Unalive Promotions

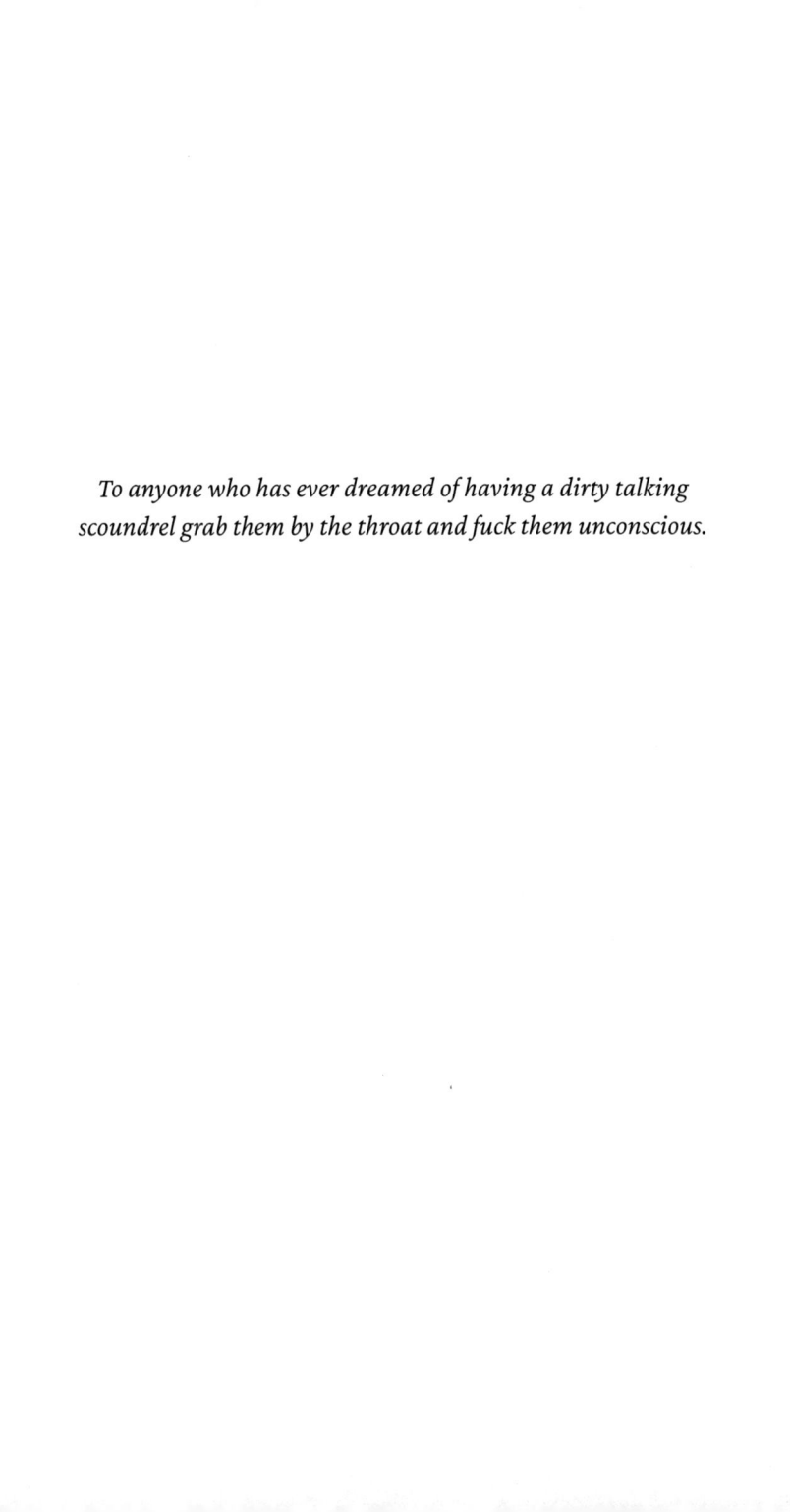

To anyone who has ever dreamed of having a dirty talking scoundrel grab them by the throat and fuck them unconscious.

Preface

This book contains very dark themes.
For a complete list visit www.macobb.com

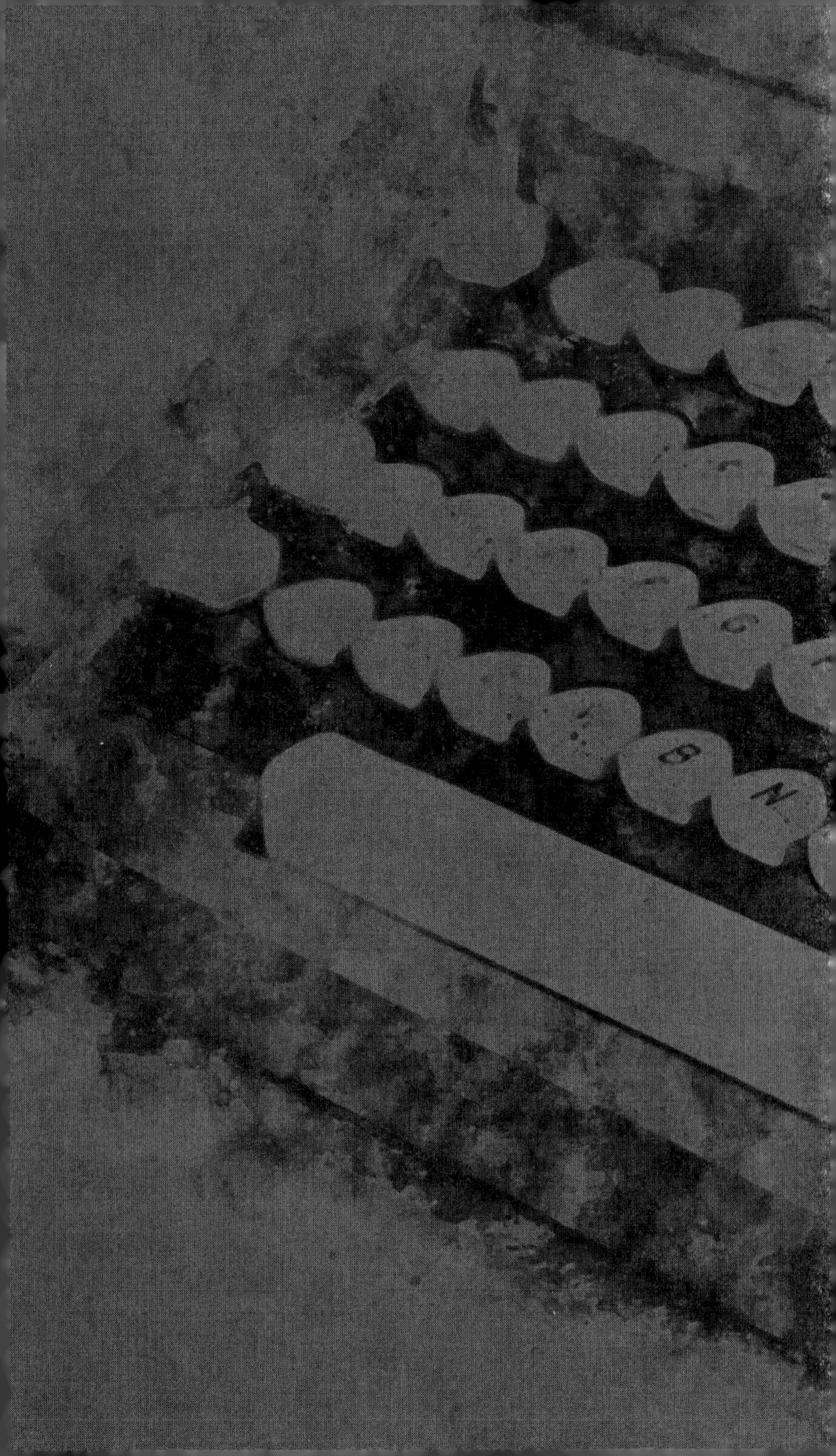

Chapter 1

Alice

"Un-fucking-believable." I read the review again. "How can someone read a book in an erotica category and say it has too much sex?" I glance at the imploring eyes of my red heeler like she'll be able to give me an answer.

Coffee. I need more coffee before I deal with any more of the bullshit. The leg of my oversized sweatpants slips below my heel, cushioning my step weirdly on the hardwood floor.

"Daisy, why didn't you remind me to get more milk when I was in town?" I can't see her through the door of the refrigerator, but I know she's tilting her head at me.

As I kick it closed the magnet holding my calendar gives, and it falls to the floor. March stares back up at me, and I scowl back. Spring in Missouri can be iffy, but I need a change of scenery.

"You know what? We need to go for a walk. Come on, Daisy, I'm cranky as fuck and need some fresh air." She's a tan blur dashing from her bed near my desk to the front door.

"Yeah, yeah. Give me a sec to put my boots on." The calf-high rubber boots push my sweatpants up in a knot against my calves. I try to push them in, but they fall out even farther until they hang loosely around the ankles of my boots.

"Well, hope I don't find any deep puddles." While I grumble through putting on my windbreaker, the hood on my sweatshirt makes an uncomfortable lump behind my head.

"Daisy, girl, I'm a mess. Let's go check the mail." Before the door is even all the way open, she pushes her nose through the crack and runs outside.

The cool spring air still has a bite to it, but she doesn't seem to mind. Within seconds, her nose to the ground, she circles the meadow ringing a large oak tree that is in my front yard before I even step off the porch.

Whew, that breeze feels good. For some reason, the house is suffocating today.

The overgrown cement path gives way to the squishy gravel of my driveway where my little Subaru is parked. Daisy doesn't seem to mind as she dances in the soft dirt sending splatters of gray and brown over her tan legs and belly.

"You're going to get a bath now." She will track that all over the house. I better remember to get ahold of her collar before we go in, or I'll have to trace her footsteps with my mop.

Again. I'm a slow learner, apparently.

Okay, the cool air felt good when I first left the house, but now it's starting to bite through me. Wrestling with the hood of my sweatshirt, I manage to bust it free and drag it over my head. Just means my whole head of hair is sticking around my face now. Better? Slightly. Except for the stray strands whipping into my eyeballs.

The freezing metal lip of the door of the mailbox sticks to my fingers when I pull it open. Grabbing the handful of envelopes and fliers, I stuff them under the flapping edge of my jacket and close it quickly.

Damn, I think I left a layer of skin behind!

Speed walking back to the house, I nearly trip over Daisy as she darts by, chasing a stream of oak leaves caught in the wind.

I thought I raked them all up last fall, but that giant tree seems to just keep dropping turds all over my yard.

They never end. It's the price I pay for building my house on an old homestead. The original foundation isn't far from here, although it's nothing but a few haphazard stones and part of the chimney now. But, the trees are what I fell in love with. Tall oak and walnut trees creak and groan in the growing gusts.

My weather app said there might be a little storm coming through tonight, but I didn't realize it would start so early.

"Daisy! Come on, girl!" Stomping my feet up the steps to try and knock off some of the mud, I open the door in time for her to sneak past me and run for her bed.

Leaving muddy doggy footprints all the way across my floor.

Where is one of those hidden cameras that I'm supposed to stare blandly into like on the sitcoms? Because that's what I feel like doing right now.

"Ugh. Again. You're too damned fast, girl. Fine, I'll get the washcloth." Kicking off my boots, my bare feet land on the back of my muddy sweatpants. They're caked halfway up my calves with the sticky clay.

"Seriously!" Jerking my pants down at the door, I use them as a welcome rug to wipe my feet off.

Whatever. In nothing but my white granny panties and my hoodie, I throw the mail down on the counter and dig out a small towel from the drawer next to the sink.

I don't even care if the water is cold. She had no issue with stomping in the icy mud, so chilly washcloth it is.

Daisy lolls on her back, her tongue hanging against her cheek as she sticks all four of her paws up from her bed.

"Yea, you know the drill. Next time I'll catch you at the door." She sneezes in response. "I really mean it this time!"

Well, nasty washcloth and dirty pants, off to the laundry you go.

When I flip on the light in the bathroom, a terrifying monster greets me. Wild black hair, red and green eyes, bright red cheeks.

Oh. It's just my reflection in the mirror. I look like one of those crazy witches in the bad children's movies. Holy crap, I never thought my hair could get that huge and frizzy without some serious hair spray. It would have to be an ozone hole-level event to get my hair that big if I tried.

Smoothing some of my wild mane, I find it turns out to be a waste of time. Well, at least my eyes look cool. The wind made them all red, but the green really pops now.

Red and green. Merry fucking Christmas. Well, with this hair? Maybe the nightmare version.

With dirty sweats in the washing machine, I think maybe I should take a shower.

And the lights flicker.

No, I'm not showering if the power might go out. The Wicked Witch of the West gets to live for a few more hours.

Fine, I can get some more writing done. At least my laptop has a long battery life.

The branches of one of the smaller walnut trees tap against the big windows in my bedroom as I get dressed.

Pouring a cup of black coffee, I put it in the microwave for thirty seconds to heat it up. Without milk.

"Daisy, remind me to get milk next time!" Why is the handle four hundred degrees, but the coffee is barely lukewarm?

"I should just go back to bed," I can't help grumbling.

THREE CHAPTERS COMPLETED, AND MY COFFEE HAS SOMEHOW transformed into mimosas as the afternoon progresses. I think it has a lot more to do with the wind kicking up, setting my nerves on edge.

Getting sidetracked watching cat videos, I finally give up trying to be productive. It's dark out and the lights keep flickering, giving me a headache. One last swallow of the sweet drink to empty the glass.

The windows are rattling, and so is the door. I can hear spattering rain, or maybe it's hard snow hitting them with every gust.

Might just have to pour one more small drink to take to bed with me. As I empty the bottle of wine into my coffee cup, I debate if I should read more of the romance novel I started the other day or watch that silly rom-com one of my friends recommended in the group chat.

A particularly large gust rattles the pictures on the walls.

Movie it is. Loud too, to dull the roar I can hear over the valley.

Wine, hokey lines, and bad acting soon lull me enough that I'm falling asleep trying to watch.

Turning off my phone, I set it on the nightstand just as a low rumble ripples through the house. The bed quakes and there's a groaning sound that feels like it's echoing off of the walls. A giant tearing crash and my mattress shakes again.

Sitting bolt upright, my heart is pounding so hard my chest hurts.

What the hell was that?

Fumbling for my phone, I switch on the flashlight and slide out of the warm sheet. I don't even notice the cold floor as I creep around the house.

I swear it sounded like the roof was being torn off, but I can't see any signs of damage. Windows rattling, yes, but still in their frames.

It doesn't take long to check each room.

Satisfied, I crawl back into bed. It takes a little while for my breathing to normalize and my heartbeat to not be pounding in my ears.

There isn't much I can do about it tonight if it happened outside. I'm dreading what tomorrow will show. Thinking of all of the terrible possibilities, I fall into a fitful sleep.

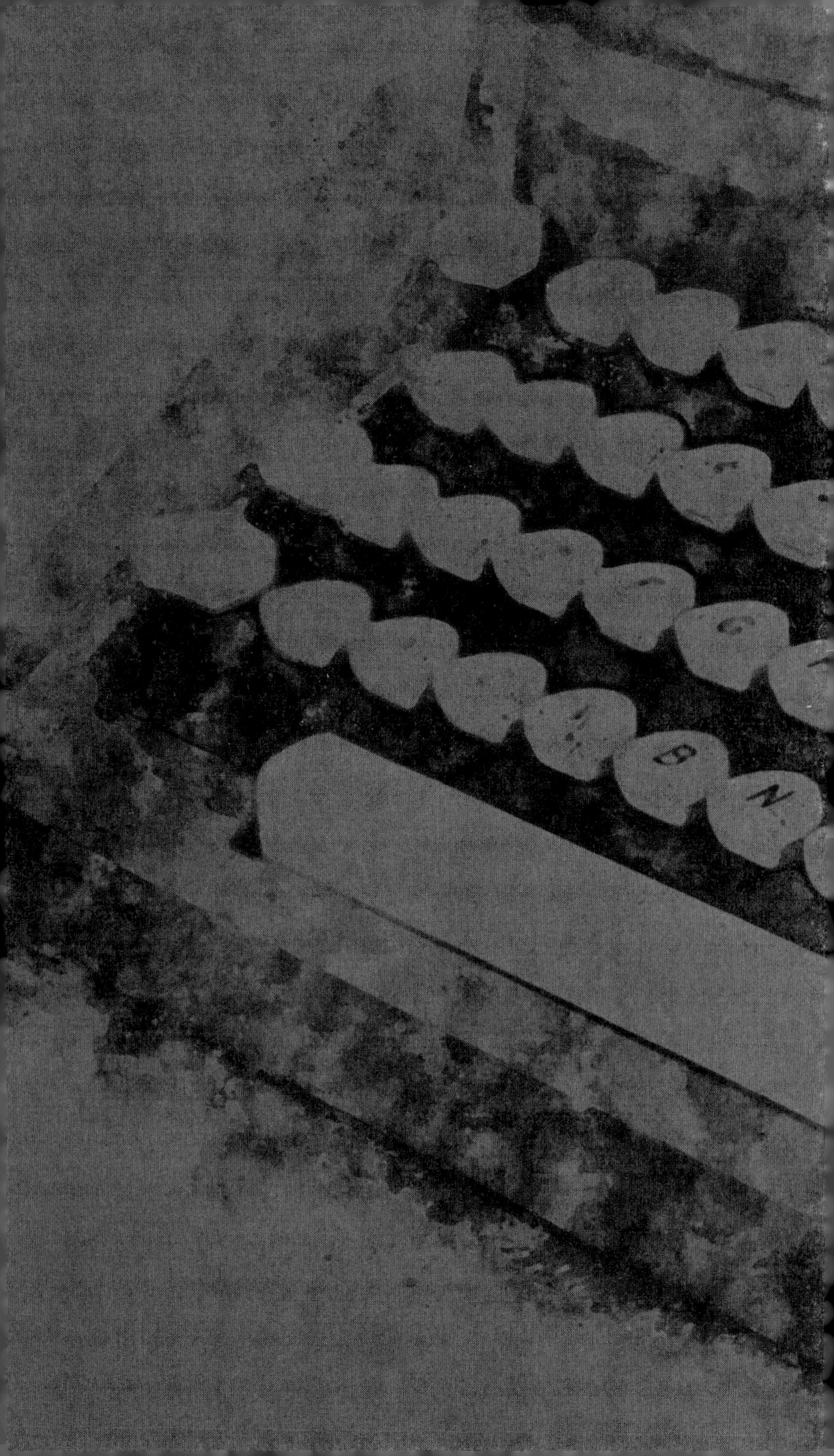

Chapter 2

Alice

Sun streaming in through my windows rips through the lids of my eyes, making me blink painfully awake.

Daisy's nails clicking on the wood floor back and forth next to my bed as she whines finally goads me to throw back my heavy comforter. I've been keeping her doggy door closed at night to keep her from tracking in mud. But, now I'm wondering if the occasional mopping might just be worth it.

"I know, I know, it was yucky outside. I bet you have to piss like a racehorse." One leg of my sweatpants is around my knee, the other around my calf, and for some reason, it makes me feel like I'm walking crooked.

Why do they say that? Piss like a racehorse. Do they hold it until after a race?

I groggily pull the door open, a warm morning full of bird song greets me, and I lose all thoughts of animals and bladders.

The giant oak tree in my front yard is on its side. Roots

taller than my house have created a wall of dirt and woody tendrils in the middle of my walkway.

Well, shit.

Daisy wastes no time diving into the cavernous hole it created to investigate.

Sudden panic hits me. I can't see my car from here, just dirt.

Stuffing my bare feet into my boots, it only takes me seconds to run across the yard to look. I never knew the trunk was that big around. It makes it impossible to see past it. Trotting farther, I finally round the end of the huge top of the tree. This thing must be forty feet long!

"Oh, for fuck's sake." One of the heavy branches has absolutely crushed the passenger side of my car.

Even the tires are flat.

Yelling at it in frustration and anger doesn't seem to help. But, I keep trying until I'm hoarse.

"Goddamn tree! You grew for what, two hundred years? Why did you pick *NOW* to fall over?" Pissy at its lack of answering me, I stomp back up the porch.

Great. Now I need to find my insurance stuff for the car. I only had two more payments and it would be paid off.

Hmm. Probably a good thing. It is still covered under full coverage. My cheap ass was planning on dropping it down to liability as soon as payments were over.

"Daisy! Come on!" She prances up the steps and through the door, muddy footprints marking her path.

I should just give up. Buy her some sort of rug that goes from the door to her bed. Her little gloopy tracks are interspersed with droplets of drool, and I don't know why until I see her circling on her bed with her mouth propped open with some dirty object wedged between her jaws.

"What did you find?" She plops down and lets it roll out

between her paws, but it keeps going and bounces with a hollow sound onto the floor.

Her little pointy muzzle reaches out and snaps it back before I have a chance to pick it up.

"Fine, you win." I have to find my insurance paperwork and start my claim. That means sorting through my stuffed desk drawers that have needed organizing for the entire three years I've lived here.

The third time she tosses her new loud toy across the floor and her nails click it back to her bed, I'm done.

"Okay, bring it here," I call in my best singsong voice.

Daisy jumps up and runs over, pushing the object at me. Her ears and eyes look like they do when we play fetch.

"Good girl. Now, go lie down." I swear she looks mad at me.

With a huff, my rambunctious heeler throws herself down on her bed and settles her head on her paws. Staring at me.

"Man. If looks could kill."

I'm almost setting it on the windowsill next to my desk when I notice how light it is and that it's almost perfectly square.

"Weird. What did you find?" Her slobber makes a great cleaning agent, revealing a seam between two dark wooden halves with a tiny brass hinge.

That's different. Trying to pry it open, it takes the right combination of cuss words before it finally clamshells open for me.

A worn and yellowed piece of paper is folded inside. When I pull it out, it reveals a silver banded ring nested beneath it.

What the hell?

"How cool is this? Daisy, you're a champ. I'm sorry I took your toy. Okay, not really."

Unfolding the paper carefully, I smooth it out on my desk.

There's writing on it in pencil, and it's very faint.

Henry, your love was fierce, but my heart lies with another. Rest in Peace, Nora

Damn. Poor Henry.

"That's fucked. She sent you a Dear John letter after you're dead." I'm shaking my head so hard my hair gets in my eyes.

Cold, Nora. Brutal.

"What a bitch," I murmur, pulling the ring out of the box. It's wide on the top, narrow on the bottom. Squinting, I can see the faint engraving of what looks like a skull on the flat wide surface.

Old time-y goth. I like it.

Stringing it on a silver chain I always wear, its heavy weight settles it between my boobs. "Found ya a happy place there, Henry." It's a nice memento for the shit storm in my front yard, too.

It takes everything in me not to scream and cry on the phone with the insurance agent. He finally agreed to have a rental car brought out in the morning and that, with the pictures I provided, he would send out a tow truck to fetch my poor squished Subaru.

Finding a tree removal service was harder than I thought it would be. For all the names listed online, only two answered their phone. One outright refused. He said they were way too busy after the storm.

The other said I could try calling back in a couple of weeks.

Great.

Why is talking on the phone with people so exhausting? It's taken all damn day just to accomplish these two basic tasks.

"Daisy, I give up. You want pizza?" Her ears perk up. She loves pepperoni. I always get extra so she can have a few pieces.

Too many though and she farts so bad it drives me out of the house.

She jumps up and spins a little circle in front of me before diving through her doggie door to the backyard

"I too have to pee when I get excited. And I was really hoping you'd be willing to call this time!" I mutter to the missing dog.

In an attempt to salvage my shitty day, I do manage to get three more chapters written in my smutty new romantic comedy.

There's nothing like writing a two chapter sex scene to brighten my mood. And, make me horny as shit. I'm just reaching the climax of the scene when the knock on the door jars me back to reality.

"I'll show you too much sex," I grumble as I walk to the door.

"Hi, Alice. Gosh, that storm looks like it did some damage to your car!" He's a sweet kid, even if he is Captain Obvious.

"Hi, Bobby. Yes, that's why it's a delivery night. Thank you." I slip him an extra five bucks for having to navigate around my fallen oak tree.

I don't really mean to slam the door in his face, but I know he'd stand there and want to talk if I don't walk away. Nice kid, but I really don't want to chat with anyone today.

Daisy tap dances next to her bed, the clicking of her nails a constant reminder that I promised her pepperoni.

"Girl! Settle! When have I never given you any?" She sits primly, waiting for me to open the box. It's almost like we've had this conversation before. Well, first time today at least.

Sliding two greasy pieces onto a plate, I only manage to burn my fingers once. Three pieces of pepperoni sit on the edge cooling for Daisy. The cheese stringers are mine. I swear they're the best part. Grabbing them where they cling to the edge of my plate, I hoist them over my head and, very unladylike, dangle feed myself until my cheeks are swollen like a chipmunk's with cheesy goodness.

Hot drops of oil dribble down my chin and drop into my cleavage, leaving a glistening burning trail on my tee shirt.

"Oh, Henry, have some pizza. Bet it's been a while, huh?" When the little pepperoni pieces are cool enough, I pinch one between my fingers and entice Daisy closer.

Her eyes look like two giant, shiny, black olives about to pop out of her head as I move the morsel closer to her nose until it's just touching.

"Okay." Her whiskers just tickle my thumb as she nimbly steals the bite and immediately looks up at me for another. "Did you even taste that? Well, here are the other two." Her food dish still has food in it. She's just a pepperoni pup. Fiend. That's more like it.

The next two follow the first just as fast, and she sits with pitiful eyes watching me stuff my face with my second slice.

"Nope, no gassing me out tonight. Go lie your pre-stinky butt back on your bed."

After I shoo her away, I manage to zero back in on the scene I was working on earlier. I don't feel nearly as in the moment now as I was before. Not with a belly full of pizza and stains on my shirt.

Scrolling back, I find a couple of places that need a word changed here, a spelling fixed there. But, nothing new is flowing.

It's dark, and it was a long day of dealing with people. I'm done.

A glass of wine, the rest of the pizza in the fridge, and I'm heading to bed. Screw the shower. That pain in the ass insurance guy can just see me in all my grimy glory tomorrow.

Well, I don't want to sleep in a greasy shirt though. It makes a fabulous towel to wipe my boobs and an extra swipe to my armpits before tossing in the corner with my ever-growing piles. My pits do say I better shower.

"Laundry tomorrow, shower tonight," I groan. Stripping off my sweats, I kick them into the pile, too.

While the water heats up, I catch the reflection in the mirror of the ring nestled against my chest. At almost thirty years old, my breasts are still kind of perky.

"Don't you think so, Henry?" I mash them together, the ring firmly wedged between. "You loved fiercely. What does that mean?"

I've never been loved anywhere close to that. There was a worthless marriage when I was barely out of high school to a guy who couldn't hold a job. And then a line of walking dildos who should all be on a bus to Loserville.

One day I'll learn to start with liking their brains before their dicks.

But, after writing smutty scenes all day, I doubt I'd choose wisely if I had the option right now.

Lathering myself up, it's so hard not to let my mind wander to the shower scene I wrote yesterday between Nathaniel and Anna. My hands run over my body as if I'm being caressed by another.

Maybe not by the pretty boy billionaire I was writing about. Perhaps a tall, dark, brooding man with a handlebar mustache and wild eyes. Someone like Kurt Russell in Tombstone.

That could be Henry.

He'd have big coarse hands that run up and down my body. Firm fingers diving between my legs and finding me wet and oh, so ready.

The hot water pours over me, undulating rivulets that tickle and dance across my skin while I'm rubbing myself faster, building the tension in my belly. Imaginary whiskers would chafe my thighs as his tongue darts over me. His breath would smell of bourbon and burn when he kisses me.

A cold shock from the tile against my face jerks me back to reality, but it's just as my knees wobble and the bubble of pressure bursts into little waves through me.

Propping my forehead against my hand, my nose is brushing the chill of the wall while I regain some semblance of control over my breathing.

The ring sits heavy on my chest. Heat radiates from it now that it isn't under the scalding spray. My thumb slides through it easily and I bring it up to look closely.

"Henry, I wish you'd come here and love me fiercely." It's shiny with soap still dripping from the smooth surface. The skull stands out a little better now that some of the years of grime have been washed away.

"I'd kill to have a fierce orgasm right about now," I mutter. Dropping the ring, it bounces back against my chest on its chain. A little shiver works down my spine and I shift so the tepid water can warm me one last time before I turn off the tap.

Fuck. Really? Not a single clean towel.

Flapping my arms like a deranged seagull, I try to air dry as much as I can before giving up and flopping naked onto my bed.

Let my bedspread dry me off. It's the only time it will see any wet spots in the foreseeable future.

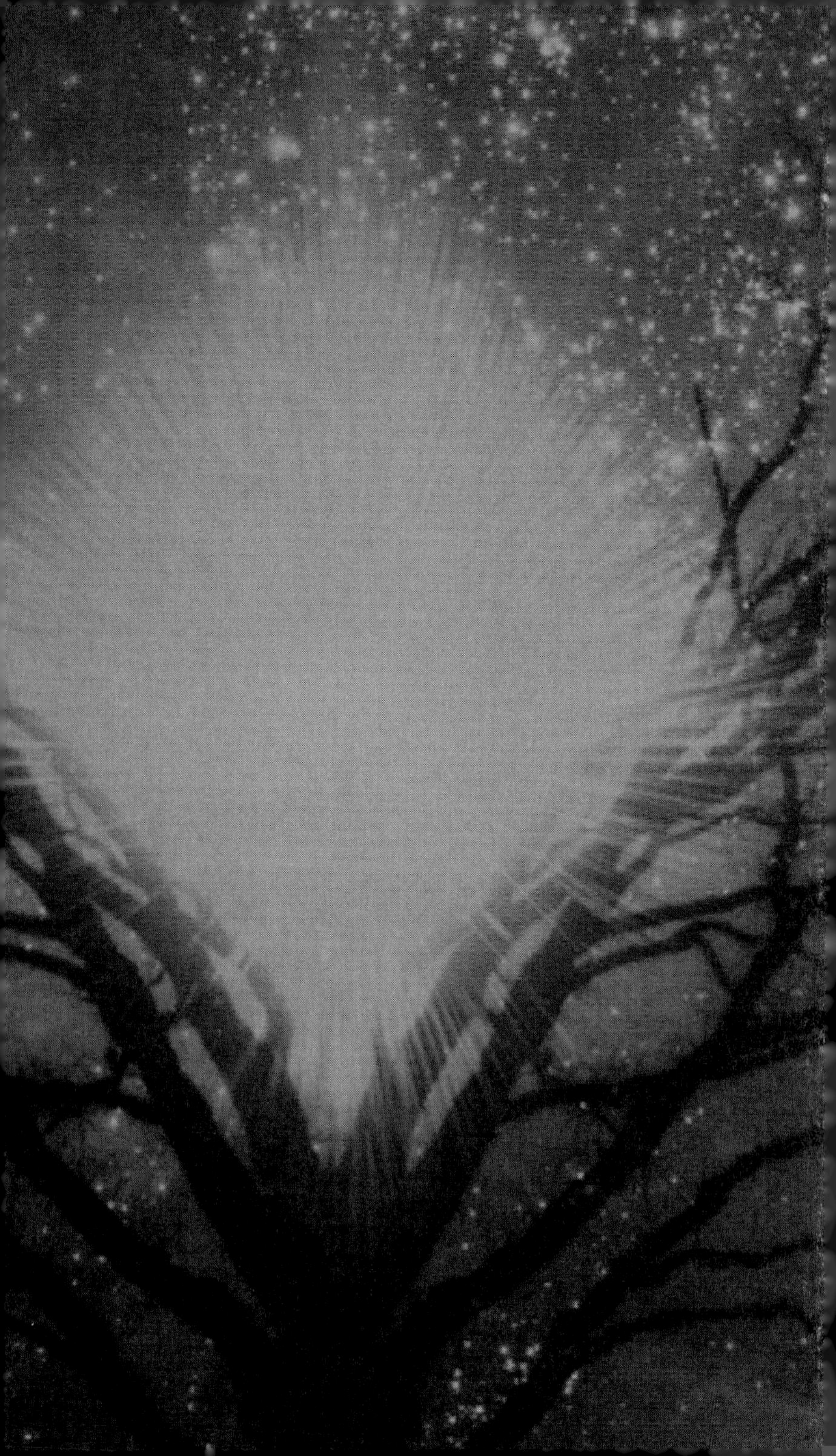

Chapter 3

Henry

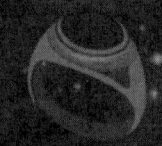

Dark.
Empty.
Floating.
Not water.
No up. No down.
Nothing to focus on.
Warmth. I'm drawn to heat.
I can feel it with my fingers. It crawls up my arm.
A tingling spreads in waves across my chest. Sensations eat through me, a thousand bees buzzing beneath my skin.
Painless fading into the darkness.
Constant.
The heat.
I want the heat.
Yearning for it, I summon my will and push again.
The heat grows and spreads into my limbs.
Blindly, I wrap my hands around it and pull it to me. The blackness of the void shifts, revealing my functioning sight. Gray gives way to outlines. Vague shapes sharpen in the opaque mist.

A room forms around me. Hard edges and flat lines transition and deepen into walls, a door, windows.

Where am I?

I still feel as if I'm floating. My feet drift through the shapes, and my hands do not arrest their movements when I reach for the wall. A trick of imagery it seems.

How?

Small pinpoints of illumination in various colors give me more clarity. Drifting around the room, I can see numbers on a small box. A glow affixed to the wall. Yet none have the flicker of a candle. Or the heat of a lantern.

Lights without flame.

Wizardry abounds.

A sound wafts through the thinning haze. Breathing.

But, not my own.

In fact, no blood rushes through my ears. No beat falls from my chest. I still cannot see my own limbs clearly. They are just faint outlines, transparent and foggy.

Like my mind.

Befuddled at my lack of tactile ability, I want to discover the source of the warmth that seems to be the only tangible object.

Moving into the shape of the bed, the shadows of my legs extend through it as if it doesn't exist.

But, I am stopped by the heat. A warmth that I can trace with my fingers. Soft supple lines of a hip are solid beneath my touch.

Firm.

Alive.

Through the imaginary layer of a blanket, I can follow that curve, the small of a back, soft widening into shoulders. Tendrils of hair over the nape of a neck. A delicate turn of a feminine jaw that moans lightly through a deep breath.

Who is she?

Why can I touch only her?

Pulling a stray dark strand from her cheek, I lean closer to inspect this unknown woman. She smells of soap, clean, but like chamomile and honey. Her exhalation radiates down my arm, and I almost feel a shiver as it brushes against my skin.

My hand has no substance. I can watch her eyelids flutter in sleep through my palm.

I can feel the texture of my clothing, yet push through it to my skin at a thought. Is it temporary? It manifests its coarse fabric again when I think about touching my sleeve.

What am I that I can touch only myself and her. Do I exist for her?

Who am I?

That gives me pause. Struggling to dig within, I search my own thoughts. Scouring for memories, elusive, small tidbits of images flicker like ticker tape snowflakes.

Faces. Emotions. Places.

So many jumble into piles; it's difficult to identify what is important.

Her. She is. I can feel it, tugging at me.

Following her bare shoulder, my fingers raise gooseflesh on her arm as I dance the tips over her wrist. When I flatten my palm over the back of her hand, she twitches.

Her low groan echoes through me as she turns over, her hand pulling from my grasp. Throwing the covers, she lies bare before me. Her legs asunder, breasts exposed to me in the dim light.

A small snore belies her slumber as she settles against the blankets.

The chain around her neck droops beneath her, and I'm surprised when I can gently pick it up from her warm skin.

My ring hangs as a small weight dangling from the silver length. I'd recognize it anywhere.

The memory plucks from the piles.

Smells of gunpowder and death. How heavy the revolver was in my hand. Limp fingers that I pry the ring from.

It's my father's face, frozen in agony. Blooming red spreading across his chest.

Anger floods through me. I have never removed that ring. How did this woman get it? When my fingers wrap around it, pain sizzles its way up my arm. As the searing metal slips from my grasp, forgotten memories fling themselves forward.

Nora. The betrayal I felt seeing her naked flesh writhing with that of my best friend. My brother-in-arms.

Bastard. My knuckles ache at the memory of bashing his teeth in when I discovered them.

How her mouth twisted my name as she told me to leave.

Henry. I remember it now.

I am Henry Sullivan. And I remember dying in agony.

But, the question still remains how my moniker ended up on a gilded chain around her neck.

It is a beautiful throat. Pale against the blanket, arched as if in ecstasy beneath me.

Unable to resist the lure of the tangible, my hand works my way over her arm yet again to the sensuous tender skin inside of her elbow and down the side of her chest.

I'm still unsure how I came to be in this room, but I am enjoying the view.

A pressure comes from within, a knot tightening. Her body being spread open before me awakens a need, a longing that is difficult to fight.

How I can feel a hardening in my cock that barely seems to exist is a strange concept. But, when my hand finds its way to it, I can feel it filling my hand. The tingle of arousal works its way through me as my fingers wrap around my near-invisible girth.

Just the lightest brush against her nipple, and it beads into a little peak for me.

Divinity.

Another rush of tingles surge through me as I watch her body react to my touch.

I'm beginning to understand. I have died and found an afterlife. My only source of entertainment is to be a naked beautiful woman whose arousal I can smell when I caress her.

If I can smell her, and touch her, perhaps I can taste her as well.

Her legs are already spread across the bed, and her belly quivers as my hand seeks hotter recesses. The damp heat of her nearly burns my finger when I press against her.

A soft moan breaks from her lips and makes my cock jump in my hand.

She's already slick when I push into the slit of her trimmed pussy, another moan cresting from her arched throat.

Temptress.

Bringing the scent of her body to my tongue, the sweet taste of honey fills my mouth and permeates my nose.

Hunger awakens in me. The urge to bury myself deep within her spurs me to touch her again. With gentle pressure, I widen her knees.

I have been summoned from the nether to her; it must be my duty to satisfy her needs. This is a wondrous hell, allowing me to succumb to my desires. My life was one of inflicting pain. There's no way I deserve peace for the things I've done.

But, this? It has to be heaven.

My lips follow my fingers, stroking the soft skin of her thigh down to the hot little center so languidly exposed before me. Whiskers tickle my chin as I whisper over her, closer to the burning sweet nectar that runs in syrupy droplets to the sheets below.

She's so fucking wet that it overwhelms my senses as my tongue touches her for the first time.

Her breath catches. Another moan escapes her as she rocks her hips.

That's it, you vixen. Raise your pussy in praise to me.

Flattening my tongue against her, I take pause. By some benevolent stroke of luck do I find myself buried between the hot thighs of a dark haired woman. It must not be a dream. She feels so incredibly real. The silken feel of her clit, the sweet juices saturating my mouth, and the rapid pants of her sleeping lust all make it nearly impossible to restrain myself.

Moving slowly, a long luxurious lick of this dripping cunt ends with a nip of my teeth against her engorged bud.

"Henry!" she gasps. Her eyes flutter open and her hand flails, glancing off the side of my head. I can feel her nails tangle briefly in my hair before I jerk away.

Her scream deafens my ears as I back away while she reaches over and touches an odd lantern that blazes bright light. I try to block it with my arm, but it shines through me.

"Who's there?" she calls. Her green eyes are wide and wild, searching the room as she struggles to cover her nakedness beneath a sheet.

Even though I stand before her, with chagrin at my intrusion, her gaze does not land on me, but rather goes through me at a glance.

"Daisy?" she calls out. A knee high red dog trots into the room, wagging its tail and sits before me, looking up.

It can see me. And does not appear to be riled by my presence.

"Oh, my god, I must have had too much wine. Girl, I had the craziest dream." The dog, who must be Daisy, stands and faces the woman, her tail whipping tight circles behind her.

She rewards the vigilant pup with an idle pat on its brow before she slumps back against her pillows.

"Fuck. That felt so real." Her arm folds over her face, covering her eyes.

My delicious lady has a dirty mouth. Honey and spice.

Doubt teases the edges of my thoughts.

She does not seem to know I'm here, nor is her reaction exactly receptive to my lavishing.

What is my purpose here? It's obvious that she is not any sort of celestial reward.

Even if she does taste like an angel.

As her breathing levels to the relaxation of sleep, the dog loses interest and returns through the door it had entered.

If I cannot festoon my oral attention on her, perhaps I can learn more about where I am.

What are these strange items in this room? A bar? Odd lights glimmer from small boxes spread throughout, reds, blues, whites.

Definition seems to fade the farther I drift from her. Edges soften and the void of darkness flirts with the corners of my eyes.

Drifting through objects may take some getting used to, but I find myself unhindered by any obstacle. My hand traces effortlessly through a dark chair with wheels. A desk strewn with papers looks as any workspace would, no matter its plane of existence. Despite the odd box with a glowing bouncing ball sitting near the back of it.

Clarity forms on a small yellowed piece of paper lying atop the others.

Nora.

I'd recognize her handwriting anywhere. That bitch. Even in death she defies me with her traitorous heart.

More memories push from the pile and blizzard within my head.

Thunderous hoofbeats beneath me as I spur on my roan horse. A toothy grin from my best friend riding beside me. Each of us holding bags of money in a death grip as our horses gallop over the rough terrain with the giddy energy of success popping through my body.

The smell of the piles of cash mixing with the earthy air of our barn hideout.

Sounds of ecstasy in tandem, moaning, and the creaking of a bed as I push the door open.

My heart shattering. The agony ripping through me at the betrayal.

The burn of the whiskey as I tried to drown the pain. Twisting my signet on my finger. A hateful realization that my entire life I have been used.

An oath I made on that ring.

Damn them all. I hope they're trapped in a purgatory worse than this.

Lightening around me signals the morning sun. How long have I been locked in my thoughts?

Groaning and a thump beckon me to her. A tether pulls at me, thickening as I draw nearer. My vision crisps the closer I drift.

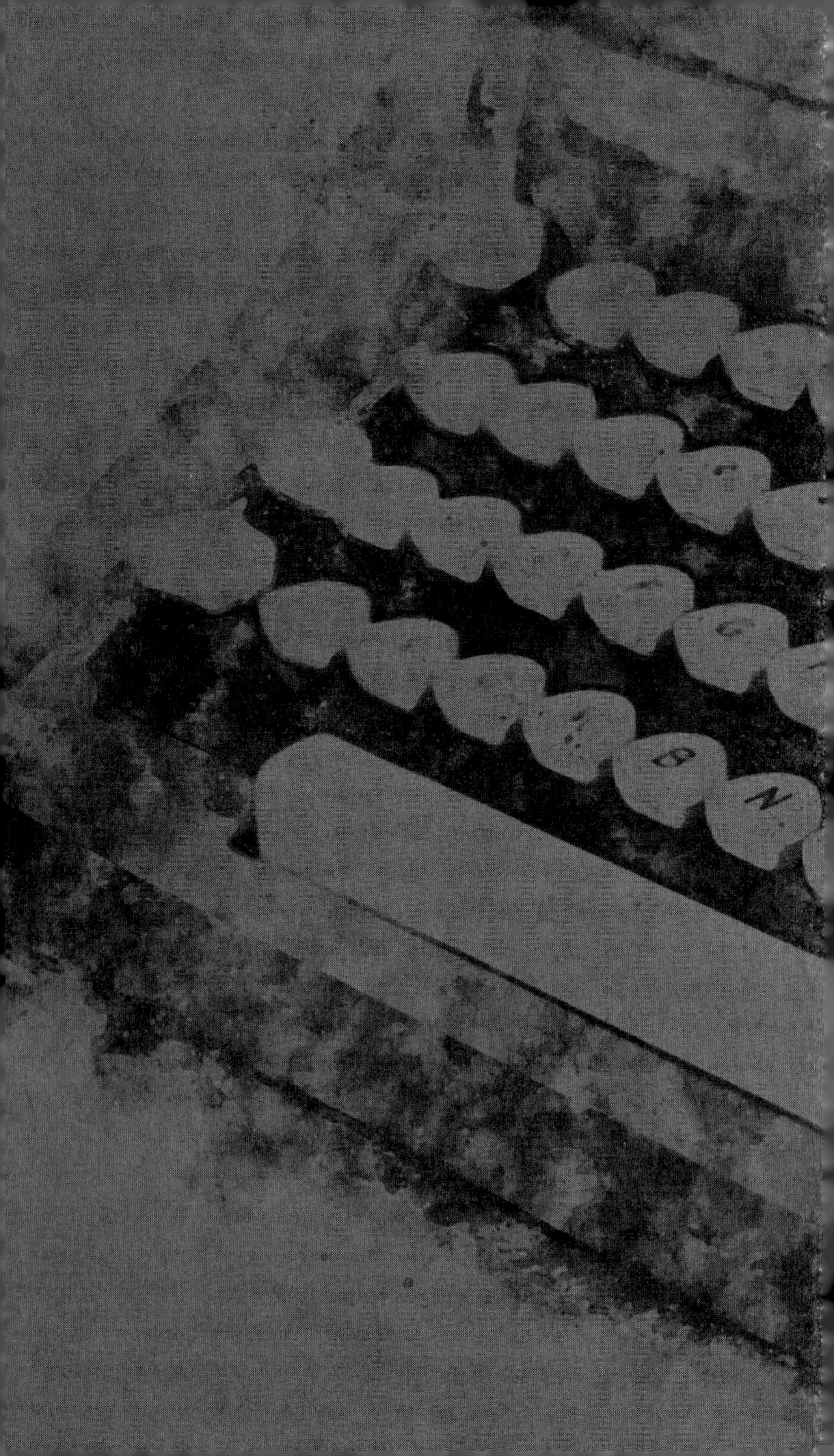

Chapter 4

Alice

My stomach is still unruly at how real that dream felt. It was like he was really there.

I swear I touched hair *after* I was awake.

But, there wasn't anyone there.

"How much fucking wine did I drink last night?" The bottle is still on the nightstand. When did I open this? Does it go bad?

Trying to shake off the feeling that I wasn't alone last night, I resign myself to slipping into a pair of jeans. I do have to see actual people today. As much as I love my stained sweats, I think I better deal with the insurance guy in presentable clothes.

He's still getting a hoodie though. I can only dress up so much.

Now, where the fuck is my scrunchie? Ah, in my mess of dirty clothes in the bathroom. Someone really should do laundry.

I swear, if I ever write a bestseller, I'm hiring a maid. Or a cook. Maybe both.

A sexy chef with an Italian accent who knows how to

make gelato from scratch. He'd warrant more than my current messy bun and no makeup.

I'd probably have to wear heels or some shit.

"Daisy, you forgot to remind me to get milk yesterday." She tilts her head and stares at me while I wait for the coffee pot to finish. Then she looks to my left and wags her tail like someone was holding a treat out to her.

Weird ass dog. It's a good thing she's cute.

Vanilla nut coffee soothes all my senses as I carry the hot cup to my desk. I wonder if my hot Italian chef could make a perfect cup of cappuccino.

I can't even remember the last time I had one. That would mean I'd have to go into public. And, I do that as little as possible.

When I hear the engine in the driveway and a door slam, my belly does a little flip flop of anxiety until the knock at the door kicks me into action.

"Hi, Mrs. Brooks?"

I didn't expect him to be kinda cute, in a tall, thin and nerdy way.

"Um, no missus. Just Alice Brooks." I try to put on my best smile, and find myself regretting not putting on makeup.

His soft smile twinkles his deep blue eyes and makes my knees a little weak. "I'm Mark. We spoke yesterday. Well, I can see that the cause of damage is pretty clear. I apologize for my skepticism on the phone." When he moves, the crisp nylon of his jacket crinkles in the chill. "Acts of God are covered, so all we need to do now is arrange for the tow truck to take it to the dealership where they can assess the total damage."

His fist makes a bulge in his jeans as he digs out a pair

of keys. They're still warm when he drops them lightly into my hand.

I get that horny little tingle thinking about them being in his tight pants.

"These are for your loaner car until the Subaru gets evaluated." He gestures behind him, and I can just see the hood and top of a silver sedan over the tree trunk.

"Thank you. Do you need a ride back to your office?" Maybe I want to linger around him. He smells good, like aftershave and a new car.

Besides, I need milk for my coffee. I swear I'll cry if I have to go another day without it.

He looks like he should be on a poster in a dentist's office when he smiles. "I appreciate the offer, but my coworker should be—"

Gravel crunches under tires as another car pulls into my driveway. A green coupe. I think this is the most cars I've had in my driveway at once since the moving company left.

"Maybe next time. It was nice to meet you, Alice." He holds his hand out facing up.

"Um. Thank you again." My fingers slide over his warm palm and he wraps his other hand over mine.

"I'll let you know when the body shop is finished. Have a nice rest of your day."

I can't stop watching his ass move until he disappears behind the tree. His hands were soft, but those cheeks look rock hard.

Whew! Walk away, girl, walk away.

With the door between me and Mr. Tight-butt, I realize I need to go find my debit card and get some groceries.

"Daisy, girl, you're lucky you're fixed. I feel like I'm in heat! Ugh! Even the insurance guy is getting me going."

Maybe I should just start writing sweet romance novels. No more steamy scenes.

Who am I kidding? I love the sultry shit. Reading it, too.

It'd be nice to have someone to participate with. Lady Palm and her five friends gets boring after a while.

Key, check.

Money, check.

Sweating my tatas off, mark that, too. The hoodie has to go. That's the best and worst part about March: some days are winter, others are summer, and my horny raging hormones don't help.

Yanking the heavy shirt over my head, it pulls up my tee at the same time. Cussing, I try to untangle myself without stripping down to my bra. I can't see a damned thing when a warm hand touches me in the small of my back.

"What the fuck!" Ripping the whole ensemble off in a heap, my racing heart pounds in my ears.

An empty room.

Holy hell, that was weird. I felt fingers. A palm. The heat is still tingling on my skin.

Goosebumps erupt over my arms and neck as I stand here in my sports bra and uni-boob.

I must be losing it. Maybe I really do need to meet someone just so I don't go over the edge.

The heavy weight of the ring hangs below me when I bend over to get my tee shirt.

"Oh. Henry, are you fucking with me? If you are, knock it off. It's creepy."

Talking to ghosts now. It's bad enough I talk to my dog like she can understand me, but now imaginary people?

Lock me up and throw away the key.

The loaner car is basic, and gets me to the grocery store

and back. Thanks to the cute insurance guy, I can finally have milk in my coffee again.

And, I bought a different kind of wine. I think the other bottle was bad or something. It had to be why I was having such strange dreams last night.

Microwaved egg rolls and a mimosa balance on the edge of my cluttered desk. My computer is calling me to finish the next chapter.

Well, first the sweatpants go back on with the hoodie. As soon as the sun goes down, the chill works its way through the house.

If I wasn't so cheap, I'd turn the heater up a little.

Now, where was I in Nathaniel and Anna's story?

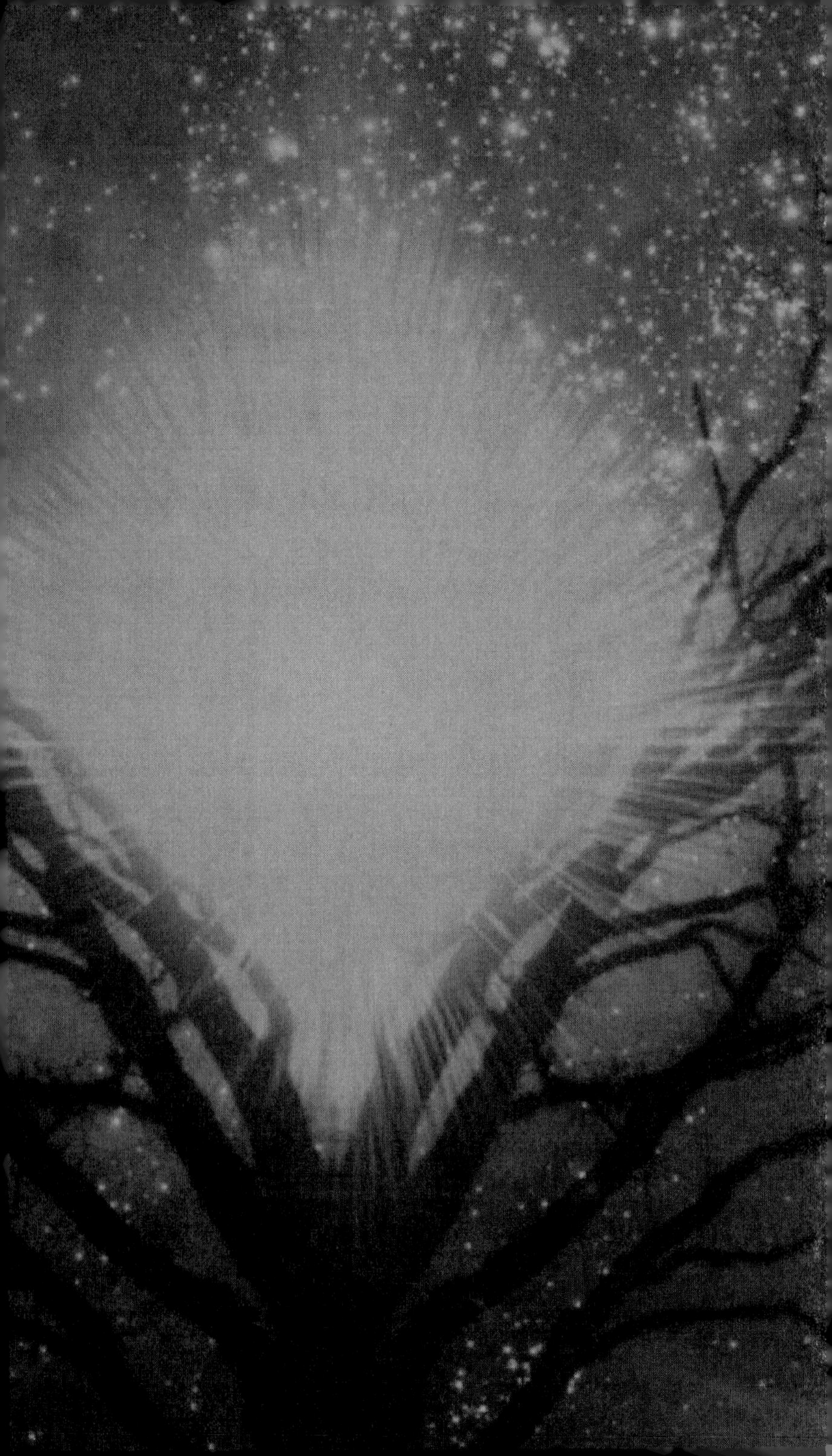

Chapter 5

Henry

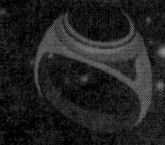

I do not understand how I can be here, unseen, with a raging cock inches away from her all day. The scandalous tight pants she wears should be illegal.

Even the bar whores wouldn't wear trousers like men. Their tantalizing legs should remain hidden until they are wrapped around a waist.

My biggest form of befuddlement came when I was whisked through strange streets of black by this tether that binds us. The contraption she rode in was terrifying in its power, yet she handled it as if she was born doing it.

Peering within it while she gathered her supplies, I saw that it houses a blinding complexity of odd shapes and pieces. All intertwined within the silver body that sits upon wheels of a black tarry substance.

She pulls me with her. Images fade around me as her proximity wanes. I let myself gravitate through the wall to reside near her side.

Ravishing is a word I don't often use, but her tousled hair and bare face reveal her vibrant inner beauty. So many women wear the garish rouge to liven their glow. But her full pink lips, the soft rose of her cheeks when she stands in the warmth of the sun, it delights me more than any painted lady.

What vexes me is that look on her face when that man touched her hand. How she twirled the dark lock of her hair between her fingers while closing her emerald eyes as she leaned against the door after his departure.

Her eyes bewitch me. What I would give to have them fixate upon me.

All day I have been weighing if I want to touch her again. It isn't until she pulls her overshirt off and that bare skin of her midriff assails me that I lose control.

She is fire. My fingers tingle from where I brushed against her hot back.

And, when she said my name…I nearly threw her on the bed to claim her.

Who knew a single word could send ribbons of desire through me?

Why am I so smitten? It's but a single day since I was beckoned to her side.

It is clear she is mine. Or I am hers. We are bound together, so she must be special.

Now, as the sunlight wanes, she sits before a lit box at her desk. Her fingers tap upon a board of letters as she mumbles to herself and drinks glasses of wine mixed with juice.

My reservations are loosening. I'm growing tired of standing and watching. At first, I thought my place was to observe. But, the only sensation I feel is the lingering scald of her skin. The only taste and smell I savor is the remnants of her.

I can't stand it any longer and summon the courage to broach the silence.

"Alice?" Her name rolls from my lips like a shot of whiskey. Burning, slaking a thirst, and igniting a need in my gut for more.

She doesn't react. Not a blink. Not a flinch.

"Alice? Can you hear me?" My feet drift over the smooth wood of the floor without feeling it.

Daisy raises her head from the bed and tilts her ears. Perhaps in response to my voice?

Clicking of buttons fills the silence. Again, there is no sway in her demeanor.

Damnation! All day have I fretted, for naught. My irrational fear of vocalizing and terrorizing her seems petty in light of a new realization.

I cannot speak to her.

Although as transparent as the air, my stomach sours and rolls. Bile tears at my throat.

But, I can touch her.

"Perhaps, one day, you will grow accustomed to me." My fingers reach for her shoulder. "So, I can convey to you just how—"

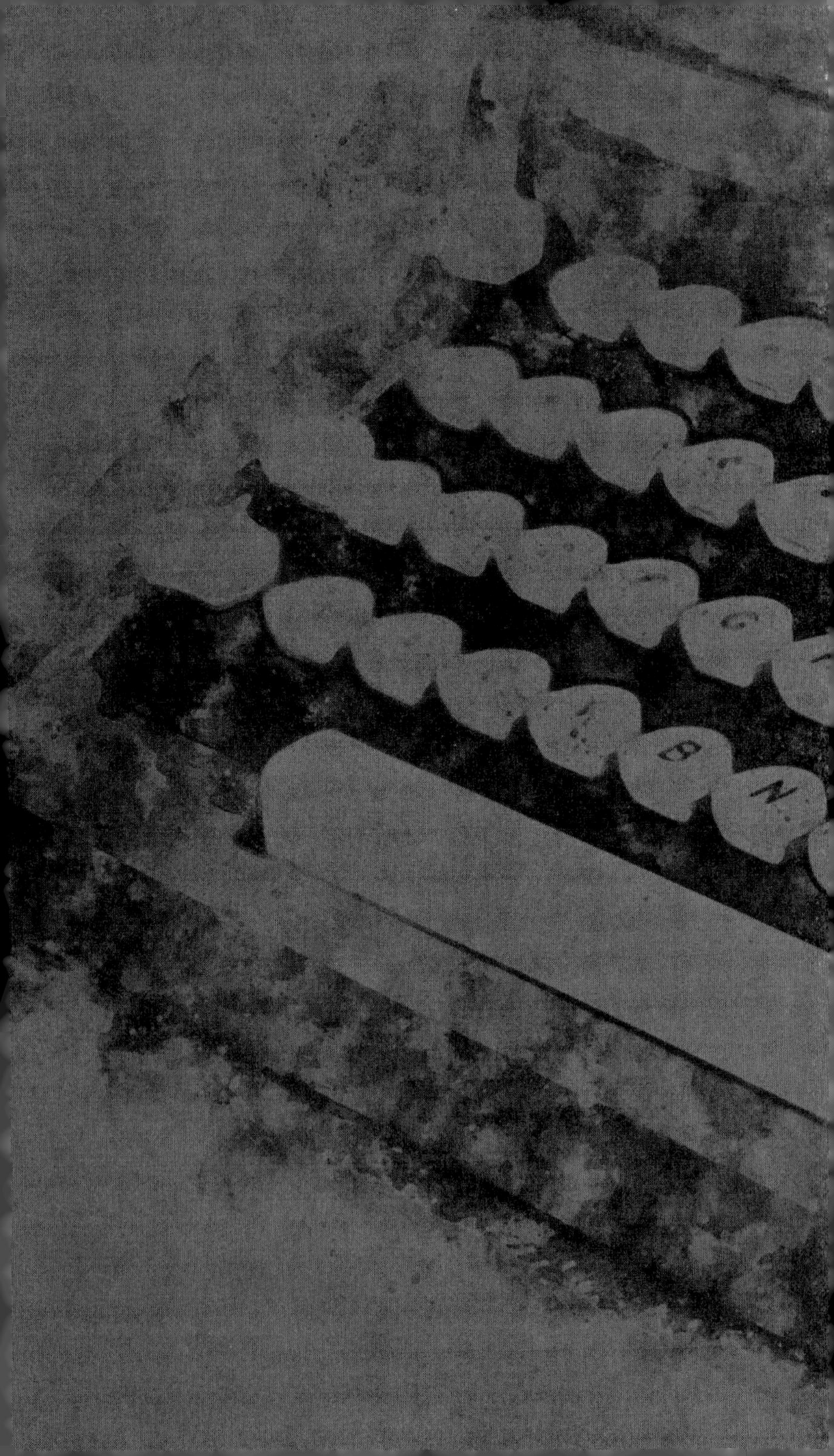

Chapter 6

Alice

"**B**eautiful you are." A deep male voice breaks through the silence as fingers brush my arm.

Holy shit, I have never moved so fast in my entire life.

Pretty sure my keyboard is embedded in the ceiling, my rolling office chair now resides in the kitchen, and I am trying to claw my way through the wall into the backyard.

Fighting back the panic threatening to bubble over into incoherent babbling, I try and see where the voice came from. There has to be some big burly dude standing behind where my chair was, but there's nothing. No one.

Daisy tilts her head and stares at me, then looks back to the middle of the room while she lolls her tongue and pants.

Certifiable. I am clearly going insane.

"Daisy, what the fuck? Did you hear that?" The cold wall presses against my shoulder blades and holds me up from collapsing into a driveling mess.

I may have peed myself a little. That was the most realistic hallucination I think I've ever had.

Not that I tend to hallucinate. But, sometimes after a bottle or two of wine and a scary movie, I'd swear the shadows move a little.

Once I was driving cross-country and was so sleep deprived I could have sworn that two people ran in front of my car in swirling snow.

But, nothing like this.

The little hairs on the back of my neck won't go down.

It felt so *real*. I heard actual *words*.

Beautiful.

Every syllable.

"I feel like I'm being pranked." Peeling myself off the wall takes more effort than I thought it would. My legs are shaky, like I ran a marathon.

Huh. Okay, maybe I have no clue about running that far. But, I bet it would make my legs all wobbly like they are now.

Why am I exhausted just pushing my rolling office chair back across the floor to my desk?

My hands are just as spastic as my legs so I flatten them on my desk to stop the tremors. I think I'll just rest my forehead and close my eyes for a second before retrieving my keyboard.

"Daisy, go fetch my keyboard," I mumble blindly. If I had a Labrador instead of a heeler, I bet it would bring it back for me.

Warm pressure falls on the back of my hand. Did she actually—

She's on her bed.

Terror laces through me and I freeze. I can't breathe as I watch the skin on the back of my hand shift and move. It feels as if invisible fingers slowly massage me and flatten over my wrist.

I'm too scared to scream again. My throat is paralyzed. Yet, I'm strangely transfixed by the sensation. Rough fingertips tickle the veins as they trace between my knuckles, sending tingles of panic and electricity through me.

If I call and make an appointment with a psychiatrist tomorrow, will that save me from losing my mind tonight? Because I think I already have.

The exploration of my hand stills. If I weren't afraid, I'd close my eyes and be able to envision the large hand that is attached to those fingers.

"What is happening?" The words are rough as they leave my useless throat.

"Don't be scared. I won't hurt you."

The deep voice echoes through me. It's like he's standing...right...

Next to me.

I'm breathing so fast I feel lightheaded. Or maybe it's because I'm seeing shit that isn't real. Or maybe I'm sleeping.

That's it.

I must be passed out at my desk and drooling on my keyboard.

"Okay. Ha. Ha. Great dream. Time to wake up now." There has to be a dragon, or a zombie, or something that will come crashing in the room.

Nothing. Just the solid feel of a hand covering mine.

"Can you hear me?"

I swear I can feel the breath from his words ruffle my hair.

"Yes. Can I wake up now?" My lower lip won't stop trembling. The tears welling in the bottom of my eyes blur my vision to the point where everything looks like rays of color. A scream keeps tightening my chest as it tries to escape.

"You are very much awake. My current situation may be up for debate." A deep exhale wafts across my cheek. I can smell...whiskey?

Is that sadness in his voice?

"Who are you?" I'm almost afraid of the answer. My eyes squeeze shut letting the collected tears run down to gather at my lips.

"I believe you know. I am Henry Sullivan."

Fuck. This can't be real.

Ghosts aren't real.

My stomach is rolling and I'm nearly in hysterics. With a purposefully deep breath, I raise my free hand to cover his.

And it does. There's even a sleeve over his wrist that my fingertips brush against. Heat radiates between my hands that hover an inch or so apart, separated by his invisible body.

When he moves his thumb against my wrist, that's too much.

I lose my shit again, jerking my hands away and standing abruptly. The chair goes rolling haphazardly behind me before it crashes against the wall.

"This isn't real!" My voice cracks into a high pitched shrill sound that reminds me of the Wicked Witch of the West.

Stars flutter in my narrowing vision. I'm suffocating. I can't seem to catch my breath no matter how fast my lungs spasm.

Staggering backward, I slam into the wall and it pushes the last of the air from my chest. The floor rushes up to meet me, but I'm stopped just before bouncing my nose off the wood slats. Booming heartbeats deafen my ears as the room fades to black.

Chapter 7

Henry

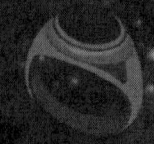

I barely managed to keep her from bloodying her mouth when she fell to the floor.

That could have gone better.

Her panicked breathing levels out in her unconsciousness. Should I leave her to revive from her vapours? Indecision stills me, my hand still cupping her soft cheek. Her lashes flick in her slumber, tickling the base of my thumb.

The sensation of *feeling* is so foreign after the agony of the day drifting without substance. A portion of me wishes to pick her up and hold her to me. So that more of me can experience the comfort of touch. A trickle of fear threads through me that I may depart at any moment to return to the void.

That determines my choice. My inability to be affected by the solidness of the floor is to my benefit as my arms pass uninhibited through the surface until I cradle her to my chest. It is peculiar that I can stand with her easily while my feet float without contact.

She burrows her face against my shoulder in slumber and her fingers thread little burning embers upon my chest.

It is disconcerting how comfortable I feel with her in my embrace. There is a part of me that is thankful she is unconscious right now. Carrying her into her bedroom would be akin to flying from her perspective. Weightless and floating, we drift into her chambers and I gently lay her upon the blanket and stand within the mattress next to her.

The little moan she looses as she snuggles against the pillow pierces through me. How I long for her to shower me with those noises within the throes of passion.

Jonathan's voice echoes in my ears. He said I fall too fast. That I wear my heart on my sleeve and give it to any girl I see.

He was right. I gave it to Nora, who only had eyes for him.

Ratbag.

Alice turns in her sleep, her fingers landing against my thigh which sends hot shivers into my groin. Her dark hair spreads over the satin pillows as she rocks her head. Furrows cross her brows and her cries grow louder.

With a start, her verdant eyes flash open. Her shoulders raise like a springboard as her heels dig into the downy coverlet, propelling her against the headboard.

"Fuck!" She jerks the chain that carries my ring from around her neck. Flinging it to the far wall, it lands in a coiled pile in the corner.

There's a small tug in my chest in its direction, but I can still feel the overwhelming pull toward her.

It isn't the object alone I'm drawn to. A ribbon I can't see is tethered to my guts that flexes and stretches with her quiet sobs.

She cries because I'm real. It tears me ragged that my mere existence can cause such a visceral reaction in her.

In an overwhelming moment of wanting to offer

comfort, I reach my hand out and rest it gently over her extended foot.

"I won't hurt you."

She snaps her leg out of my touch and buries herself deeper against the pillows adorning her bed. "Go away!" Her muffled voice digs through me. "Just leave me alone. Please," she whimpers.

"I don't know how. I am tied to you somehow."

Damnation. There is no movement of recognition. It seems only when making contact with her smooth delectable skin can she hear me.

I am not opposed to touching her. Quite the contrary. But, her trembling reaction does not exactly convey reciprocation.

My longing to brush my fingers against her wars with the fear I know I instill. Desire wins. My hand reaches again for her ankle.

"I am tied to you somehow. I would leave if I could."

Would I? Perhaps.

She freezes. I'm not sure if it's my words or the warmth of my palm that causes it.

"How?" I finally hear her squeak out.

"How am I tied to you? I sincerely wish I knew."

Her breathing slows from its frantic pace. "No. How are you here?" She turns her face from the corner. Her flushed red cheek and the tip of her nose sneak into view.

"It is a mystery to me as well. I also want to convey my apologies, ma'am."

Her eye opens and wildly looks around the room at my words, then quickly squeezes shut.

"It seems the only way in which we may converse is through direct contact." I fight the urge to circle my thumb over the hollow of her ankle. The quiver running through her leg betrays her stoic jaw.

"So, let me get this straight. You don't know how you got here or why you're attached to me?" The green gems of her eyes open. Bloodshot from rubbing them, she looks in my direction. "Why can't I see you then?"

A smile pulls at my lips. "Whatever prankster has orchestrated this must not want me mesmerizing you with my handsome features."

She raises her head and tilts it a little to the side, giving me a small lift of the corner of her mouth. "Handsome, huh? Well, that remains to be seen," she snorts.

Clever girl.

It lightens my mood to see her no longer quivering in panic. But, a little knot forms in my stomach when I see her eyes darken again.

"Ghosts are real," she whispers. "Are there more?" The creep of doubt clouds her features as she sits up and wraps her arms around one of her pillows.

Habit finds me shaking my head despite the fact that she can't see me. "I do not know the answer to that question. I came from nothingness."

Her face scrunches up with her lower lip in a petulant looking pout. "So, I should either buy a lottery ticket or go get myself committed. Because this is the strangest shit to happen to me this week."

I can feel my brows twist in confusion. "You've had a more tumultuous occurrence than this last week?"

"Oh, hell, yes. I had a Tik Tok video go viral last week. Strange, huh?" Her smile grows marginally. "And I thought *that* was freaky as fuck!"

When her voice drops at the end, I'm not quite sure she's talking to me anymore.

"I fear I have no idea of what you speak."

Except fuck. I know very well what that means. Dirty girl.

For the first time, I'm thankful she can't see me. Being this close to her with her overwhelming scent of citrus wine and that filthy mouth combine to have an uncomfortable swelling effect in my pants.

"Don't ghosts only come around if they have unfinished business? Is that why you're here?" She stares at her ankle where my hand rests. She doesn't seem to be balancing on the edge of terror anymore. At least her breathing has leveled.

The oath. It must be the oath I swore on the ring that is tying me.

"It's possible." I can never tell her what it is. I'll surely be doomed to wander through walls forever.

"Do you have unfinished business, Henry?" The green glitter of her eyes focuses through me as her chin tilts up. They're pink and swollen from her biting them and they torment my gaze as I struggle to answer her.

"I think everyone does, in some fashion. Do you?" I immediately regret giving in to the urge to move my thumb over her warm heel. Her eyes darken with a flash of fear as they dart back to where my hand rests.

Her breath hitches. "You know this is freaky as shit, right?"

"Freaky? I'm not familiar." She speaks so strangely sometimes, so it is hard to follow.

The long exhale she gifts me with washes over me in sweet warmth. "How old are you?"

"I remember my thirty-fifth birthday. I don't remember another." I spent two weeks in the jailhouse because of it. Damn Jonathan.

"Oh, wow." Her hand moves out, almost like she is going to reach out to mine. But, after a pause, she settles it to the pillow on her lap. "I'm sorry. You weren't much older than me. When were you born?"

Images of my father, his face twisted in anger, flailing me with his horse whip jerk my hand from her foot. The vivid bite of it across my back and flank. My palm, red and wet with my own blood. He beat me so badly I pissed myself. I vowed to kill him that day.

Onslaughts of memories besiege me. My mother pleading for him to stop. Wagons and horses and endless walking. The fire of fever and the shadow of her praying over me.

I peel away from the bed and from her. Chaos brims too near to the surface as I fight the rage simmering within me.

As the distance grows, distinction fades into rounded edges and darkness.

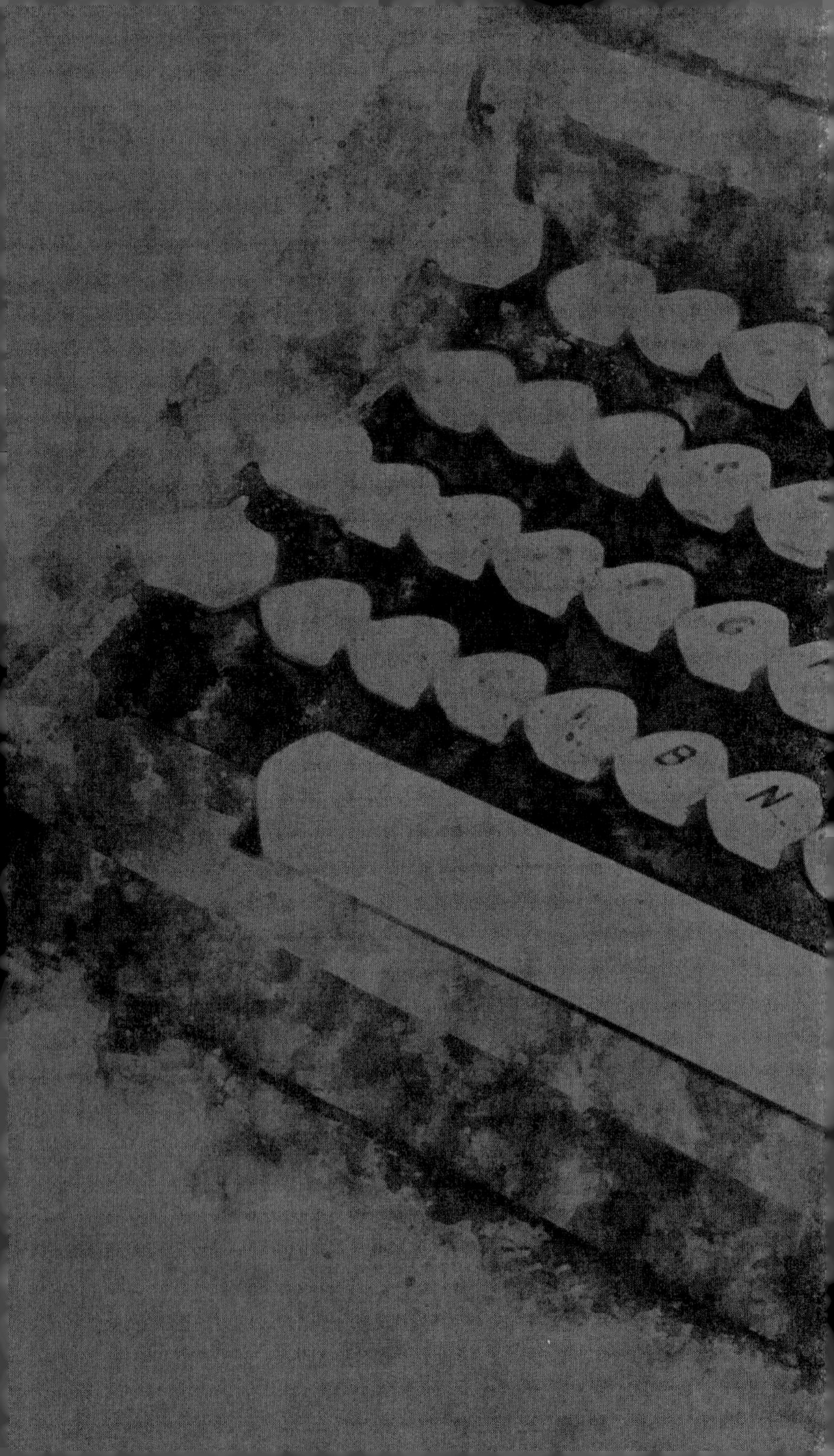
B
N

Chapter 8

Alice

Well, if that didn't win the "what-the-fuck" trophy, I don't know what will.

Ghosts. They're real. And, I have one.

I think I sat on the bed for nearly an hour, unsure what to do and still too scared to move. When he told me he is "tethered" to me, that pretty much nullifies being able to run away from him.

That would make a pretty good book idea. Haunted by a ghost who chases you across the country.

A shiver runs up my spine. No. That doesn't sound nice at all. Not if I'm the one doing the running.

In a weird kind of way, there is a small part of me that wants him back. He smells like horses and leather, with a little bit of whiskey and gunpowder.

I think that's what danger smells like. If that were true, wouldn't he have hurt me already?

My mind is reeling. Or maybe it left, and I'm imagining this entire thing.

I should have my house checked for mold. I knew Daisy makes too much of a mess when I give her a bath in the tub.

All that water is probably ruining my floor and I have a secret infestation of toxic mold.

That has to be it. Mold spores are making me hallucinate.

Damn, it felt real. His hand was large, calloused and hot on my foot.

And, his voice. Fuck...it's like hot fudge. Thick and heavy with a tinge of southern sweet.

I'm turned on by my own crazy.

When I'm brave enough to leave my bed, I nearly trip over my desk chair outside my bedroom door. The keyboard to my computer is laying on the floor against the kitchen counter.

Shit, I hope it isn't broken.

Wait. I remember that part and falling to the floor when I couldn't breathe. What I don't recollect is going to bed. How did I get there?

A frigid wave washes over me. Did he carry me?

Nope. Nope. Nope. This is not me losing my shit. A tremor rolls through my belly and clamps down, drenching me in a cold sweat. Lightheaded and woozy, it feels like dinner is fighting to come back up.

I barely make it to the bathroom before the remains of leftover pepperoni pizza and the acrid burn of orange juice and wine scorch their way out through my nose into the toilet.

After I clean myself up and track down my phone, the bed is calling my name. It's exhausting being haunted.

Tossing and turning all night is not conducive to looking like a supermodel. Not that there was a threat of that ever happening. There's a reason I chose writing and not the spotlight.

But, only an hour of sleep over the course of the night has me vibing like a troll today.

Lovely.

Google directed me quickly to a local mold inspector who said he could send someone over this afternoon to gather a few samples.

It didn't guide me as easily to find someone I could talk to about ghosts though. So, I'm stuck randomly picking someone to confess to that I'm nuts now.

Because that's the only explanation. Or mold.

Please, let me have a nasty house that can be cleaned and bleached so I'm not crazy.

I'm furiously scrubbing down every surface I can reach. When I'm elbow deep in cleaning the toilet, there's a little part that is grateful to hear someone at the door.

Daisy barks while running in a small circle near my feet.

"It's okay, I heard the knock. Shh, girl!" She moves back when I reach for the handle.

Shit, I still have the toilet brush. The mold guy already came and left. Who else would be stopping by?

"Oh! Hi, Mark! I wasn't expecting you."

He looks as perfect as yesterday, and flashes me a dazzling white smile that lights up his milk chocolate colored eyes.

"Hi, Alice. I have the estimate for your car repairs and some paperwork for you to sign. I hope you don't mind me dropping by unannounced?"

Heat floods my cheeks over my smile. "Of course not!

Please, come in. Coffee?" I do my best to hold the dirty brush behind my back without letting it touch me.

"That would be nice. Thank you."

He smells like aftershave as he brushes past me to the couch.

I don't even want to think about how badly I smell right now. Dodging behind the kitchen counter, I stash the nasty toilet cleaner under the sink and scrub my hands like Lady Macbeth.

Daisy prances to her bed and circles a few times before landing where she can watch our guest. He stretches his legs out to the side of the low table and begins laying out his papers.

"Cute dog. A collie?" His jacket crinkles as he leans over the folder and drops his pen.

"Daisy's a heeler. And a primadonna. But, she keeps me in line. I have milk and sugar?" All of my cups are the giant ones. Small cups do not exist in my world.

"Is it soy milk? If not, black is fine, thank you," he says without turning.

Okay, black it is.

Balancing both mugs, I set them gingerly on the table away from the documents he brought.

"Sorry, no soy milk." I hope at this end of the couch he won't smell me. "I don't get much company." Did that sound like a desperate cry for attention? Shit, I hope not. Even if he is cute.

The small frown at the corner of his mouth disappears into his practiced smile. "Totally fine." He picks up a yellow page and hands it to me. "Unfortunately, your car was deemed a total loss."

"Shit." It just slips out. "Sorry. That's awful." My cheeks heat up and I stare down at the mechanic's receipt.

Stop apologizing to this guy!

He raises his eyebrow slightly, but continues as if I hadn't spoken. "The good news, you still have full coverage, so you're eligible for full compensation up to the value of your Subaru." He leans toward me with another sheet in hand.

I get a drift of the smell of whiskey as he does. Weird.

"This shows you what the value of your vehicle is and has the payout value. We should have the check cut later this week." He flashes me a broad grin and picks up his cup. "Toast! Usually there is a lot more red tape, but I made sure to push this one through for you."

Did he just wink at me?

I hold out my full cup, and he carefully clinks his against it.

It feels like a miniature version of Daisy is running circles in my belly.

"Thank you. I really appreciate it." Fighting the urge to bat my lashes, I give him my best smile.

The number on the paper he hands me makes the tiny puppy in my gut jump up and down.

He looks even cuter giving me money.

"Wow! I guess this means I get to go car shopping!" Am I bouncing in my seat? Maybe.

Crap, I'm also not wearing a bra. That slows my roll a little. I may be single, but I'm not going to bounce my tits in front of him like a cheerleader. My shirt is heavy enough to hide most of the nip action, I think.

"It does! I just need your signature here." The pen he hands me is warm from his hand. "And here." He points at the two lines for me to sign, his dark head leaning over near my shoulder.

He smells good. Like hair products, and, is that gunpowder?

"Thank you." I really, really hope I don't stink too badly. I know I worked up a sweat scrubbing around the bathtub earlier.

He straightens, his expression unwavering as he watches me. When he leans back and puts his arm across the backrest of my couch, I forget how to read. Pretending to look over the details of the contract, I'm highly aware of the proximity of his hand behind me.

Do I like it? Kinda.

Okay, I'm a little excited. A long forgotten little tingle between my legs tunes in to his lanky frame only an arm's length away.

"There. All signed. So, if I start shopping for a car, when would I be able to pick it up?"

His fingers brush mine when I hand his pen back. The couch cushions help to cool my damp palm.

"How about, when you find a car, you call me. I'll drop you off at the dealership and bring that bottle of champagne to celebrate." He drops his fingers against the back of my hand where it rests between us. "Maybe even dinner afterwards?"

It's hard to say no when he raises his eyebrow like that.

"Um. Yeah. Maybe, that sounds nice." I sound like a complete idiot as I stammer through the single most confusing reply in the history of answers.

Did his eyes narrow just a little? I'm such a mess.

"It's a date." He gathers the papers from the table into his folder and stands.

I have a perfect, eye level view of his ass when he walks to the door.

Manners, Alice.

"I look forward to it. Thank you again for helping me with this." Am I supposed to shake his hand now? Hug him?

As he pulls the handle, he turns back and gives me another wink. His cheek pulls up in a lopsided smile. "Call me when you're ready." Then he's gone.

A wash of hot breath, heavy with the taint of whiskey, washes over me and a warm hand weighs upon my shoulder.

Fear freezes me to the sofa.

"Are you letting him court you?" a deep voice rumbles. It feels like it's only an inch from my ear.

"Henry." I thought he was gone. "Have you been here the whole time?"

"It isn't appropriate for a woman to sit with a man alone." His hand moves closer to my neck until his thumb rests against my collar bone.

I love and hate how it feels. Terrifying and possessive.

"I don't know what things were like when you were alive, but nowadays there's nothing wrong with it. He's just the insurance guy for my car." This whole thing is so strange. A bossy ghost?

"There is no time where it's right for a man to be alone with a woman who isn't his." He squeezes slightly, and it makes me cranky that my insides go jiggly.

What the fuck is wrong with me?

"Well, you're alone with me right now, Henry. And I'm not yours." I don't even know where he is. I'm arguing with an invisible hand that's on my throat.

A trill of panic runs through me. He's never given me "gentleman" vibes, but what if he's on the other end of that spectrum? The villain from the old west movies.

"It's different with us." His voice is husky and low as his

breath brushes over the small hairs of my neck. "We are bound by a greater force."

My stomach flip flops at his words. This isn't right. It has to be some perverse daydream.

I didn't see any mold when I was cleaning. The short bald man who was here earlier seemed skeptical as well.

"Why?" My voice is squeaky and cracks at the word. "Why me? I don't understand? Anyone could have found the ring. Would you have been bound to them the same?"

His warmth disappears, and my skin feels cool without his touch.

Breathe, girl.

I wish I could see him. It would be easier if he didn't just randomly grab me and scare the shit out of me.

It startles me when I feel him grasp my hand, pressing it into the firm cushions of the couch.

"Have you ever longed for something," he says from my right. His voice carries to me as if he's sitting where Mark sat just a few moments ago. "Wished so viciously, that you would give your very soul for it to come true?"

Oh, my god.

Flashbacks of two nights ago in the shower. I wished on his ring.

I did this. I brought him to me.

"Your color is pallid. Are you peckish?" His fingers tighten around mine.

"I—I believe I'm beginning to understand." I am not going to admit that I wished for *him*. "What was it like? When you, um..." How do you ask that question?

"Ah. The death part." He loosens his grip, barely touching my knuckles as I nod. "You read the note that Nora left with the ring." I can hear his teeth grit when he says her name. "My brother-in-arms, Jonathan, took her and everything from me. He is also the rabble-rouser who led to my present condition."

"That's shitty. With friends like that, who needs enemies?" My voice still sounds off-key but not quite as shrill as before.

Daisy tilts her head when he gives a deep laugh. It sounds so rich and alive that it's hard to believe it's a ghost making that noise.

"My enemies never killed me. It was the guise of friendship that cost me my life." His fingers slip from mine, and the room goes silent.

Minutes pass, and he doesn't return.

I need wine. Badly. No more cleaning today.

The big glass seems appropriate. It's on the top shelf, but if I push against the counter, I can just reach it. The tall flute wobbles as I brush it on the very tip of my grasp.

Dammit. One more lunge upward.

It teeters on the edge before tumbling to me. Shit! My reaction time is just a fraction too slow, and it falls end over end before shattering on the floor next to my bare foot.

"Fuck!"

There is glass *everywhere*.

I can't move. If I take a step in any direction, I'll be stepping on razor sharp shards.

Before I can even decide what to do, I feel warm hands on my upper arms. "Don't move," he breathes across my ear. One hand disappears, and without warning, my legs swing up into the air.

"Oh, holy shit!" I'm floating. And even stranger than that, I'm being held against a *chest*. A big hard one with a heavy lapelled jacket that rubs against my arm.

He carries me smoothly out of the kitchen. It doesn't

even feel like his legs are moving. It's more like we're drifting across the floor.

I didn't know there was a chest attached. For some reason, I just thought maybe it was only his hand. Smells overwhelm me. Leather. Horses. Woodsmoke. They all blend into a strangely pleasant scent that reminds me of the outdoors.

Holy fucking shit on a stick. There's like a whole *him*. I'm teetering on the edge. I can't catch my breath, no matter how fast I breathe. Stars flash in front of my eyes and I squeeze them shut.

"Alice, relax." His chest rumbles with my name.

My hand flies against him, gripping the fabric of his shirt. I don't want to open my eyes as I trace a seam and a button. The heat from his skin pushes through, almost scalding my hand.

"I just don't understand..." My mind is whirling. I thought he was just a voice, just a touch. But, he's carrying me as if I'm weightless. Every piece of me is touching so very much of him.

My god.

The firm cushions of the couch push me gently out of his arms as he sets me down. Before I can even settle in, I feel one of my feet being lifted, and his hands work their way over the sensitive skin on the top of my foot, around my heel, and rubbing every toe.

"That feels so good, but what are you doing?" I can't stop the little moan that escapes as his thumbs push against the arch.

"I am inspecting you for injuries. Feet are hard to heal, and yours appear delicate."

He isn't treating them gingerly, and I'm starting to

believe he's a fucking angel with his strong hands moving slowly over every inch.

"You're being very, um, thorough. I don't think I was cut."

I should have kept my mouth shut. My heels are still tingling from his absent touch and they feel amazing.

"Thank you, Henry. If you can hear me?" Does it work like hearing him?

His fingers brush my hand. "I can always hear you."

Huh. I'm not sure if I should be creeped out or thankful. He did save me after all.

"Can you, um, hear my thoughts, too?" Oh, fuck. I hope not.

The heat of his palm moves up my forearm, making the little hairs raise on either side. "You're thinking how much you appreciate me rescuing you. And how delicious your seductive little ankles felt in my hands."

He can read my thoughts. And he thinks I have seductive ankles. Why does that make my belly clench in a good way? I didn't want him to stop because his hands felt so good. I wonder what they would feel like if he worked his way — oh, shit. He can hear what I'm thinking?

The rich baritone of his laugh echoes again through the room. I'm starting to like it.

"I cannot read your thoughts, Alice. But, the look on your face says they were suddenly quite salacious."

Heat moves up my neck and sits firmly on my cheeks. He might as well have been able to read my mind. Pretty sure I have a bright red billboard shining from my face right now.

"So, ankles? Is that a thing for you?" Is that enough of a subject change? I need to stop thinking about his hands.

"Ah. Well, women wore long dresses and high shoes.

Even the saloon whores kept their boots on." His laughter fades into a sigh. "It was a special treat to see a woman's ankles. A rare treasure."

And here I've been running around barefoot all day. It must be like spring break in Miami for him.

"I can't imagine the heat without shorts and flip flops. What year was that?" Last time I asked him, he disappeared.

"Flip flops? You use such strange terms."

He rotates his hand so the pads of his fingers tickle below mine. Why am I getting little sparks radiating through me with his movements?

"I remember when Missouri became a state," he continues. "There was chaos in the streets for days."

"Hold up. You were *there*? Like, when it actually happened?" I need my phone. Google to the rescue.

It was 1821.

Two hundred years ago.

My stomach twists painfully. A little stabby pain that bends me over.

Welcome back to the land of disbelief. This isn't possible. He's been trapped in that ring for centuries? Like a genie in a lamp...wait.

"Can you grant wishes?" I should really think before I just blurt things out. But, it's there now.

"Pardon?" His hand stills, the heat leaving scorch marks where it rests.

"Well. I mean. The stories say that genies trapped in lamps can grant wishes. I was just curious if it worked for ring men. Ring genies? Ring ghosts?" I can't stop talking.

Shut up, Alice.

Silence eats away at me.

Daisy rolls over on her back and resumes snoring lightly, her legs splay in the air.

"What would you wish for?" he asks quietly.

Dammit. I already wished for the impossible, and it's stroking my hand right now.

"Oh, I don't know. The usual stuff, I guess." Me and my mouth. "A bestseller would be nice. A maid." A sexy sounding ghost who has a big strong chest.

I need to simmer these hormones. He could be like Hellraiser for all I know, just stringing me along until I do something stupid. Or, maybe he's an invisible Predator and my spine is going to end up in a display case. I wonder if he has tentacles?

Apparently, I watch too much TV.

"What do you mean by 'bestseller'?" His voice snaps me out of my movie reverie.

"Oh. One of my books. It'd be great to make it on the top one hundred list." Heck, top thousand would make me happy.

"Like, Jane Austen," he says quietly.

"Yes! You know her books?"

"I do."

He doesn't add anything else. His hand has even stilled on mine.

"Henry? You don't like Jane Austen? She wrote amazing romance stories." Sense and Sensibility is what inspired me to become an author. A really smutty one who puts "too much sex" in my books.

"What is romance? Is it the longing for what we cannot have? The dream that never lives up to reality?"

He sounds so bitter. Nora must have been a real bitch.

"I think it's the mystery. The anticipation. Hope. And maybe a little bit of being swept off their feet."

The vibration of his chuckle moves through his fingers. "I swept you off your feet. Does that make this old scoundrel a romantic?"

Now, it's my turn to laugh. "This is officially the strangest week ever. I need to clean up that glass so I don't walk on it trying to make coffee in the morning." That thought gives me pause.

"Henry? Do you sleep? Or do you just hang in the shadows watching me?" Holy shit, I'll never have privacy again.

"When I drift from you, time and objects fade. It is the tie that leads me to return."

I have no idea if he's telling the truth. Maybe he'll get bored watching me pee. It's usually when I get lost scrolling on my phone. Even Daisy did, when she was a puppy and in her clingy stage.

"How do I know I can trust you?" He scares the ever-loving bee gees out of me. But, he did rescue me from the kitchen. If he can pick me up, he can hurt me if he wants to.

"You don't."

A shiver runs through me that melts into a dull heat in my belly. He can do anything he wants to me.

Good or bad.

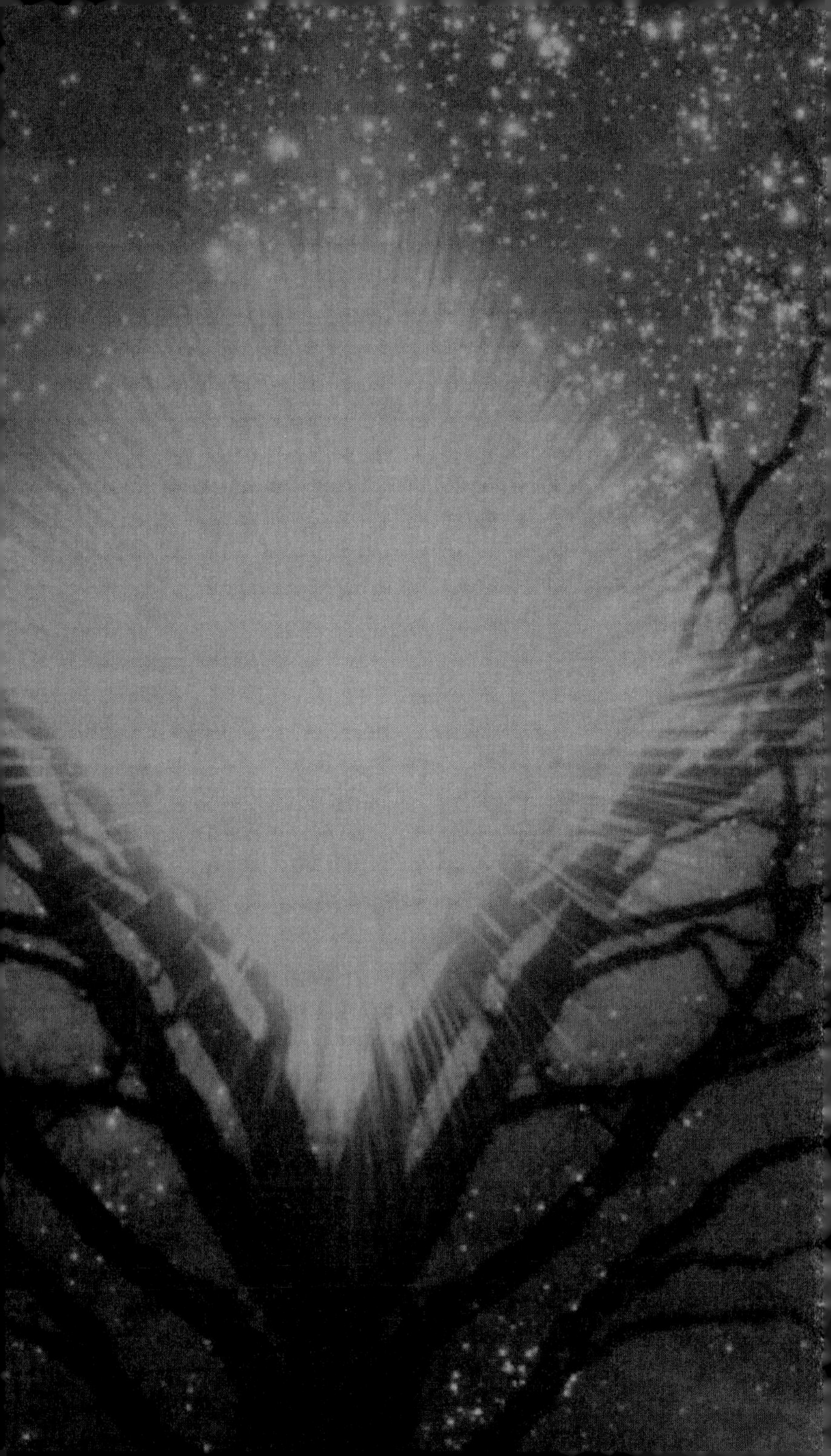

Chapter 9

Henry

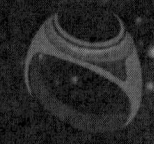

My body still burns where I held her against me. It took everything within me to relinquish my hold on her. Harder still was letting myself drift away from the heat of her skin.

It is addictive. Worse than the opium that dulls the mind and softens the senses. She makes everything crisp, my every sensation acute and piercing. I *feel* when I am with her.

My cock longs for her. I find myself constantly fighting the drive to indulge in her. To partake of every inch of her. Her taste still lingers on my lips. My raging prick begs to be tempered. No amount of stroking into the aether relieves the pressure building within me every time I touch her. A secret caress of her exposed ankle while she was sleeping was enough to have me spewing as if a geyser was erupting from my loins.

I want her.

She is mine, I am sure of it. This bond we have is for good reason. Her wit and chaos draw me to her. The mischievous glint in the gemstones of her eyes sends sparks of fire into me.

I'd be content to hold her hand forever. But, there is so much more I'd rather do.

So, for now, I will bide my time. Learn everything about her and the strange world she lives in.

Like this contraption she rides in that whisks us down the blackened paths into town.

"What is this buggy you ride in?" She only startles a pittance when my hand covers hers resting on the protuberance between the seats. Such a strange carriage without horses.

I miss the wind. My air is always still now. Except those moments when her breath brushes over me.

She is my entire universe now. I struggled through the evening and night, watching her sublime form in repose. Keeping my distance was a level of hell I didn't know existed.

"It's called a car or automobile. They've been around for over a hundred years." She does not quite hide the small tremor in her tone as she releases a deep breath.

My presence is still jarring it seems. Ironic. In life I was told I was intimidating as well. She can't even see me, yet is still put off by me.

Perhaps it's better this way. She can't see the scars I've carried since I was young. The memento my father left that shied the respectable folk from my path.

No one gives a shit what your face looks like when they're staring down the barrel of your gun.

"Car? It rides much more smoothly than my horse. Are you returning to the grocer's for more supplies?" Buildings pass by in a blur outside the curved window panes. My gaze is drawn instead to the soft pulse of her neck. Her dark hair is pulled back, exposing the long arch of her throat that disappears into her jacket.

Her lip pulls between her teeth as her eyes dart in my direction. "No, I have an appointment." Her fingertips dance across the wheel in her grasp. "Did you really stay away last night?" The pink tip of her tongue flicks over the angry red marks on her swollen bottom lip.

I would willingly relent to those teeth if that tongue were to follow.

"I did. I'm a man of my word." I'll never tell her I stood over her bed and loosed my invisible seed onto her floor while lightly touching the smooth skin on the hollow of her ankle.

Her shoulders relax at my words, the lie that flowed too easily. I cannot resist her, but I don't want her to continue to fear me.

"Have you always been? A man of your word, I mean?" Her eyes face forward while her fingers tap an erratic pattern on the wheel.

"I've been a man of my word, although my actions have often been questionable."

She swallows hard. "Were you a criminal?" Her voice drops as the color fades from her cheeks.

I'm not sure how much to divulge. My mere presence is terrifying enough for her. Should I reveal how much of a monster I've been?

"I always had a hard time adhering to the rules. And I've spent my time behind bars, but in my defense, it was mainly for brawls and drunkenness." Fights that Jonathan always seemed to start, expecting me to finish. He had a propensity for pushing my loyalty to its limits. I wish now I had walked away much sooner.

I'm fortunate we were never caught for our more heinous acts.

Unbidden, images of standing over a man while I cave in his features with my fists flash behind my eyes. A rage festers in my gut that has my fingers leaving the soft back of her hand. Struggling to contain the boiling within me, I watch in silence as she stops her carriage in front of a long rectangular building.

Drifting behind her as she enters, I eavesdrop as she asks a young woman of serene face directions. A rigid and boring hallway leads to a wooden door with frosted glass.

Alice seems almost hesitant as her knuckle raps softly against the name of "Dr. J. Myers" patterned in gold over the dark grain.

Her timid affect tightens my stomach. Her demeanor is reluctant when a woman's voice beckons her inside.

Unable to resist the urge to check the room before her, I drift through the wall before she enters.

It's an office, simple in furnishing. A lone woman sits behind a desk. I am confused by Alice's trepidation. I don't see any threat to her.

Perhaps it's the power this woman holds. This new time is remarkable in the flamboyance that they can exert themselves.

Ignoring their pleasantries, I prowl the room to ensure there are no hidden dangers. My ears pique when I hear the older woman say, "Now, tell me why you're here."

"Well, a couple of days ago, there was that bad storm," Alice begins. "My dog found a ring. And since then, I've been, well, um..." Her voice tapers as a crimson blush fills her cheeks.

"Your request for this consultation said you were hearing voices?" the woman prompts.

She's here because of me.

"Um, yes. One voice really. A man named Henry. I think he's a ghost." She fidgets with the zipper on her jacket and slumps into her seat.

"I see." The older woman glances down and makes a note on a pad. "And what makes you think he's a ghost?"

"He said he was alive when Missouri became a state." Alice sits up straight. "I had my house checked for mold. I've never heard voices before. I actually *felt* his hand."

I cannot resist, my fingers drift to her, finding the skin of her left wrist through her jacket. Her clothing offers no obstacle to my touch.

She shies only slightly, but keeps her eyes forward.

"Sometimes, our minds work in strange ways. Perhaps the storm was a triggering event. Did anything else happen during this storm?"

"Yes, my car got smashed by the tree I found the ring under." Her right hand crosses her body and covers mine, stilling the movement of my fingers.

"Hmm." The woman pauses. "That can be traumatic. Did your insurance cover it?" She jots down more on the paper before her.

"Yes. In fact, I met the cute insurance agent because of it. His name is Mark."

A spear of pain twinges into my chest, and my grip tightens on her arm. She thinks he's cute. I wonder if she's saying that to purposefully rile me.

If I were able, I would make sure he would never want to smile at her again.

"Oh, okay. When was your last relationship?" The woman's large brown eyes look up from her desk to Alice.

Her hand tenses around mine. "Four years ago. That was my last relationship. I dumped him."

"May I ask why?" The woman is back to making notes.

"He cheated on me." Alice closes her eyes, her cheeks tightening in a grimace.

The dog. Causing such pain to her. I know the agony of having your heart thrown back into your face. It's an indescribable ache that dredges shadows of self-loathing.

It draws a protective growl from my bowels, and my other hand drifts to the small of her back.

She stiffens, her eyes fluttering open as she glances at the older woman.

"She can't hear me, nor can I make her. I tried to get that buffoon Mark to hear me. You're my only one." My lips are only inches from her ear.

She gives a tiny nod before that damned lower lip goes between her teeth. The heat of her long exhale cascades over me, heavy with the scent of coffee and vanilla.

The sterility of existence away from her may draw me closer, but it is the heady intoxication I feel that beckons me to want to touch and caress her constantly.

"How long were you with him?" The woman's questions are almost clinical and entirely too invasive.

"Two years."

That traitorous man had her for two years and philandered her love away. What I wouldn't give to have two years by her side. I can only dream of having her look *at* me.

"He's a cretin." I say it low, slipping it through my teeth. The tiny upward curl to her lip it elicits is a reward I'll covet.

"No one since?" The older woman's eyes raise. I almost feel she is looking at me as I hover next to Alice.

"Not, um, a relationship." A flush of pink escapes from the collar of her shirt and works its devious way up her delicate throat.

The woman behind the desk gives a flippant wave of

her hand. "A casual sex life is normal. Did you use a condom?"

"What is a condom?" I've never heard such a word. Conniving? Conundrum?

"Oh, my god." Her eyes dart toward me, then back to the desk. "Yes. Every time."

"Very smart. Well, that removes several options. Syphilis has been known to cause hallucinations. I'm assuming you've had regular health screening since?" How matter of factly that woman discusses such a crude disease. Alice isn't a whore.

But, by her own admission, she has carnal needs.

My cock twitches at the thought of sating her appetites.

"Yes, I do my annuals. Everything is good as far as I know. That's, well, kinda why I'm here. I know this isn't, um, normal." Her hands twist on her lap.

A knot forms in my gut watching her writhing uncomfortably.

"It sounds like you have a good grasp on what's going on. Sometimes when someone says they hear voices, other factors become apparent. You don't seem to have any of the obvious markers, so we're going to explore more physiological reasons why you may be experiencing what you say you are. Sleep schedule okay? History of cancer in your family?" The woman rattles off several other words with which I am unfamiliar, so my eyes instead drift back to Alice.

Her expressions change with each inquiry. Sometimes her brows shoot toward her dark bangs, sometimes they furrow with a small crease between them. Her answers are short and clipped, yes or no.

They settle on a future date for another unfamiliar request.

"What is a scanning of cats?" I hold my curiosity until she is back within the confines of her carriage, er, car.

"Uh, a cat scan? It's a picture of your insides. She wants to see if I have anything going on with my brain." She is pale as she navigates her way back towards her home.

"How is that possible? Do they open your skull? That's barbaric! Do not let them do this to you!" I can feel my chest tightening at the thought of her being hurt.

"What? No! Geez, Henry, chill. They aren't opening my skull. It's just a picture. I have to lie in a tube, and it sends light at me. That's it. Fuck, no, they aren't cutting me open." She stops the droning noise of the car and stomps up the short steps to her door.

Musing at a distance, I watch her peel out of her jacket and lean against the door with her chin arching to the ceiling. Her eyes squeeze shut and it rends my heart to see the flutterings of pain etch her features.

My fingers brush her elbow. "Why are you putting yourself through this grief?" Her discomfort is palpable. The entire morning she has appeared on the verge of tears.

"I need to find out why I'm hearing you." Her voice is soft, nearly a whisper.

"I am bound to you. You're special." It's obvious, isn't it?

"No!" Her voice raises and the green of her eyes seems brighter as she looks in my direction. "You aren't 'bound' to me! There isn't a 'you,' don't you see? There's something wrong with me!"

When she throws her hands up and paces away from me, a knot of fury forms, simmering beneath the surface. She is testing me, but she will learn my ire runs shallow.

Harshly, I grab her elbow and push her back against the door. "There is very much a 'me,' just as much as there is a 'you.'"

She flails, panic shifting her lips into a flat line. In her struggle, she manages to push against my chest. "No! Ghosts aren't real! You aren't real!"

My tenuous hold on my rage snaps. Before I can stop myself, my hand finds her throat, pinning her to the door. Driving my hips into her, the heat of her body sears into mine.

Terror flashes through her eyes as she claws at my hand. Holding hers above her head with my other hand, she is trapped between me and the wooden door.

"Does this feel real to you?" The tip of my nose grazes her cheek as I tilt my head enough to meet her lips with my own.

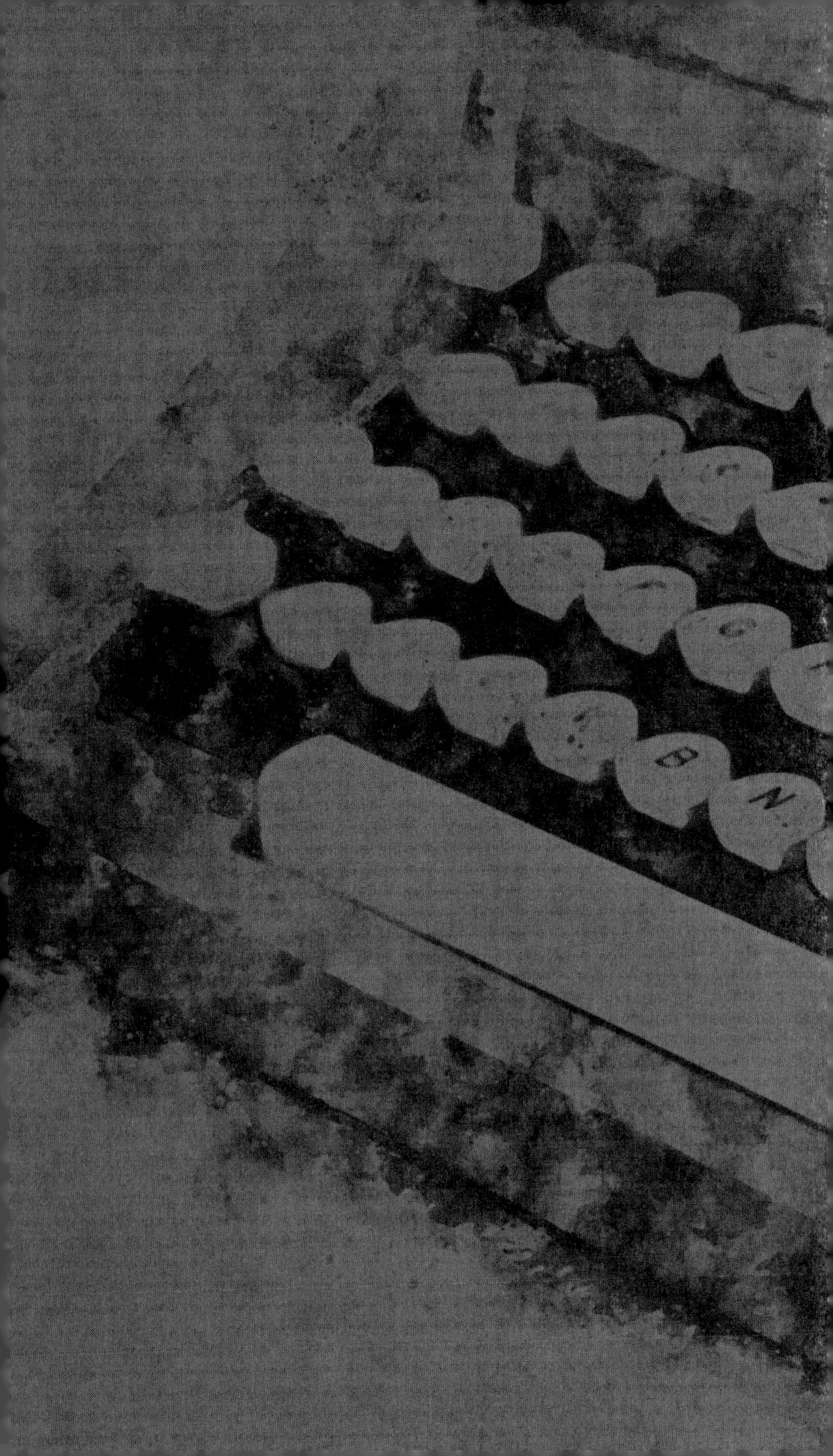
B
N

Chapter 10

Alice

I can't move. All I can feel is him, all of him. The grip of his calloused hand around my throat is squeezing me hard enough that it forces my chin up.

If I close my eyes tight enough, maybe I can wish him away. This can't be real. He isn't real.

My feet kick out, but his knee is wedged between my legs so firmly that it feels as if he's merged with the door digging into my back. He's bigger than me and holds me propped on his meaty thigh like I weigh nothing.

But, the press of his mouth against mine, the tickle of whiskers on my cheek, and the subtle taste of whiskey overwhelms me. Heat begins to spread through my body with the persistent movement of his lips.

Oh, my god. I can feel him. He's hard. And huge. Jesus, I didn't know that ghosts have dicks. Giant ones. Or, maybe that's just him.

The hot wet flick of his tongue probes my lips. And, fuck me, if I don't relent.

A deep groan vibrates from his chest and my traitorous nipples act like little lightning rods, transforming it into bolts of electricity coursing through me. His tongue invades my mouth like troops on the beaches of Normandy.

I've never been kissed like this. He's devouring me. Tickling along the inside of my teeth, he explores with every reach until I push back. Pressing against him, we battle for ownership of my mouth, and I fear I am losing.

I feel myself giving in. He's pinning me so tightly, and consuming me so ravenously, I can hardly breathe. Stars dance behind my eyes and I can feel myself getting light-headed. But, it doesn't stop my hips from grinding against his thigh, or the little moans that work their way from my throat.

When he pulls away, I'm absolutely gasping for breath.

"Do I feel real now?" How can he be breathless, too?

I can't even talk. All I can manage is a zombie-style groan.

"I've been wanting to taste your perfect lips for days." He tenderly kisses me while his thumb burns a line from my neck to cup my jaw. "You make me feel alive."

A weird shiver runs up my spine. I just made out with a dead guy.

The best kiss of my life was from a ghost. That says so much about my previous partners.

"Henry—"

No inner logic! Do not step in now!

"—This isn't right."

Dammit.

The friction of his thigh is arguing with my brain. His hands still hold my arms above my head and my fingers start to tingle in his vice-like grip.

I'm completely at his mercy. And I don't know how I feel about it. There's a flutter of panic in my chest, but a whole different feeling deep in my belly. His hard-on is still digging into my pelvis.

My horny, haven't-been-laid-in-ages body wants to see if he's as big as he seems.

Fuck.

"It feels right." His words brush over my neck before his lips follow. Gentle nibbles start at my collarbone while his whiskers skim over my sensitive skin.

When he takes a firmer nip, the shockwaves course through me and any resistance I felt melts under his hot breath.

As he works his way up to my jaw, each taste is deeper, harder and more voracious than the last.

Tingles turn to pinpoint arcs of lightning racing through me as he takes the lobe of my ear between his teeth.

"Deny it," he growls.

If he isn't real, and I am just imagining this, it's like an elaborate masturbation fantasy, right?

Totally.

I can hear myself letting out a manic giggle as some sort of dam on my sanity cracks.

Fine. I'll play the game. It feels too fucking amazing to want to stop.

My sex deprived body shuts my brain off.

"It does. It feels good." I give. I concede. I throw myself off the cliff of doubt and tilt my head to him, letting my own lips explore the edge of his jaw.

"Just keep your eyes closed, my little minx, and I'll make you feel better than 'good.'"

There's no way I'm opening them. It would be a douse of cold water to see the emptiness in front of me. It would be like standing on the edge of the Grand Canyon and feeling a push between my shoulder blades.

"Why me?" The question escapes my lips and morphs into a moan as his hips gyrate against me.

"Perhaps you needed me—" He peppers small, zinging bites down my neck as his hand releases my chin. With scorching heat, he drags his palm down my chest and cups my breast. "—As much as I needed you." Sizzling barbs of sweet pain erupt as he pinches my nipple. His touch is directly on my skin, as if my clothes don't even exist.

"We are bound together. Destined to be as one. I'm sure of it."

I've never heard such certainty. It's been my experience to be the pursuer, the beggar, the needy one. He must be a figment of my imagination to be so sure he wants *me*.

"I don't even know what you look like." I can't stop myself. There's still some place in my head screaming that this isn't real. If he looks like what I envisioned, then I know I made him up.

While I fixate on the thought of Kurt Russell, his grasp on my numb hands loosens. Letting my left hand free, he carries the palm of my right to his jaw.

"Know me, as I know you." His words are soft as my fingers brush against a short beard on his cheek. The muscle clenches as he tightens his jaw. Feathering my hand across his ear, a curl of hair teases across my knuckle.

"What color is your hair?" It's thick as I trail my fingers through it. Not long, but enough I could grab a handful if I wanted to.

"Dark as mud. It lightens in the summer." No longer holding my hand, his whispers down the skin of my side. The light touch of his fingers through my clothes raises goosebumps across my belly.

Tracing his jaw on both sides, I feel his mustache is thicker, but not long.

What is that?

A roughness covers his right cheek. Deep crevasses furrow into his skin. Following blindly, I find it leads up his cheek, over his eye, and onto his forehead.

"Henry? What happened?" I can feel him wince beneath my investigating touch.

"I was a dog that bit at my father." There's a hard edge to his voice.

"Wait, your *dad* did that? My god." So long, Kurt Russell. There is definitely zero resemblance.

A cold rock forms in my stomach as I realize I feel sad for him.

Can he actually be real?

"When you're defiant, there are consequences." He leans closer, his lips grazing the shell of my ear. "Pain makes the best teacher."

There must be something wrong with me. My heart beats faster and my panties get a little more wet at his words.

Don't say it. Don't say it.

"What would you teach me?" I can feel my lips turn up in a teasing smile. I might as well enjoy this insane ride.

"Oh, you're a vixen." His lips find the quivering flesh of my neck. "I am going to teach you that you are mine." His bite draws the skin into a sharp pinch that radiates through me.

Pressure builds between my legs with each nip.

"I am going to mark this pretty little neck—" Another shock ripples through me as his teeth sink again. "—So every time you gaze upon your reflection and see my marks—" Sweet pain has me writhing against his thigh. My hands knot in his hair, clutching him to me. "—You'll remember that I did that to you, and how good it felt."

He wraps one arm beneath mine and grabs my hair, tugging my head back while his mouth assaults my throat. The other works its way down my hip, my thigh, and traces its way between my legs.

I might as well be naked. The rough pads of his fingers work their way over my skin. It's like my clothes don't exist for him.

"How can this feel so good?" My breath comes in tiny pants. He has me teetering on the brink. I've never been into any kind of pain, but each time he covers the sting with the push of his tongue, I feel closer to the precipice. Pressure flows through my limbs. My belly is so tight I feel like I'm going to explode.

The hairs of his beard tickle my jaw as he works his way closer to my mouth.

"It is because you and I are as one. Fate has answered our call and brought us together." His fingers push between my thighs, teasing along my slit.

A vibration rumbles through his chest again, working its way through me. "You're drenched for me, filthy girl. There is no denying it." He cups his hand against me, and my hips move on their own, begging for the friction of his fingers to delve into me.

"I don't believe in fate." My voice sounds so whiny in between gasps.

"You don't believe in ghosts either. Yet, here I am." His lips crash against mine as he pushes a finger into me. His thumb finds my throbbing clit, triggering the cascading wave of orgasm to rocket through me. Stars fracture behind my eyes, and my cry flutters through our battling mouths.

Clinging to his neck, I know he is the only thing keeping me from crumpling to the ground in a liquidy pile.

"Henry...I, oh fuck." I can't think straight. His body burns where he presses against me. He pulls his hand from between my thighs and pushes his wet finger into my mouth.

I taste myself as my lips reflexively close around him. My tongue dances over the calluses while he takes hold of my jaw.

"Your tight little cunt is begging for me. Take off your clothes so I can see you naked and impaled on my cock." He pulls his hand from my hair, but keeps a firm grip with his other still in my mouth.

Holy fuck, he talks dirty. And I love it.

This train to Crazy Town is missing *all* the stops.

I still have the numbing euphoria of climax buzzing in my limbs when I start peeling off the layers of clothes.

He curls his finger behind my teeth and tugs at my jaw, dragging me toward the bedroom door.

"I want you spread before me so I can worship you as you deserve." He gives another pull just as my damp pants fall around my ankles. Off balance, I stumble forward and my eyes fly open.

The sobering absence of seeing the empty room knocks me to my knees.

A cold splash of doubt and panic seize me as his hand still tugs at my mouth.

The invisible hand that is very possibly a figment of my imagination.

Daisy watches me crawling on the floor. She lazily tilts her head like it's a Tuesday.

Fat lot of help she is.

The sting of his hand on my ass surprises the fuck out of me, and I lurch forward.

"I told you to keep your eyes closed." His hand rubs over my sore butt for a moment before the heat of it disappears and he smacks the other side with a matching slap. I hate how it sends bolts of ecstasy through me.

Okay, fine. Squeezing them shut, I'm at the mercy of a ghost. Or my own mental state.

I have no idea what is real anymore. I'm naked, except for my pants knotted around my ankles, on my living room floor.

I'm glad I live alone. This would be hard to explain.

"Good girl. You look fucking delectable. Perhaps I'll leave the worship for later and rut you right now." His hand frees my mouth and both of his large palms stroke hot coals down my sides until they settle on my hips.

He's behind me.

Oh, fuck. My thighs clench as he raises my ass and shoves his knee between my legs. I can feel the bare skin of his chest against my body as his whiskers punctuate his hot mouth nibbling down my spine.

Did he take his clothes off?

"Spread that beautiful cunt for me. I've been waiting lifetimes for this."

Why do my arms listen to him and give? My chest falls to the cold smooth floor as one of his hands disappears from my hips.

Then I feel it.

Pressure.

He rubs the head of his hard dick against me. Long languid strokes from my dripping clit all the way up to the star of my ass and back down.

I can't quite stop the small involuntary pull away from him every time he pushes against my backdoor.

His hand finds my throat, and he pulls me up until my back is against his chest. "I'll have every part of you. And when I do, I'll have you screaming like a mountain lion. Your body will quake like an old empty cart on a cobblestone road. And then you'll beg me to do it again."

My heart races, the thumping in my ears nearly drowning his words.

He's naked. He has a hairy chest. He's going to fuck my ass.

There are at least three things I didn't expect today.

Getting railed by a ghost on my living room floor didn't really make my list today either, but, well, plans change.

One hand still on my neck, his other positions the giant head of his erection at the entrance of my very needy and willing pussy. In one movement, he pulls me backward, and drives himself forward.

Filling me.

Stretching me.

Impaling me.

Holy fuck.

His groan spills his hot breath over my shuddering body. "My sultry vixen." He takes my hand and flattens my palm over my lower belly. "Feel me fuck you."

When he pulls back, his engorged head ripples along my tight walls. My belly sinks with his withdrawal. Then bulges as he drives back into me. He's pumping the air out of my lungs into a long moan.

The head of his cock pulses behind my belly button every time he pistons into me.

His hand leaves mine, pushing its way down until he touches my stretched clit.

I can't help it. I scream. I'm so fucking sensitive. It's like he's rubbing a live wire and raw voltage runs rampant through me.

"That's it. Scream my name as you squeeze my cock." His finger moves faster, as does his hips, thrusting into me.

A funnel cloud swirls within me. The force of him rams me closer to the tornado of destruction. Churning, his grunts feed the chaos until I'm exploding in debris, screaming his name. The sporadic twitch of his hips as he joins me sends me shattering into starry-eyed oblivion.

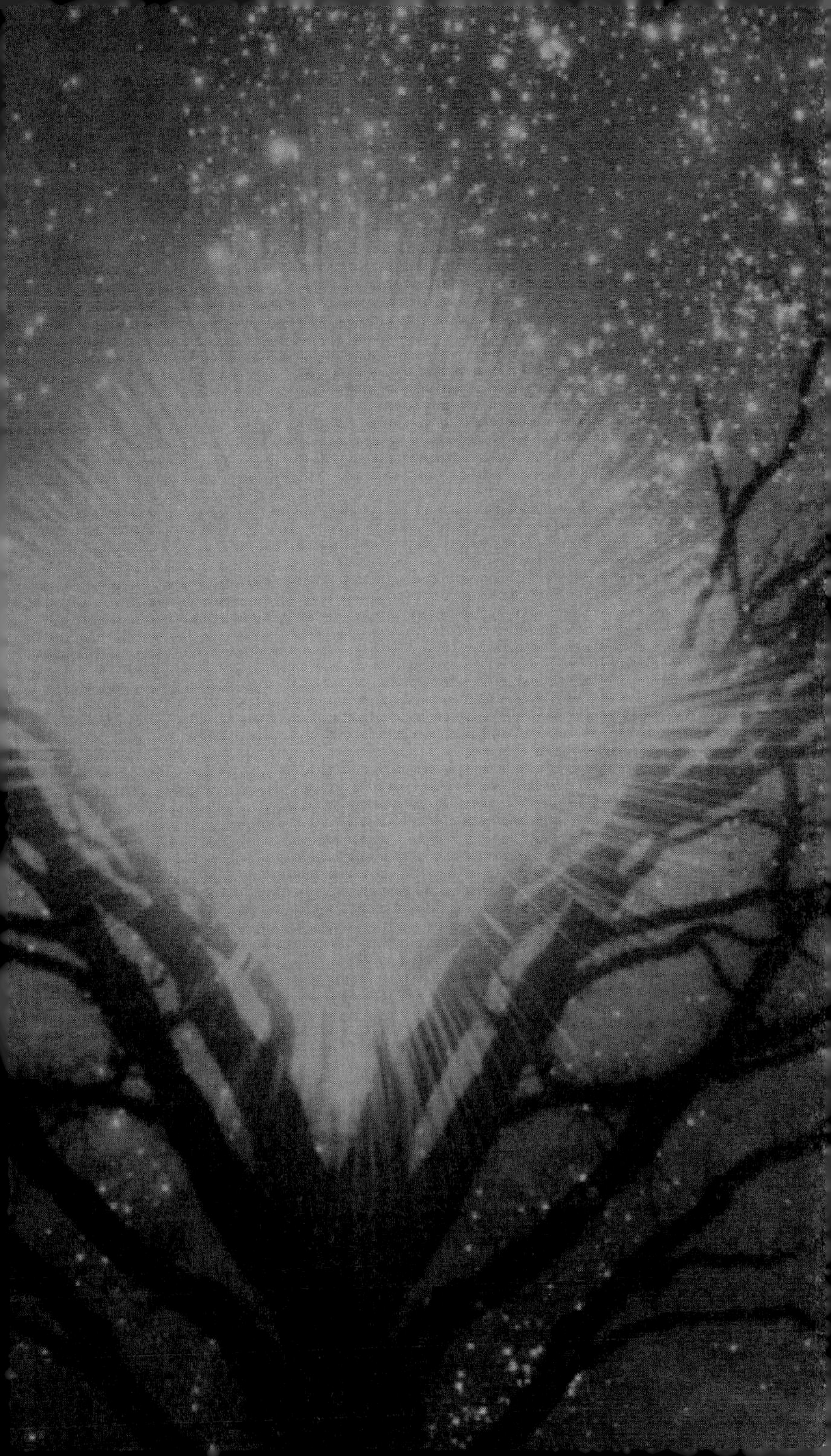

Chapter 11

Henry

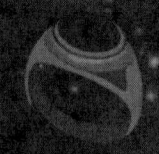

She's limp in my arms. The back of my thighs shake in the aftereffects of release, but I manage to hold her tightly to me.

I don't want to let her go. It would be a fine eternity to remain buried in the tight confines of her pussy.

Feeling weaker than before, lethargy tugs at my limbs. It's almost reminiscent of my living times. Spent, sedated and relaxed. She gives me this contented warmth. The heat of her body, the scent of her soaps, it almost gives me the illusion of life.

I wish I were. To alleviate the fear in her eyes. To meet them with my own. I would give anything to have her *see* me.

Holding her in my arms is a grand substitute. She may not be able to lay eyes upon me, but she is mine in every other sense.

For the first time, I feel naked as I unsheath myself from the scalding hold of her body. Even in slumber, her glorious muscles fight to keep me embedded within her.

"Do not fret. I'll return what's yours soon enough." My

lips find her neck as I lift her. She's weightless in my arms drifting her into her bedroom and laying her onto the sheets of her bed.

Instinct has me grabbing at the blanket to pull over the goosebumps forming on her cooling skin.

Damnation. I cannot offer the solace I crave to provide. Useless to interact with her world, frustration builds within my chest. Even if she is mine, she will still have to face this world alone as I watch. Helpless.

Mundane tasks, opening the door for her, pouring her coffee, all impossible for me.

I'm useless. Unfit. A waste. A mongrel.

The biting ire of my father's words sizzle through me. Memories of the pain of his whip punctuate each word.

Rage without focus coils its vile serpentine knot beneath my skin. Seething, it rolls inside me, battering to be free.

Distance. I need space from her. She is my only tangible; I'll not unleash this darkness on her.

My hands spasm to grip her, to squeeze her and watch her writhe.

Pushing away, the room fades. The tether that binds me to her thins as details fog and blend into gray.

The fervor within me lashes out into the void.

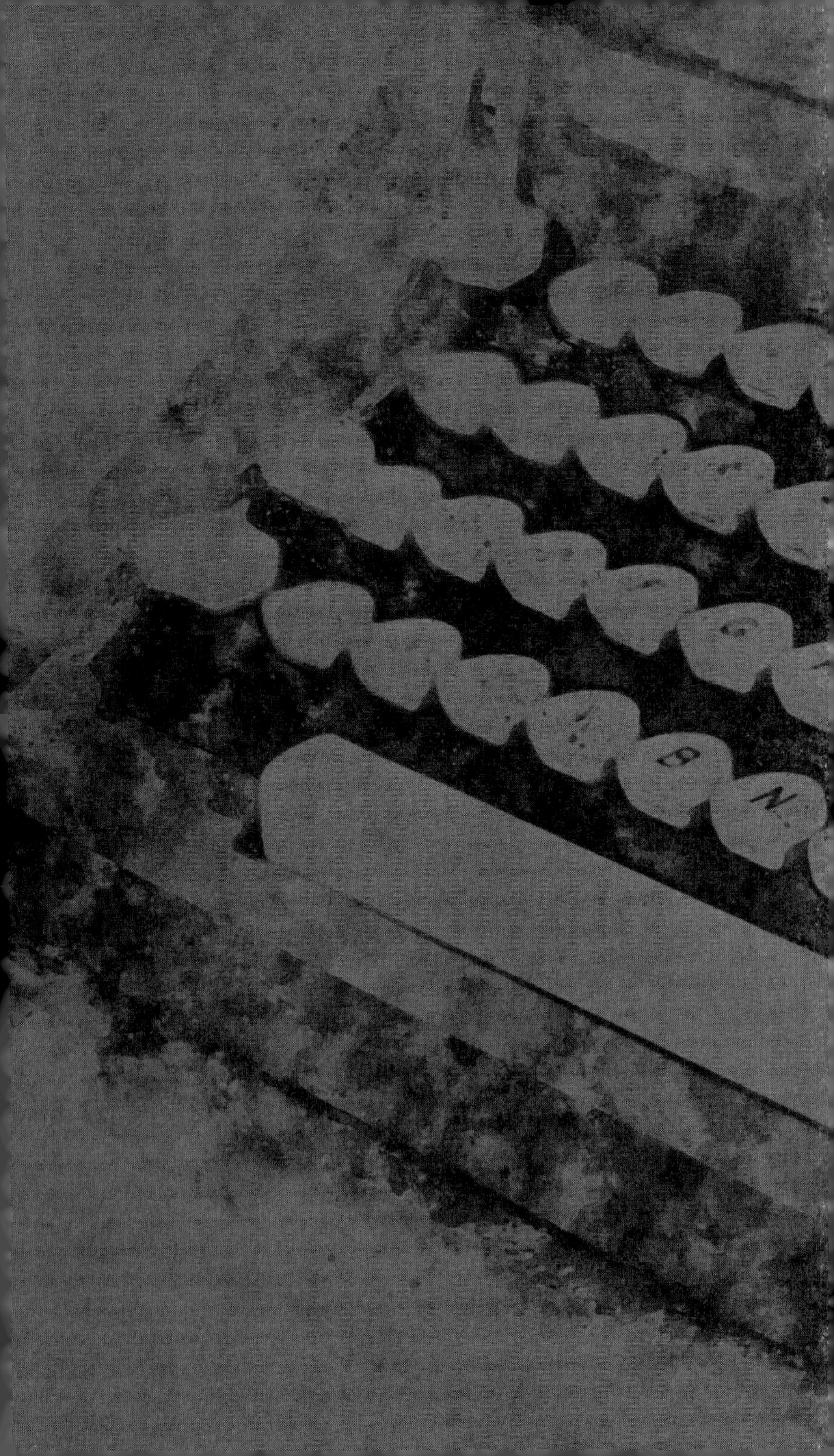
B
N

Chapter 12

Alice

Where the fuck is my cell phone? I can hear it ringing.

The blanket is wrapped around me like I'm a damned chimichanga.

I had the craziest dream about Henry.

Wait. I'm naked. My legs are trapped in the sheets because my pants are still around my ankles.

Ice grips my stomach. It was real. And, holy wow, I can feel it as I fight to free myself. My lady bits are aching, but not in a bad way. More like dusting off the ol' cobwebs.

I'd call that a house cleaning. No more dust mites for me.

Although, my living room needs a maid now. I have pieces of clothes scattered everywhere.

It's half a second away from going to voicemail when I slide to accept the call.

"Hello?"

"Miss Brooks?" A woman's voice asks.

"Speaking." I remember one time reading scammers try

to trick you into saying yes on a call. Now, I never say it. Not sure if it's true though.

"My name is Kathy. I'm calling from the radiology lab to schedule your cat scan. We had a cancellation and can get you in tomorrow at nine am if you're available on such short notice?"

"Tomorrow would be great, thank you." What is dripping down my leg?

"Sounds good. We'll see you then. Please dress comfortably and don't wear any jewelry. Have a nice evening."

My eyes flick to the window where the sun is setting behind the trees.

I slept for almost three hours.

Wiping the inside of my thigh absentmindedly, there's not really anything on my fingers that I can see.

But, I can feel it. Thick and viscous.

"Fucking ecto-jizz, Henry?" This is the first time I've had sex without a condom. Can someone get pregnant by a ghost?

That would make a weird book.

Who am I kidding, this whole thing would be unbelievable even as fiction. I've never written a paranormal romance, but there's a first time for everything.

My tummy rolls, and I'm not sure if it's nerves knowing I have to go to the hospital tomorrow or hunger.

Wine will fix either one.

TOO MUCH WINE MAKES THE ALARM CLOCK EXTRA SPECIAL THIS morning. It's probably good Henry never came back.

"He's a wham, bam, thank you ma'am kinda ghost, Daisy. I'd like it if you could bite him in his invisible nuts when he returns."

The way she tilts her head must mean she completely understands me.

It's not that I really expect him to be a snuggler, but it always feels strange when there are crickets the next day.

"Don't let me say it, Daisy. It's so fucking bad." Her ear pops up with her nose remaining on her paws.

"I knew you'd make me say it, the worst pun ever. I got ghosted by a ghost." Ouch. It hurts to verbalize it. "Terrible. Look at what you're encouraging. I hope you're proud of yourself."

I may have no afterglow hangout time with him, but I do still feel *good*. My limbs feel light, and a good night's sleep has a little pep back in my step.

Comfy cat scan clothes on. Day old microwaved coffee in hand and I'm starting to feel human.

"No parties while I'm gone, Daisy." Her other ear pops up before I close the door.

There isn't much paperwork to fill out at the hospital. It doesn't take long for the older woman with an array of badges hanging from her scrubs to usher me into the coldest room I've ever been in.

"I'm sorry, the heater is on the fritz. I have some blankets you can use to bundle up in. The table always seems to make the chill worse."

She's right. The table is sub-zero and I think I'm frozen to it. The paper-thin polyester blanket does nothing to curb the cold.

As the table slides slowly into the biggest metal doughnut I've ever seen, her tinny voice garbles out of a small speaker near my head. "Just remember, you have to stay completely still. It's normal to hear a clicking sound."

"Got it. I'll try not to shiver too hard."

"I'm sorry, hun. If you can stay still, we will be done much faster." The static sound disappears when she keys off the mic.

This sucks.

The soft smell of horses and leather makes my heart beat a little faster.

"Are you in pain?" Henry's rich baritone washes over me as his fingers brush my hand beneath the eggroll wrapper they are trying to pass off as a blanket.

"Um. Uh-huh." I hate it when he asks me questions when other people can hear me. Real or not, I really don't need *everyone* thinking I'm off my rocker.

"Is everything okay?" The static kicks out around her words.

"Yes, I'm sorry, I'm a writer and thought I would take advantage of the time to work through a scene." Everyone knows authors are a little eccentric.

Henry's touch disappears, but her voice continues. "Oh, fun! What kind of stuff do you write?"

Fuck. I hate that question.

"Smut. Lots and lots of sexy romance." There's a fifty-fifty chance she will either be intrigued, or look down on me with disdain.

"Smut," Henry growls, his finger tickles along the lobe of my ear. "That sounds filthy. Sm-ut." He emphasizes the "T" and I feel his beard pop against the skin of my cheek.

"Oh. That's nice, hun." The speaker goes silent. I've never been happier to be judged so she will leave me alone with his hands.

"Can they see you?" His finger trails down my chest and

circles my breast, ignoring the layers of fabric. It takes everything in me not to jerk at his touch.

"Yep." My answer should be ambiguous, but even talking to him brings heat to my cheeks.

"But, they can't see me. Or what I am doing to you."

Oh, fuck. He's right. I'm stuck having to be completely still. "Please, no."

"Don't move, my little minx, lest they express their ire." His lips close around my hardened nipple. Electricity courses through my body as I feel him rolling it between his teeth.

"Stop, please!" I try to hiss it quietly, but the speaker must be more sensitive than I expected.

"Is everything okay?" Her voice breaks through the static.

Shit. "Yes, I'm sorry, my leg is spasming." A cold sweat is breaking out on my forehead.

He tightens his jaw, pinching then licking the pain.

"Please try and stay still. We're almost halfway through." The exasperation behind her words drips through.

"Yes," Henry adds, his hot mouth leaving my skin. "Be still, but I'm just getting started."

His hands find my wrists, pinning them to the table as he settles his body onto my legs.

How can he weigh that much when he's not even there?

"Henry, don't." I hope squeezing my eyes tightly doesn't mess up the scan. His torturous mouth keeps traveling down my belly, plucking the skin between his teeth as he moves. Each time he releases a bite, it's like I'm getting poked with a knife. But, his hot tongue that follows takes the sting away.

"Now, this," he pauses. I can feel his whiskers tickle

against the mound of my pussy. "I neglected to indulge in this dessert last time. I need to make up for that travesty."

His words almost drown out the clicking of the cat scan machine. Please, let this be over soon.

As he frees my left wrist, my arm reaches up involuntarily to be blocked by the useless blanket.

The only thing it's good for, apparently.

"Please remain still." Badge lady is starting to sound irritated with me.

I don't care. All I can focus on is the fiery trail of his finger as he follows the curve of my hip.

"You should be bare before me. I can't wait to see you spread before me again." The very tip of his finger teases the apex of my thighs.

"Again?" Cold floods over me. That night, it wasn't a dream. He was there. it was really him I felt between my legs. It was *his* head.

"Mhmm. From the moment I saw you, I knew you were my heaven. Eternity seems a short amount of time to be buried—" He slides his finger down in a slow thrust, rubbing against my clit in sweet friction. "—In the luxury of your tight little cunt."

I wonder if he was this intense when he was alive.

I'm sizzling. And when he pulls back his hand and slips in his tongue in its place, I feel like water thrown in hot grease. I can't stop my hips from trying to buck under the fervor of his ravenous mouth. Even with his elbows framing me and holding me in place, my back arches and a moan escapes my lips.

Pressure builds in my belly as he licks and sucks. His chin is pressing between my thighs so hard I think his beard is rubbing me raw.

A hard nip with his teeth and I'm shuddering through an orgasm when the table whisks out of the cat scan.

Angry Badge Lady is glowering over me and peeling back my eyelids while she shines a flashlight in my eyes.

Her sidekick is on my other side, grabbing my hand out from under the blanket, and I can feel him taking my pulse.

"Are you okay? Can you hear me?" She flicks the lights between my eyes.

"Yes, I'm fine. Is there something wrong?" Fucking Henry is still on my hips, chuckling. My legs are shaking with his laughter.

"It appears you had some sort of seizure. Do you know where you are?"

Funny how she can sound concerned and pissy at the same time.

"Yes, I'm at the hospital."

"Very good. What is your full name?" The way her eyes pinch says she's leaning much harder on the cranky side now.

"Alice Nicole Brooks."

She gives me a curt nod and straightens before turning to her helper. "Call Dr. Evans and tell him not to worry about coming down."

He hurriedly leaves. Great, now I'm going to make some doctor I don't even know mad.

When she looks back at me, the furrow in her brow is so deep, I'm pretty sure I could plant corn in it. "I think we're done for today. Your doctor will call you with the results."

Her ass was not clenched that tightly when she left the room last time.

"Henry, you're making me look crazy," I hiss at him as I struggle to get up.

"My pleasure." His words fade with his touch.

Fuck.

Cold seeps back into my bones as I whip the thinnest blanket in the world off, grab my stuff and stalk out of the room.

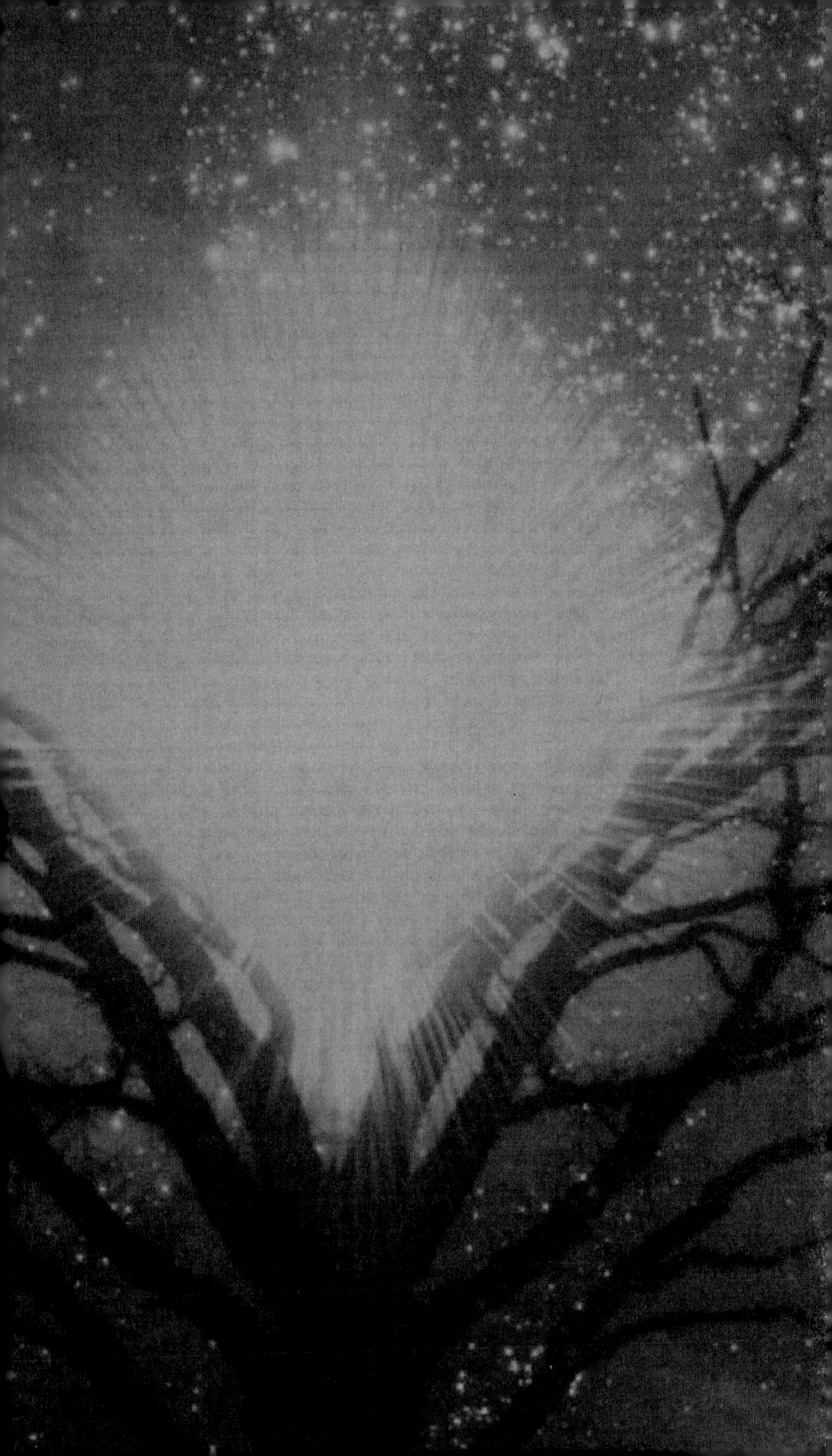

Chapter 13

Henry

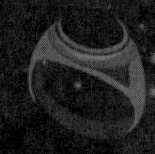

I'm enjoying this view of her. Anger brings fire to her eyes and a set to her jaw. It awakens a need in me to break her. To have her fury screaming in passion. I want to see her unleash her wrath on my cock while I fuck that tightened mouth.

Perching in front of her while she drives, she stares hard enough through me, I can almost fool myself into thinking she can see me.

No longer able to resist, I alight a touch on one of her whitened knuckles gripping the wheel with which she steers.

"You're beautiful when you're angry."

She doesn't startle. I'll take that as a sign she is growing used to my presence.

"If you're real, I wish you'd learn some manners. If you aren't real, I wish I could learn to turn you off sometimes. They're going to think I'm nuts, for sure." She pulls the corner of her lip between her teeth and transfixes me.

"I'm not a rule follower. And I'll use every advantage I have to remind you that I am here for you and you alone."

My fingers follow her wrist and I idly stroke the inside of her elbow. "Did you not enjoy yourself? You appeared to be rather chilled and quite bored just lying there."

That petulant lower lip juts out. "Yes, it was boring."

I can see her nostrils flare minutely as I drift closer. "Can you smell me?"

Her nod assures my curiosity.

"What scents do I carry? Do I smell of death?" I can't draw my own scent. It would be terrible if I reminded her of a corpse.

"No." She takes a long inhale, the corner of her mouth rising. "You smell like leather and horses. A hint of whiskey and gunpowder."

I'm pleasantly surprised to hear I don't smell of rot. "How does such a modern woman know the smell of gunpowder?"

Her cheeks redden as she pauses. "I took some shooting lessons once for a book I was writing and remember that smell." Her gaze unfocuses as I watch her reminiscing.

"What, pray tell, summons that blush?" I must know everything about her.

"The shooting instructor." A burst of red floods her cheek, and I feel the knot of envy grow within me.

"Did you love him?" My teeth ache as I grit them.

"What? No. We just flirted. Does that make you jealous?" She silences the car in front of the grocer's and unbuckles the restraint belt.

My grip tightens on her arm, preventing her exit. "Of course, I'm jealous. I envy any man who can catch your gaze. Any lips that have caressed your body. I wish only to keep you for myself, but I cannot so much as bring you a drink or help you don your coat." I make myself loosen my hold and drop a gentle kiss against the blemishes still marring her neck from my teeth. "Therefore, I will lay claim to your heart, as that is the ultimate treasure."

Her mouth opens and closes without sound as she pauses. "Henry, this can't be permanent."

The truth savages its way through me. But, I am determined to prove to her otherwise. Fate would have not brought me here for any other reason.

She pulls away and I am left to stew in the frustrations of my very existence.

I RESERVE CONTACT UNTIL SHE RETURNS TO HER HOUSE. THE glower she carries exudes her resistance to communication.

At least the dog seems happy to see me. It perplexes me how she can see me, but Alice can't.

Fitting. My father always called me a mongrel. Somehow, it's appropriate.

Once she changes into her baggy gray pants and finishes her glass of wine, I dare a soft rest of my palm on her shoulder.

"Do you despise me so vehemently for my urges to bring you pleasure?"

Her fingers are still their tapping on the strange lettered board she holds on her lap. She looses a long sigh before she answers. "No, I don't hate you. But, do you have any idea how bizarre this entire situation is?"

"Imagine how strange it is for me?" Rubbing concentric circles with my thumbs where her neck curves to her collar elicits a delicious moan that has me hardening behind her. "Thrust from darkness into the room of a beautiful woman who was spread in the glorious nude before me." She lolls her head forward onto her chest as she relaxes.

Did she just giggle?

"Did I say something amusing?" My lips brush the exposed skin behind her ear.

She shivers with another small laugh. "You said 'thrust.'"

This draws a chuckle from my own chest. She can be so clever, then so crude. It's always a surprise what she will say.

My fingers splay and work their way slowly down her back. Not the chair, nor her clothes, offer any obstacle to caressing her skin.

"Mmm, Henry, that feels so good."

That low moan of pleasure tickles through me until my pants bind my cock uncomfortably. With a thought, the restriction is gone. There are few benefits to being invisible, but I'll indulge in drifting naked and hard while working my hands over her supple form.

The smoothness of her skin draws me up to the curve of her breasts, which I cup in my hands, kneading steadily as the heat of her body burns against my chest.

"Show yourself to me as you were that first night." I must taste her. "Taunt me with your beauty." A small sample of the sweet sensitive lobe of her ear. "Let me define the word 'thrust' so you forever have the thought of me buried in your sweet cunt when you hear it." My teeth find the memory of my marks on her throat and she shivers against me.

When her fingers dig into my hair, a triumphant ribbon winds through me. She abandons the board on her lap to clatter to the floor as she arches into my hands. I reward her with a firm tug on her taut nipples and my tongue finds the clevis of her neck.

"Oh, Henry...your fucking...mouth..." She's panting and writhing beneath me. I can't resist the allure of her any longer.

"Take." I pluck the thin skin of her neck between my teeth and release it. "Your." Another nip, harder. "Fucking clothes." I draw closer to her ear, pulling the tender flesh so tightly my incisors snap when it slips free. "Off."

She claws at the hem of her baggy shirt and leans away from me to pull it over her head. Her dark hair cascades down her bare shoulders in a bold contrast to her pale back.

It wraps elegantly between my fingers with which I entwine the tendrils into an unforgiving knot around my fist. The way it gloves my hand is almost the first sign of my substance I've actually been able to see. The angry red marks I have tattooed on her throat are barely a glimmer of the brands of possession I long to cover her with.

Her hips raise and lower to her chair as she slides the offensive knickers from her body, leaving her fully exposed.

A blank canvas.

"On your knees." The slightest tug on her hair has her spilling from her chair before me. Her eyes fly open as her hands land on my bare thighs, her cheek brushing the throbbing cock between us.

The fear returns as her eyes focus across the room, through me.

Anger prickles through my chest and I lash forward to grab the neck I had been kissing so feverishly.

Forcing myself not to squeeze as hard as I'm wanting to, my frustration pushes my words through my teeth. "Keep your eyes closed, or I'll choke the light out of them."

Panic flutters across her features, her cheeks flush red

and her nails dig sharply delicious pain into my thighs. But, she closes her eyes.

"Good girl." My fingers loosen and sweep an errant tendril of her dark hair behind her ear. "Now open that mouth. I want to see your lips stretch around me."

With one hand still knotting her hair, my other positions the tip of my rock hard cock against her waiting mouth.

Wet fire races through me as her hot tongue works its way under and she sucks the head into the burning embrace of her throat. The sweet agony of her ministrations spears lightning into my belly. Seeing her stretch and gag around my invisible girth when I push deeper is a new experience, but one I'm enjoying.

"That's it, take more." Pulling her hair forces her closer and drives me deeper. Tears seep from her eyes as she fervently sucks. When her hands work their way up my thighs and she latches them around my shaft, I nearly lose control.

"Do you want me to come in your dirty mouth?" The vibrations of her begging moans quiver through me. She's squeezing her legs together and grinding herself on her heels.

My perfect girl. Getting off just by having my cock down her throat. That sends a twitch into my legs that has me pumping into her face and rips a groan from my chest. Cinders flow through my limbs as her pace quickens. Her teeth roll over the edge of my mushroomed head and I can't hold back any longer.

Erupting into her greedy mouth, she twists and pulls on me as if to rip my length from my very loins and swallow me whole. With each spurt into her, she mewls and shakes with her own tremors of release.

I'm so fucking sensitive it hurts. She's drained me dry and still clings to my softening cock like a laudanum addict reaming a bottle for one more drop.

Jerking her head back, my lips find hers, and I can taste myself on her tongue. "You're such a good cock whore, Alice." Gently, I kiss away the salty tears that still rest on her flushed cheeks. "My sweet vixen." Freeing my hand from her hair, my palms find their way down her trembling sides and cup beneath her thighs.

She's weightless as I wrap her legs around my waist to carry her to her room.

"Now, it's my turn to make you scream until you're hoarse." My teeth find her neck as we drift toward her bed.

Her lips leave trails of fire on my jaw. The nails on her fingers rake my back, crossing the furrows that reside there. Each bump sends tendrils of heat into me, breathing life back into my spent cock.

"Oh, Henry. Are those scars?" Her palms flatten as she explores the ridges across my shoulders. She doesn't pause her exploration when I lay her on her bed.

"It's nothing. Still those hands, woman, or I'll pin them above your head." The last thing I want is her pity.

"Please. I want to know more." Her petulant lower lip juts out, still red and swollen from the friction of my cock.

I can't help but nibble on it.

"I do not wish to dwell on painful memories when I have your wet cunt pressing on my belly." My voice is low as the words slip out against my bite marks on her neck.

Her body is warm and writhing beneath mine. Wrapping around her, I want to envelop her, to absorb her to become one with me. To always feel her hot breath on my chest.

Tracing the line of her collarbone with my lips while her

fingers knot into my hair is a heaven I'd die again for. The dual coals of her nipples bead against my chest, calling to me. Taking one of those taut buds into my mouth tethers a succulent moan from her as she arches to me.

"Oh, my god!" She digs her nails into my scalp. Clasping her luscious breast in my palm, I simultaneously suckle on one nipple while pinching the other. The triumph of her cries hardens me against her thigh.

When both nipples are red and raw with lush marks, I work my way down her belly.

My fingers lead my mouth closer to the soaking recesses of her alluring pussy.

"I love how you've trimmed for me. I can savor the view of your dripping arousal before I feast on your needy cunt." The fact that I can taste her and that it can linger on my lips for hours creates an insatiable drive to devour her.

Teasing the short hairs with the tip of my nose, I let my whiskers mingle in her honey scent before treating myself to a long slow lick.

I long to be able to rub myself against the sheets while I covet her hard clit with my tongue. Ignoring the ache in my rekindled cock, I focus on the delight of her slickened slit. The twisting of her body and the music of her moans tell me she is more than enjoying this.

Her fingers tangle in my hair as she tugs me deeper into her.

For the first time, I'm thankful I'm dead. I'd suffocate between her thighs as tightly as she's gripping me against her.

Sweet purgatory.

Knotting two fingers deep in her violent depths, I roll them and make her hips jump in frantic spasms.

Her moaning grows louder and more impassioned.

Short rapid breaths are a staccato as she twists her body in a rhythmic gyration while she face fucks me. Her ankles clasping behind my head wedge me against her as her back arches through a harrowing climax.

"Henry...!" She draws my name in a tremulous wail until her mouth gapes silently and her body shudders.

My tongue never ceases. She may think I'm a figment, but I will shatter her resolve. One rending orgasm after another to tear down her denial.

Sweat pools along her belly and her legs are slick with it where they limply lay over my back.

"No, I'm not done with you or this pussy." Pushing her thighs up so they press along her chest spreads her before me. A decadent pie, hot and sweet.

I attack her like I'm starving. As if I've been chased across the country by bears and she is my first respite.

Salvation lies in the depths of her cunt and I will eat her whole to reach it.

"Oh, my god! It almost hurts...please...I just need to catch my breath..." Her voice cracks with each word, but I show no mercy.

I will devastate her with my tongue. Long probing licks until I bury my nose in the snug opening and lick around the starred muscle below. The back of my knuckle pushes against her ass and her thighs shake as she tries to pinch me off.

"Henry, I, um."

I can feel her stiffen.

"Mine to ruin, my minx." The heat of my breath presses past my cheeks as I bury my tongue within the tightened ring.

"Oh, fuck!" she screams as her hips rock against me. It

sends a jolt through my body and a need in my stones for my own release.

I know she will love it when I own her every orifice.

Perhaps not tonight. I don't have the patience. My cock is leaking into the void to be seated within her.

"I need you." My voice is raspy as I climb her supple body. Puckering her flesh with my teeth on my journey, I feel the heat of her palms which beckons me to hasten.

Poised and dripping at her entrance, the wet friction thrusts our hips in tandem and we join in a gasping pause.

Her eyes flutter open as I pierce her to my hilt.

There it is. The whisper of fear again.

I cannot contain the growl in my chest as my hand finds her throat. "I told you to keep your eyes closed."

The gentle pressure tightens as my belly slaps hers. She undulates with each of my forceful surges and I feel her body begin to tense beneath me.

Pressure within my loins coils as my hand on her delicate neck squeezes. Her rhythmic grinding on my cock grows erratic as her cries sneak past my grip. The muscles of her glorious pussy spasm and lock down around me as she screams.

Silencing her throes, my own roar fills the room. Ribbons of hot cum spurt from me, milked by the vice-like pulsations of her air deprived climax.

As I soften my hold, she takes a gulping gasp.

Neither of us move, our chests heaving, bellies still twitching. My cock is locked within her until she lowers her legs clasped around me.

"Holy shit." Her deep breaths punctuate each word. "That was amazing."

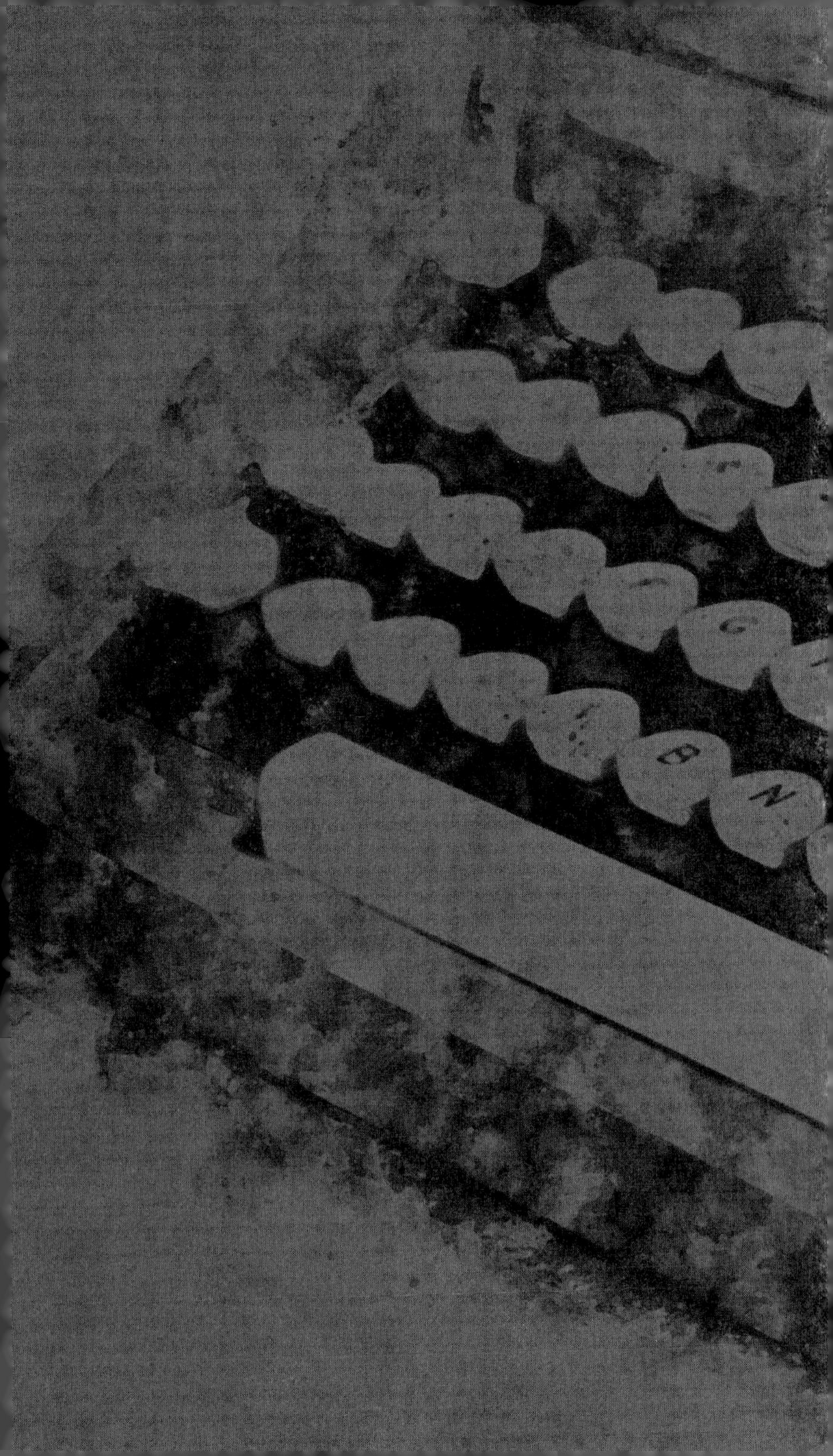
B
N

Chapter 14

Alice

My bladder is screaming at me to wake up, but the warmth of his body wrapping around mine is too nice to want to crawl away from. It's a nice surprise to find him still here. I don't really want to get up. I wish to just enjoy the feel of him against me.

Long slow breaths flutter across my cheek. Did he just snore a little? I didn't think he slept? Don't ghosts haunt all night?

He sure as fuck haunted me. He possessed my pussy like it was a lifeline.

A pussy poltergeist, scaring me with his wicked tongue until I scream. My throat is sore from it. I'm almost positive I'll lose my voice. Or maybe it was the way he was ramming his giant dick into my tonsils.

My god, I'm achy all over, but in the best way. Like after a worthwhile workout at the gym. Except squats don't make my legs all noodles like they are this morning as I stumble to the bathroom.

Shit, the toilet is cold!

"Are you hurt?" His rough palm warms my shoulder just as I am starting to pee.

"Henry, seriously? I'm fine." This whole touching to talk thing has its weird moments.

"Your squeal could wake the dead." He has the gall to laugh at his own horrid pun.

His lips brush my head before I can't feel him anymore. "No watching me on the toilet. That's a new rule," I groan. He might be standing right in front of me, but at least he doesn't have his hands on me *while* I'm using the bathroom. Gross.

Of course my phone rings while I'm in here.

My hands are still wet and it takes three swipes before my stupid cell accepts the call.

"Hello?" I manage to croak out. Crap. Did I miss them?

"Oh! Miss Brooks?" A light pitched woman's voice has surprise lilting her words. "I was afraid I'd missed you. Dr. Myers would like you to come in to go over the results of the cat scan."

Heat blooms across my cheeks as I'm reminded of the debacle in the machine. "Um, yes. Next week sometime?" I still have to find a replacement car. It's easy to forget I need to leave the house with Horny Henry attacking me.

"Well, I'm afraid Dr. Myers was quite insistent I get you scheduled as soon as possible."

A cold stone drops into my stomach.

"Why? Is it bad? What's wrong?" My heart is pounding in my ears.

Henry's big arms embrace me from behind and I feel myself leaning against his broad chest.

"I don't have access to your charts, I'm sorry. You can go over that with the doctor. Will today work?" Her tone is suspiciously neutral and it's making the room feel like there isn't enough air.

"You can't just tell me if it's good or bad?" Why does my voice sound squeaky?

Henry runs his hands up and down my arms. I surprise myself by reveling in the comfort he's offering.

"How does one this afternoon sound? You'll be able to go over all of your questions with Dr. Myers."

"Yes. That's fine. Thank you." Bitch.

"What distresses you?" The soft baritone vibrates through me as his words trail over my ear.

"I have to go back and see the shrink. I hope it's nothing. But, I don't think they usually call so quickly. Fuck."

Why am I just realizing we're both naked? He's hugging up against me and I can feel him getting hard. He rolls his hips, dropping his dick to bury it between my thighs.

"Mmm," he rumbles. "If you insist."

"What?" I can feel my senses dull, and my eyes close as he presses himself tighter, his hands roaming to my belly and breasts.

"You said to fuck." His whiskered lips tickle the back of my neck. "Your wish is my command."

"You're a pretty accommodating genie." I'm losing myself in his hands. He feels so damn good, it makes it easy to forget the stress of the world.

Shit.

"Henry. I have to shower before my appointment." Despite his distracting touch, the thought of what she might say has my stomach rolling.

"I can feel the distraction in your body. Why do you fear that woman so?" His thumb flicks across one of my nipples that is still raw from his teeth. It sends a little zip to my knees that nearly makes me buckle against him.

"It isn't her as much as what she might tell me. It's scary." I might as well admit my fears to him. Who would he tell?

His hands still and he wraps me snugly with his lips to my ear. "You should wear my ring. It brought me luck."

"Henry. You're dead. That doesn't sound very lucky."

"It brought me to you."

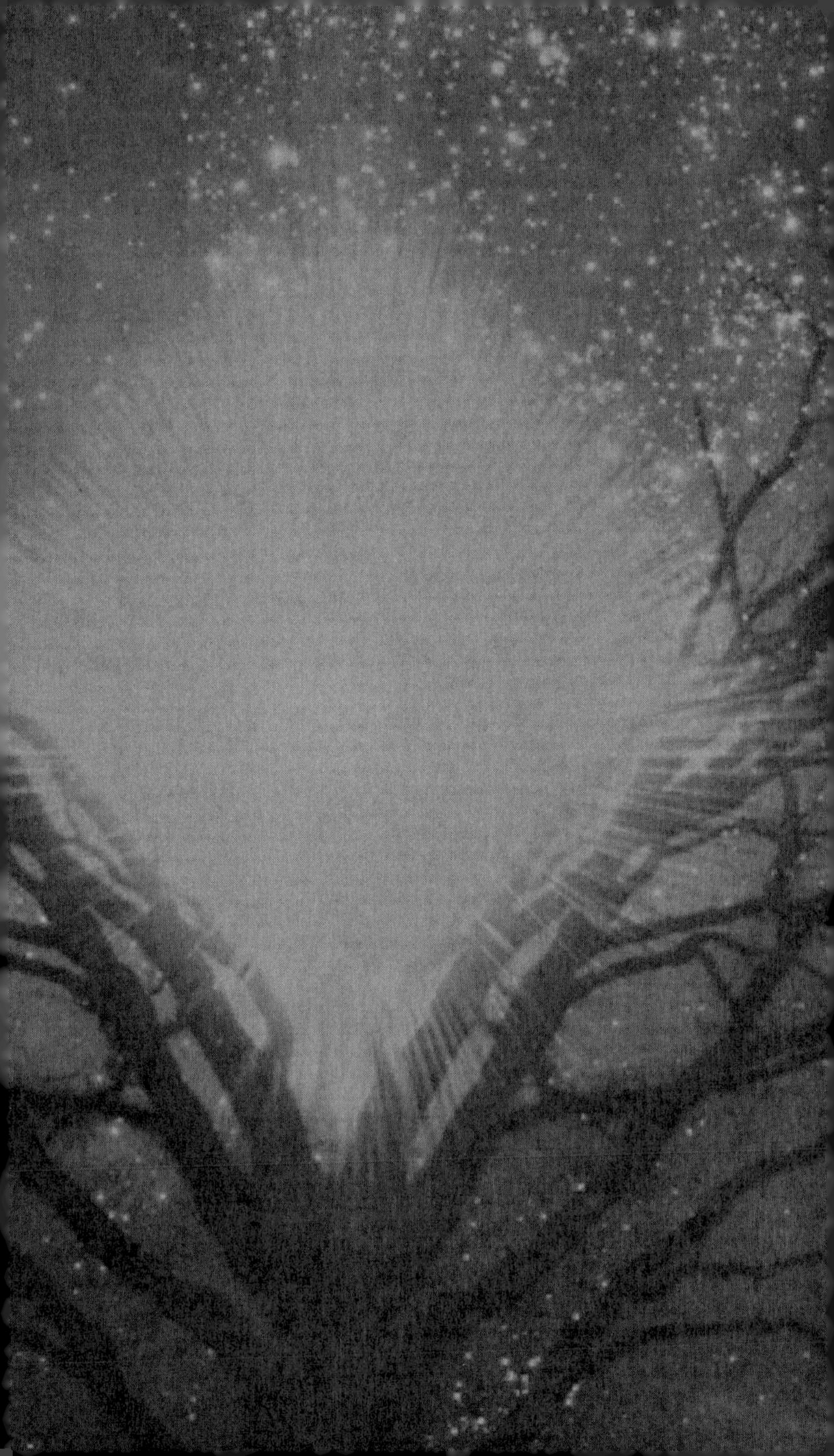

Chapter 15

Henry

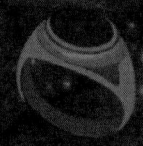

The nervousness that Alice exudes has me hesitant to relinquish my hold on her. It is a pleasant shift in her affect from fear to seeking comfort from me.

But, it twists like a knife in my guts to see her uncomfortable. If I were the man I used to be, I could precede her into any room and use my size to mollify anyone she meets. Now, I am just a shadow, a wisp. She can cling to me only in a sly link of her smallest finger, or subtle touch of my leg.

Her knee bounces under my palm as she awaits the doctor's arrival.

When the old woman arrives, her face carries a disgruntled twist to her features.

"I'm terribly sorry to keep you waiting, Alice. I was going over the results again with the radiologist." She tucks her dark skirt as she sits behind her desk. "And the report indicates you had a small seizure episode while getting the test done? Your health questionnaire didn't indicate a history of seizures or epilepsy. Did the ER doc look at you afterwards?" Her eyes pinch as she stares at Alice who is picking at the hem of her pants.

"I didn't have a seizure." She's so quiet I can barely hear her and I'm only inches away. I want to tuck her strand of loose hair behind her ear, but manage to restrain myself. "I had a muscle spasm in my back. The table was very cold."

Her finger tightens over mine when I laugh. The corner of her mouth turns up as she fights a smile.

"I see. Well, I wanted to show you why I called you in so quickly." She turns a flat black rectangle that looks like a school slate around to Alice. Muddied grays and whites are drawn on it.

Oh, the picture changes when the woman slides her finger over it.

More sorcery. So many strange objects to get used to.

"This is a view of your brain. Each of these slides represents a cross section." She flips through several more images, pointing to a lighter area. "See this area of white? This shouldn't be here."

Alice looses a small gasp. Her hand moves to squarely cover mine. My ring on her thumb burns pleasantly on my wrist, not the scald I experienced the last time I touched it.

"What does that mean?" she whispers. The tone of her skin pales and I worry she may faint again.

"Well, it appears to be a mass affecting your temporal and frontal lobe. If it is benign or malignant, we won't know without further testing. But, this explains the hallucinations you've been experiencing."

When Alice leans back, she draws her hand from mine and rubs her temples.

Anger boils within me that that woman's words have rattled my girl so intensely. Why has a picture caused such a response?

"I understand this is a lot to take in. I'll send a referral to a neuro-oncologist I know who can get you started." Scribbling something on a small square of paper, Dr. Myers leans her thin arm over the desk and hands it to Alice. "This is his office number. Give him a call soon." Sitting back in the high-backed chair, she sets the rectangle down before intertwining her fingers.

"This may be a good thing. Chances are you've caught it early. Any headaches? Difficulty sleeping? Vertigo?"

Alice's warm breath drifts across me as her hand seeks mine. "Not really. Just a little tired." She gives me a subtle squeeze.

That's my girl. Happily exhausted because of me.

"I'll also call in a script for something to help you sleep. This may be a turbulent time, but rest is very important. Remember, this is just a preliminary finding, and isn't a diagnosis. Knowing is the biggest hurdle. Please make another appointment with me after you see Dr. Richardson."

"Thank you, Doctor. I appreciate you letting me know." Alice stands stiffly and leaves the office.

I drift a few feet away before I realize she's stopped outside the door and is leaning against the wall.

A tear on her cheek catches the light from the ceiling. It sends a stabbing pain into my chest and I rush to her.

Kissing it away, I wrap my arms fully around her. The cinder block offers no resistance to cocooning her with my body. Relief floods me as her stiff shoulders sag when she relaxes.

"What is it she said that troubles you?"

Alice seems to grasp fully the weight of the doctor's words.

Damn my ignorance. My wisdom lies in my hands. If

only this were a brawl. To win or lose by sheer will and tenacity. The words are still a jumble to me, a confusing assortment that may as well be a foreign language.

"It means you're not real, Henry. You are a figment of my fucked up brain." Teary emerald eyes look up and stare through me. Her hollow gaze rends my heart from my chest.

"I wanted you to be real." The words are soft that feather across my neck, but they burn white hot as if she's holding a branding iron against me.

My fury flames within me. I want to pin her again, to force her to accept me. This fetid feeling of helplessness plagues me.

If only I could prove to her, somehow, that I exist. I'm here *for* her, *because* of her. Ineptitude freezes my movements.

Do I exist? Am I just a figment? How would that be possible?

No. I must figure out a way.

"Then, indulge me in the charade." My forehead drops to her shoulder. "Pretend with me. What harm is in a fantasy?" My begging voice cracks into the hollow of her throat.

Please, don't ignore me. It is my greatest fear that she abandons me to the periphery. To become a lingering nuisance condemned to an eternity of watching her live her life. Losing this feeling of holding her, breathing her in: it would be hell.

When she rolls her head back, her eyes close and a small smile plays on her lips. "There's no harm in fantasy. I make my living on it."

Faded pink blemishes still mar the smooth skin of her exposed throat, proof of my teeth that lives on her body.

Yet, she denies my heart because of what that foolish old woman said.

"I'll be your waking dream." My hands move down her body and she arches into me. "It is a fine purpose to fulfill your every desire." The gravel in my words turns to molten kisses as my tongue works up to her ear.

"You know, even if you aren't real, I'm glad I have you." Her eyes squeeze tightly, pressing out fresh tears. "You're my favorite kind of crazy." The cool tickle of her fingers in my beard turns my cheek so she can touch her lips to mine.

The ghostly echo of my heartbeat rushes through my ears as a blaze of heat fills my belly. Part of me wants to push further into her, to claim her here in this hall. Another falls into the gentle ferocity of her tender lips.

A sweet tinge of coffee lingers on my tongue as the approaching clicking of shoes forces us to stop.

She pushes away from the wall and wipes the dampness from her reddening cheeks before making her way to the door.

The entirety of her voyage home she is an eruption of information. She talks of her youth as an only child, the loss of her parents, and triumphs in her writing. Stories of her past endeavors with men rankles me so much my knuckles pop when I squeeze my fist, but I remain quiet. My other hand remains placid in her grasp as I cling to every word.

This is my opportunity to learn more, so I can find the tendrils that lead to her heart and bind her more tightly to me. I want more than just the bond that drew me to her. I want her to crave me in return.

After a few stops, we return to her home.

I can't help her with her bags. Nor open the door to welcome her in. Perhaps I'm not really here. Maybe the fantastical properties of her amazing mind manifests me to be her companion.

Daisy rolls and boils in manic excitement when Alice pushes through the door.

"Yes, yes, hi, girl! Let me put my stuff down!" The dog doesn't seem pacified by her pleas, instead weaving around her legs and nearly tripping her.

"Dog!" My tone comes out gruff, but I'm not touching Alice for her to hear.

With a startled pause, the heeler abruptly turns and faces me before cocking her head to the side.

"Ah, so you *can* hear me. Go to your bed and stay out of the way."

She trots to me and I try to pat her, but my hand drifts through her ears. With a half-step sideways, she climbs onto her cushion and lies down.

"Good girl, Daisy!" Alice calls with her head in the cooling machine.

What a marvel a cold drink on a hot day would be. They were often too rich for my abilities, available in only the finest restaurants. Finding an icy creek was usually my only option.

"Henry?" She tosses a small pill into her mouth, then holds her hand out expectantly until my palm finds hers. "Do you want to watch a movie with me? I don't think I'm in the mood to write tonight." A drop of condensation runs down her wine glass as she takes a sip. "I'm thinking of Tombstone. Have you ever heard of Wyatt Earp?"

"I am very familiar with a tombstone. But, I don't know any Earp."

"Oh! I'll need to look up when he was born. He was a famous sheriff in the old west. Kurt Russell is so fucking hot in it."

The thought of her pining over a sheriff brings bile to my throat. "I've never found common ground with the law." Her arm stretches behind her as my pace slows. Is she inviting him in?

Tinkling laughter, she turns to me with a broad smile. "It's on TV, Henry. It isn't real. Make believe. Theater. Have you ever seen a play?" She gives me a persistent tug, coaxing me to the couch.

"There was a fine show in one of the whorehouses in St. Louis. They had fifty girls." Afterwards, they'd be auctioned for the night. I only won once and she stank of rot between her legs. The ripe bastard of a manager wouldn't give me a refund either.

"Wow! That's a lot. This isn't like that, but you might like it." When she stretches out on the couch, my cock stiffens at the glimpse of her bare belly beneath the hem of her shirt.

"I like everything I do with you." Sliding up her body, I drag my hardened length against her so she can feel what she does to me.

"You know, Henry? It's easier now that I know you aren't real. It's like...I can indulge in you and I know you're safe." Her eyebrows pucker and she frowns. "I just can't get over how fucking real you are to me."

When her fingers find my hair, she rakes sparks through my scalp with each pass. Her reluctance to accept me as anything other than her imagination does have some benefits.

I'll win her over with time.

For now, I'll let her pretend. This level of comfort she's exhibiting is addictive. It's as if she treats me as more real now than when she was doubting.

With her eyes squeezing tight, a grimace teases the edges of her lips down. "What's it like to die?"

If I wasn't lying next to her, I wouldn't have heard.

"Well." How do I answer this? "It went quickly. I don't really remember the moment."

"What happened? Wait, let me guess. A shootout?" The way she nestles against me is maddening. My pulse races with my body pressing to hers.

"Nothing quite as glorious, I'm afraid. A double cross." With a delicate trace down her arm, my fingers draw gooseflesh from her skin.

"Please tell me." Her nose finds the hollow of my throat and she burrows in with a sigh. Our legs intertwine, her arm loops across my chest, and I have never felt such a perfect moment before this.

"My partner took my girl, my money and my life. I thought he got all the best parts of me. I'm just glad he can't take you."

"Me, too." Her breath is warm against me. "You're all mine." Her body arches in a yawn.

My heart lurches. She may not believe I'm real, but I'll relish this for eternity. "And you are mine."

Gentle sleep takes her in my arms. As her slumber grows, the tether of our bond grows hotter.

At first, it's a pleasant burn. But, where her hand rests wearing my ring, it soon becomes a scorching fire that feels as if it's melting my very skin.

"What in tarnation?" I have to get her arm off of me.

Tugging it away, she rolls in her sleep exposing the strangest thing I've ever seen.

A soft glow erupts from her chest. Pale gold that shimmers a trail to her arm and centers on my ring.

The pull in my chest is violent, urging me closer to her. A grating need to draw closer has my fingers tracing the smooth skin of her neck to the apex of the aperture of light.

When my palm flattens against the flat of her chest, the world rushes in a vortex of swirling lights. My body prickles in sensation. Rough fabric, heat, cold. A tangle of clothes binds my chest. My feet are bare and I can *feel* the supple contour of the couch.

My eyes fly open, and I'm no longer in repose looking down at Alice.

I'm within her.

Her hand waves as my own before my eyes.

My fingers tickle across my scalp and pull at the long dark strands.

What wizardry is this?

My lungs hurt. With a spasming breath, I can smell the room. The dog. The wine on the table. There is old wood ash in the stove. A sour smell of rubbish drifts from the bin near the kitchen.

How in the fuck?

When I sit up, her breasts shift on my chest.

Unable to resist, I explore her body as if it were mine.

It is mine. Is it? How is it possible that I can inhabit her?

A glint of silver catches my eye.

My ring on my, well, her finger.

It's hard to sit up. Vertigo has the room spinning and I struggle to maintain my balance.

Daisy tilts her head and her nose raises, testing the air.

Tentatively, she rises from her bed and slinks closer. Her head is down and only the tip of her tail moves.

"Good girl." My voice is not my own. Alice's sweet sound echoes in my ears.

Daisy takes another step to me, her ears perking higher until her nose rests near my knee. Alice's knee.

This is so confusing.

My arm feels heavy as I lift it to pat the silken fur. Running my fingers over her head, I watch as she lolls her tongue and her tail picks up frequency.

It feels fucking amazing to touch. I've been bound to only Alice as my only source of sensation. But, this, this is incredible.

"You're a fucking good girl, Daisy. Now, don't laugh when I learn to walk."

Wait. What happened to Alice? Is she still within? Can I talk to her?

Squeezing my eyes, I try to conjure images of the woman I've grown so fond of.

Where are you?

My hands still buried within the ruff of the patient pup, I give up on my internal search. An urge to explore overtakes me. On wobbly legs, the solidity of the cool floor is an odd obstacle.

Like a child in the grocer's, my fingers trail over every surface. All of these foreign devices have intrigued me. Cold steel, smooth stone bar tops, small buttons are all textures I have pondered but now can feel.

The cool push of air is a surprise when I open her chilling box. One side is frozen as if winter is locked inside. A biting freeze burns my fingers, but I cannot resist dancing them over the frosty surfaces.

There is a tingling in my chest as the frigid temperature

basks over me. Looking down, I see that her nipples are erect and pointed beneath her shirt.

I can't resist. To know what she feels is an extraordinary opportunity of insight. My fingers close over the firm buds, causing lightning to jerk pleasantly through me to my belly.

Her belly.

Fuck. This is confounding.

But, the sensation is pleasant. And, when I cup them in my hands, the sides are nearly as responsive as the tips.

A new map of areas to lavish my tongue across aligns as my palms explore this body of hers.

That I now will know inside and out. She is mine completely.

A flare of possession simmers within. I know her better than any other. The gloating pride bubbles rich at the claiming of her. No other has ever been this intimate.

My hands trail over the full swell of hips, tracing to plunge beneath the snug band of her pants to her wet heat.

Holy hell, that feels good. Just a light touch with the ends of my fingers and it sends shivers of heat into my limbs.

I had no idea her beautiful cunt was *this* sensitive. And yet it can withstand the raging flogging my cock gave her last night. Or the teeth I used to make her scream into her own elbow.

One hand still idly stroking her wet clit, my other rummages amongst the unfrozen side of her cooling machine.

My knees buckle and tears well into my eyes as the overwhelming flavor explosion of a strawberry slides across my tongue. I never thought I'd ever experience such a simple indulgence as eating again.

Savoring the sweet tartness and the burning ember of

arousal, I wander her home while dragging my palms over every surface.

Heaviness eventually grows. This possession is exhausting.

The soft blankets of her bed beckon for me to relax into.

Still palming her hot pussy, lazy curiosity shifts into a pulsing heat as my fingers increase the speed with which I flick her dainty fingers.

Unlike when I draw near eruption and I feel the tightening in my stones and belly, hers begins as a heavy pressure that then rolls waves of molten iron through her limbs.

I'm a tad jealous now.

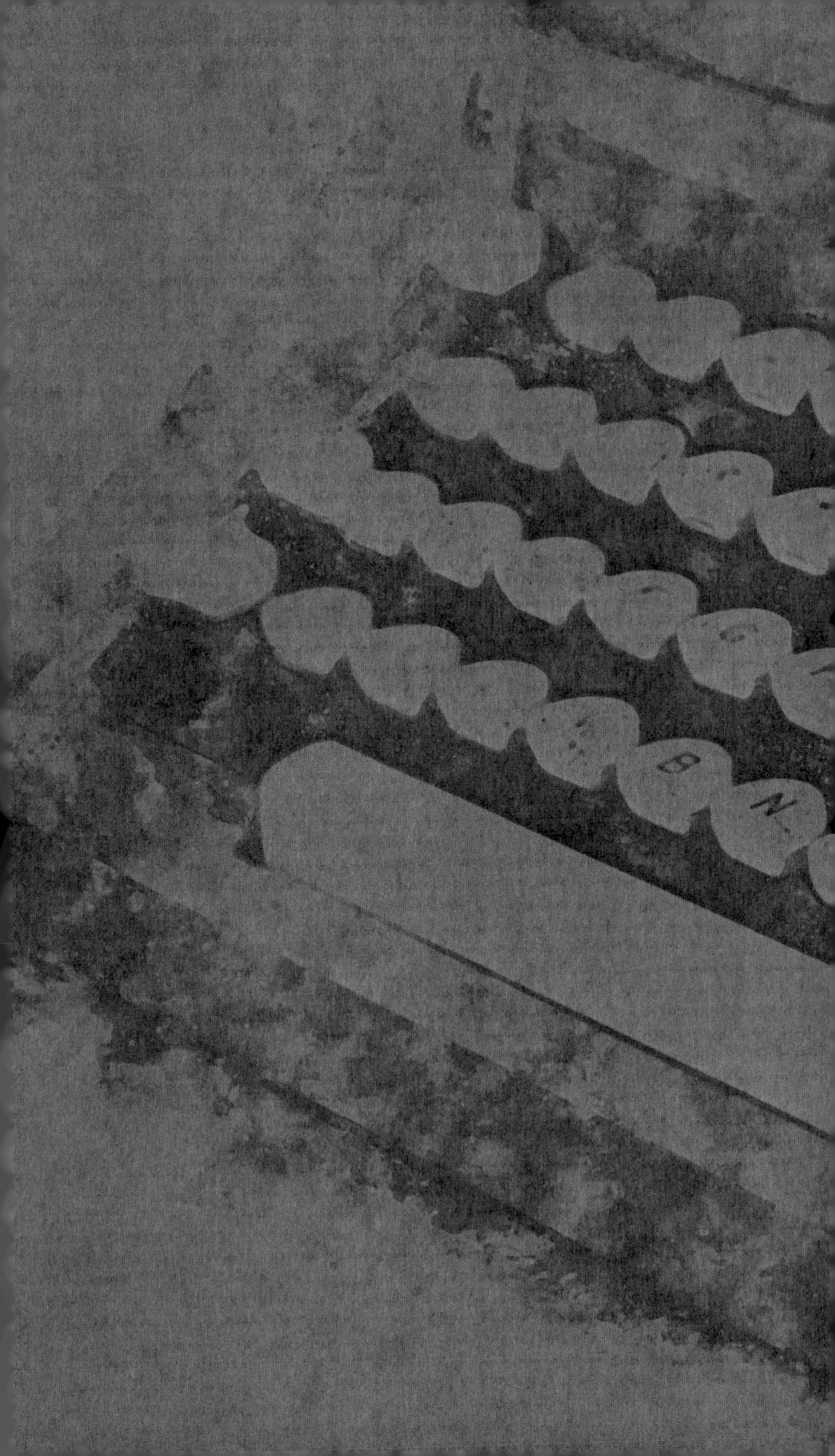

Chapter 16

Alice

ALICE

That sleeping pill kicked my ass. I feel more tired now than before I crashed out.

It's no longer a surprise that I ended up in bed. Henry must have brought me here.

Fuck. No. He's imaginary. I must have walked here in a stupor.

His arm slung across my hips and warm chest pressing against my back sure feels real though.

My lines of reality are all blurry.

Maybe once whatever this is in my brain is taken care of, I'll stop conjuring Henry.

Pain seizes my chest.

Why does that hurt to think about losing him? In just a few days I've gone from being terrified to being comforted by his presence. I wanted him gone. Now, I just want him.

Dammit.

Clinging to the sliver of insanity that he might be real will be my choice. Pretending that he is really another being. Soul? That is here because he is *mine*.

I've read some shitty shifter romances that had all the fated mate stuff. Someone who is devoted absolutely, completely to you, no matter the flaws. I always thought it was bullshit. There's no such thing as a bond like that, is there?

I wish it was true.

Why does my phone always ring when I don't want to answer it?

Flinging off the blanket, I roll to get out of bed when Henry's strong hand encircles my arm.

"No. Stay."

It's hard not to glance toward him. The emptiness makes a hollow rock in my stomach.

"I have to answer it. It might be the hospital." I'm nervous enough about the news.

"You aren't a dog, trained to respond to every whistle." His touch moves a warm path down to my hand and brings it to his lips.

It's eerie, watching my hand float in midair while his whiskers tickle my fingertips as he kisses them.

"But—" He moves my hand down to his stiff erection and runs my palm firmly up and down the length. "—I have a whistle you can blow or come to, whichever you may choose."

My cheeks heat when I feel the drop of pre-cum dampen my fingers.

"Tempting. Save your ecto-jizz for me." His chuckle is cut short as I pull away contact and rush into the living room to try and find my phone.

"Hello?" I barely caught it in time. Again.

"Alice, this is Mark. How are you?"

Shit. Is it bad I forgot all about him?

"Hi, Mark. I'm good, thank you. What's up?" No. Deep

breath. He's real. Henry isn't. I need to focus on what's real. "It's great to hear from you." Maybe that will smooth my initial curt tone.

"Great! I was wondering if you've had a chance to do any car shopping?" His voice sounds hopeful.

I knew I was neglecting something. "Oh! I haven't really found anything I love yet." That's true. But, I also haven't looked.

"I gotcha." He sounds a little disappointed. Wait. We were supposed to have a date.

Henry has me all fucked up.

"Well, why don't we plan on this weekend? I think I can find a good one by then? I still haven't made it to the Parker Dealership to see what they have."

I haven't made it to any dealerships. I haven't even looked online. Too busy getting railed by an invisible dick on my floor.

Or was I?

My head hurts.

"Sounds good. Why don't you pick me up at my office on Main Street at two on Saturday? That way if you find your car, I can take care of your rental for you."

"You're very kind. Okay, it's a date." Did that sound as cliche out loud as it seems?

"See you then."

Something is stuck between my teeth. I hadn't even had a chance to brush them this morning. A small seed? What did I eat yesterday that had seeds?

Maybe that salad before the doctor's appointment. But, all I remember afterwards was taking a sleeping pill, pouring a glass of wine and curling up with Henry on the couch.

Twisting his ring on my thumb, I head into the bathroom to take care of my morning routine.

It isn't until I'm grabbing the milk out of the fridge when I see the top for the strawberries are open.

A lot of the containers in the fridge are open. What the fuck? I must have really been out of it last night. Maybe those sleeping pills aren't the best option if it makes me binge eat.

"A man in your little box asks and you agree to a date?" Henry's hands move heatedly up my arm.

"Henry. You have no idea how much I wish you were real. But, I can't stay in a pretend world. Not when there's a flesh and blood man who is interested."

His grip tightens like a vice on my arm, fingers digging deeply into the tender flesh behind my elbow.

"But, you are mine," he growls. He actually sounds like a feral dog. It's both hot and scary.

"Ow. Look, I am absolutely yours when we're alone. I've never had someone make me feel like you do. You'd be my perfect guy." My heart pangs. Damned right I wish he was real. Being wanted like the way he wants me is what little girls dream of. Turning in his arms, my hand seeks out his cheek and I nestle against his chest.

"There is every piece of me that wishes this were real. But, you saw the same thing I did at the doctor's office. My brain is wrong. I'm seeing, feeling and hearing things that aren't here. I love that it's created you. You're amazing." I take a deep breath. "But, I can't lose myself in an imaginary world. I'd like to have kids someday, Henry. How do you think that would work with a dead guy?"

I'm not sure why I feel the need to rationalize with him. Secretly, I think I love having him to myself. He can't cheat on me, or even talk to other women. He's someone to talk to. And he makes me orgasm like no other.

I hate that my head did this to my heart.

"I would have been a rotten father. I'm no role model." His grip lightens and his other hand trails through my hair.

"It's just a date, Henry. Maybe he's a bigger scoundrel than you." My lips turn up against the lapel of his jacket.

"I'll find a way to kill him if he hurts you." That growl is back, but this time it's super sexy since it isn't aimed at me in anger.

"I'm sure you would."

By Saturday I have a car picked out.

I've also been fucked by Henry on almost every surface of my house.

I'm starting to wonder if I have the energy for anyone else. He's keeping me exhausted, but I'll admit I've never slept better.

"I still do not understand why you would follow through with spending time with him. You fell unconscious in my arms last night on my cock. I don't think that is what an unsatisfied woman does." His disgruntled tone shines through his words.

"Maybe I'm just up for a threesome." I can't fight the sarcasm as I squeeze the steering wheel. Why am I arguing with him?

Oh, fuck.

His fingers tighten around the back of my neck and I can feel his lips draw closer to my ear.

"You have cuckolded me from fucking your little virgin asshole, but now are begging to have this man take what should be mine? Or do you fancy being speared from either end like a boar on a spit?" His strong arms encircle me from behind and I can feel his chest pressing against me through the seat of the car.

"Maybe I shouldn't give you the choice any longer." Hot lips touch the nape of my neck just before he shoves two of his fingers into my mouth. "Get them good and wet like you do when you suck my cock."

Nearly gagging under his invading force, my horny animal brain kicks in and summons a pool of spit around him.

His other hand works its way down and buries itself between my thighs. Sometimes, I wish my clothes offered a barrer. As he rubs against my clit, he sends shivers through my belly.

"Good girl. So ready already." With a sweep of my mouth, his hand leaves my jaw and I feel him pressing against my asshole.

Jesus, I almost wrecked. Swerving the car into a wide spot, I barely have a chance to throw it into park before he's shoving fingers of each hand into me.

"Holy fuck, Henry!"

Undeterred by the car seat, or my clothes, he begins a slow rhythm of pushing into both of my orifices.

"See. I know you like it." His voice is husky as his teeth find the soft skin of my shoulder through my shirt.

Cold sweat prickles on my brow as I lean against the steering wheel like it's a life preserver. And I'm on a churning ocean of thrusting hands and quivering thighs. A tumultuous pressure builds in my belly. When he presses a second finger into each hole, I feel like I might explode.

"Oh! Oh, my god. Oh. Fuck. Please." I can't breathe. He's kneading the air from my lungs with every upward stroke of his hands.

"If his cock gets to go here—" The fingers in my pussy curl and I start to scream. "—then my cock gets to go here." He twists the fingers in my ass in the opposite direction and I erupt in a shuddering climax that soaks through my panties and has me clinging weakly to the wheel.

"Henry. I...I..." I can't even catch my breath.

"I don't give a fuck what you say." He slides his fingers out of me and I melt against the seat. "There are consequences to your choices. I will teach you that you are mine."

An icy ball forms in my stomach as the heat of his touch disappears. I know he's still close, but sulking.

My hands are still shaking as I pull the car back onto the road.

Mark has a pleasant smile on even though I'm a few minutes late.

I can't exactly tell him I had to take a break while my imaginary ghost finger fucked me on the side of the road.

"Hi! It's good to see you again!" I swear he has magically white teeth. He fills the passenger seat with his long legs and the smell of aftershave.

"Thank you for going with me to the dealership." Why do I feel awkward around him?

Maybe because my panties are still wet. Crap, I hope I didn't soak through my pants.

"Of course! I wouldn't want you to be taken advantage of by those salesmen. They can be very pushy." He turns a little in the seat to lock his baby blues on me. "What did you end up finding?"

"Another Subaru, I'm a sucker for them. I found a silver one." Why does it feel like I'm trying to force happiness? Maybe because my limbs are still tingling from Henry's attention.

"Silver is a great color. I'm glad you found something

you like." His hand covers mine briefly before he rests it back on his lap. "I made reservations at the Mexican restaurant on fifth street for later. A margarita always makes a good celebration drink." He flashes me that perfect smile again and settles back in the seat.

He seems nice. His hands are soft, but I know he works a desk job. Polite is a good term.

But, so is boring.

Dammit.

"That sounds wonderful. I haven't been there in ages!" Now I sound like a homebody.

"So, I noticed on your paperwork it said you are self-employed? What kind of work do you do?" His question is innocent, I hope he isn't judgy.

"I'm an author."

"Nice! What kind of stuff do you write?" I feel his eyes burning into the side of my face.

"Fiction."

"Smut." Henry's voice tickles across my ear. "Tell him about the scene we recreated yesterday. Where I fucked you across the table while you pretended to be a barmaid."

Heat flushes up my cheeks. So, yes, I've been taking guilty pleasure in acting out fantasies with Henry. But, he isn't real.

It's getting harder to believe. My brain couldn't come up with half the stuff he's told me about his life.

I hated history in school.

"Fiction? What kind of fiction?" Mark seems relaxed. He can't tell I'm fighting an internal war.

"This and that. I've written some college-based books." It was a bully romance. "And, some contemporary fiction." Office romance. "Um, oh, I wrote some agricultural-based adventures." Cowboys and super steamy. I loved that series. The dude ranch I visited had the hottest wranglers.

They were very inspirational.

"Those sound great! Must be nice to stay home instead of having to work a real job."

A real job.

When I get to the dealership, Mark steps up and does almost all the talking with the salesman. I get the impression he's been here before.

"Well, aren't you a cute one!" The short bald guy is named Randy according to his nametag.

I don't like him already.

"This is Alice. Her last car was totaled in the storm last week. What do you have in silver?" Mark tosses me a wink as he talks to Randy.

"I thought this was your decision," Henry grumbles in my ear. "Is he paying for the new carriage?" I squeeze the finger he slips into my palm and do my best to shake my head discreetly.

"A girl with an eye for shiny! Right this way." Randy waddles toward a line of cars on the far side of the parking lot. The roll of red fat across the back of his neck is slightly transfixing as I follow him.

The row of sporty sedans are bright and colorful. But, it doesn't take long to see that the Subaru coupe I have in mind isn't here.

"Now, take a look at this one! Fully loaded, room in the back for car seats, extra storage in the front. Perfect for a growing family." He smacks the hood like he's in front of a camera and leaves a sweaty handprint over the fender.

Henry growls.

"I, um, I don't have kids." The only thing I like about it is the color. It sits too low to the ground for my gravel road.

I just need room for Daisy and a few groceries. It's not like I'm moving furniture. "Is it all wheel drive?"

He has the audacity to scoff at me. "You don't need that around here! We almost never get snow!"

"Well, I drive to Colorado twice a year and they do." This guy is starting to make me cranky. I'm pretty sure it's coming through in my tone.

"Two wheel drive works well in the snow, too," Mark pipes up.

He isn't helping.

"This is a pretty car for a pretty girl."

Randy, you can kiss my ass.

Henry's fingers tighten on my wrist so hard that I know he'll leave a bruise. "I wish I could give him a ripe pretty pummeling." It sounds like he's gritting his teeth.

I can't fight the laugh. Breathlessly, I walk away from Randy the schmuck and head toward where I see the Subaru parked.

"I want this one." The price tag hangs clearly in the window. It's even three thousand less than the payoff for my car.

"Are you sure? It's a little small." Randy. I swear to fuck, I'm killing you in my next novel.

"Yes. Mark has the check." I turn away from both of them and head toward the main building.

The paperwork doesn't take long since I'm not doing a loan. I wish I could bring cash every time I buy a car; it makes it go so much faster.

"Still on for dinner?" Mark looks apologetic. It's not his fault the salesman was such a chauvinist. But, he didn't have to play it up either.

"Sure. A margarita will get the dirty taste of that prick

out of my mouth." Oops. That may have been a bit much for poor Mark. His face freezes and his smile thins.

"Ah, yeah. Margaritas for everyone. I'll meet you there." His shoulders are stiff as he walks back to the rental car I had been driving.

Henry's deep baritone laugh brightens my mood. "That knob looks like he has a prick up his ass." His body wraps around mine when I climb in the car. It takes me a moment to adjust the seats and he folds himself under me.

It's like I'm sitting on his lap, but it's pokey.

"He doesn't appreciate your filthy mouth. I'll put a taste of a prick in it that you'll swallow down. Over and over." His words stoke a fire in my belly. My addiction to him is becoming dangerous. Consuming.

I can't let him replace reality.

"Maybe he just likes his women a little more demure? There's nothing wrong with being soft and sensitive."

'Your fucking cunt is soft and sensitive. But, it locks me down like a noose around a rustler's neck." Both of his hands bury between my thighs where he lightly strokes me as I drive. "But, I enjoy that biting tongue of yours. It whips me in all the best ways."

"I fucking love you, Henry." Why can't he be real? Of course my brain makes up the perfect man for me.

I am my own tease.

"Alice. You still think of me as imaginary. If you knew the real me, you would not be so quick with your love. I'm not worthy." His breath is warm against the back of my neck.

"You always know what to say or do. You're perfect for me." The parking lot to the Mexican restaurant isn't overly full. "Now, let's see what Marky Mark has in store for this evening."

Henry's hands move up to my chest and he pinches both of my nipples. *Hard.*

"Ow! Not fair!"

"Remember who you belong to," he growls before his touch disappears.

Mark stands up from the table when the hostess guides me over. What a gentleman.

"Alice! I'm glad you made it. I wasn't sure if you still wanted to join me." He slides my chair out and helps me with my jacket.

His smile is infectious as he folds his tall lean body into the seat opposite me. "So, are you happy with your new car?" His eyebrows raise as he takes a drink of water.

"Very much. I love the new car smell. This one has a little more pep than my last one." That might have been me peeling out of the car lot. I had to test that baby out.

The waitress arrives with two large margaritas complete with little umbrellas.

"I went ahead and ordered drinks. You mentioned them a couple of times. Cheers." He holds up his broad glass and I mirror him.

It's delicious. "You remembered the mango! Thank you!"

His smile grows and we manage to find a comfortable conversation while we order our food and eat.

We don't discuss my books again, but I do learn that he's a recent transplant to the area. And that our parents both lived in Illinois at different times in their lives.

The alcohol helps to loosen us both up a little, but also goes straight through me.

Finding the restroom, I'm not surprised when Henry's touch settles on my arm.

"You should bring him home."

"That's not what you said earlier." Touching up my makeup over the sink, I can't help but enjoy the feel of his hands on my hips as he pushes his hard dick against me.

"I've always been the sort that when I'm told I can't do something, I'll move the rivers to do it." His hands stroke up my back and down to my thighs. Trails of fire simmer in their wake. "I've a feeling you're the same. I want you to *choose* my cock, not pine for another sod."

"You should know by now, if you were real, I'd only choose you. I'd stay home, exhausted and dehydrated and thoroughly fucked."

A toilet in the next stall flushes and heat flares up my cheeks. Shit, someone heard me!

An elderly woman swings the door open with a knowing smile on her face.

Pretending to end a phone call, I scramble through a game of charades acting like I'm putting an ear bud into my purse.

"It's okay, dear. But, it sounds like you aren't where you should be." Her eyes twinkle at me in the reflection as she washes her hands.

"I'm so sorry, I didn't know you were—" My cheeks are on fire.

A mischievous grin tickles through the wrinkles around her mouth as she turns to me. Her gnarled hand is still damp when she pats my arm affectionately and she leans closer. "It's hard to find a good fuck."

The lingering scent of some pungent ointment remains after she ambles out the door.

Henry laughs so hard it sounds like he's peeing himself. His chuckles fade. "I despise this. I do not want to lose you." His gentle fingers brush a strand of hair before he breaks contact.

Why do I feel like my heart is breaking? I hate the sound of disappointment in his voice.

This sucks donkey nuts. He's not real.

But, as I walk back toward the table, the pain in my chest is real.

I'm determined to see this through now. If it doesn't work with Mark, I want it to be because of us. Not Henry.

He shouldn't have anything to do with my choices.

Then, why are tears pricking my eyes? I feel like I'm on a precipice.

Mark's forehead wrinkles when he sees me. "Is everything okay?"

"I think so." Cleansing breath. "Hey, do you want to come back to my place for a drink?" Off the cliff I go.

Those perfect teeth reveal themselves in his wide grin. "That sounds nice. I'll get the check and meet you there."

Nice, he says.

The way he said it sounds like we were going to take a stroll in a park and feed ducks. Not get drunk and fuck like bunnies.

If only he were more like Henry. Self-assured. Dominant. Determined.

Instead, I have the slightly nauseous feeling I get when I feel like I'm the one begging for attention.

Henry's hand sits lightly on my thigh while I tell him about my reservations about Mark.

"It took everything in me to not bend you over that table," he huffs. I believe him. He strikes me as a bit of an exhibitionist if I'd let him.

That would be awkward. Images of me making out with an invisible man in a public place flicker through my mind.

I'd be locked up for sure.

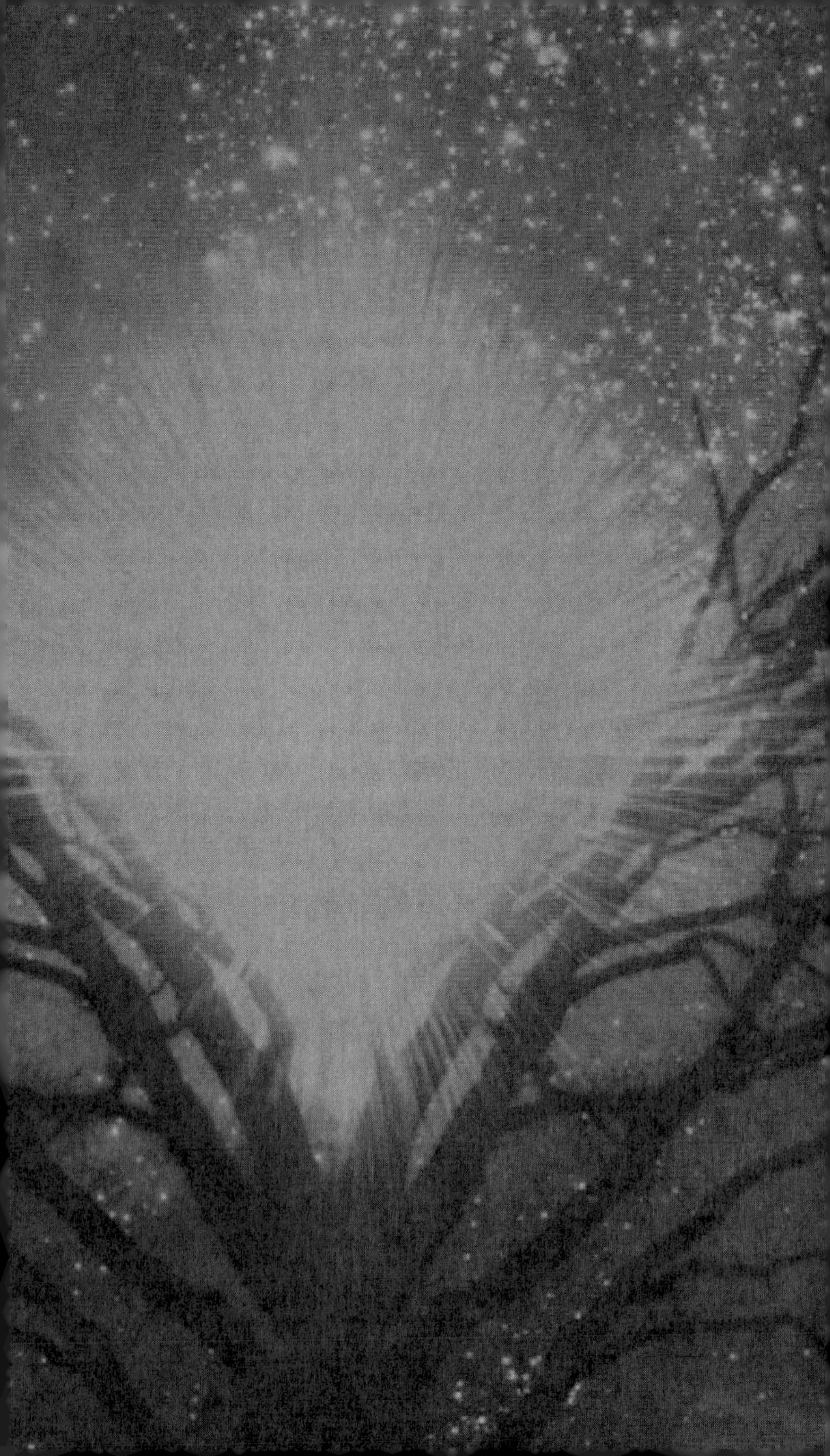

Chapter 17

Henry

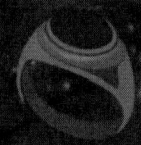

It isn't easy watching this. Her laughing at his poor attempts at humor makes my teeth grit.

The alcohol seems to have loosened their inhibitions.

Rage bubbles within me as I watch Mark lean in for a kiss.

And she fucking lets him.

Letting myself fade away is my only recourse to sanity.

This is hell and damnation. The last week has been the preparation. A cock tease of happiness and satisfaction. Watching this is not how I would picture the perfect eternity. Heaven ripped from my grasp by a garish bastard with his dapper breeches and slicked hair.

Separated only by her being able to see him.

Perhaps I should pluck out her eyes. If only she didn't already know I'm made of aether that only she can touch.

The void absorbs my screams of fury, but sends Daisy into frantic pacing. Her nervous steps seem to distract that pompous ass. It pulls me closer to keep her running circles around them on the couch.

"Daisy, on your bed." Alice points emphatically, but I playfully leap at the dog to send her skittering for another round.

Her ears climb and her tail begins to wag. She is enjoying this game I'm indulging in. Little does she know its nefarious intentions.

Listening to Alice's laughter, I know it's genuine. My chest aches knowing he can give her what I can't. A family. A helping hand. Someone who can perhaps protect her when the need arises. Who can dampen her brow with a cool rag. Or even something as simple as pour her a drink or make her a meal.

All of those fall outside of my grasp. They're tangible. Even though I've been able to don her body as she slumbers, there are so many things I long to provide while she's awake.

Something in me shifts. All I want is for Alice to be happy. If this brings her pleasure, perhaps there is still a way for me to be a part of her life.

My seed may be useless, but sowing it in her brings screams of ecstasy.

That part I can do.

Letting Daisy settle on her bed, my touch drifts to Alice. She startles against Mark's mouth and lets loose a little gasp.

"Keep kissing him." I settle behind her and begin to move my hands over her body.

My cock swells against my breeches, so I let them disappear. Rubbing my bare length on her hip sends embers into my belly.

The flush of pink that surges up her neck and across her cheeks tells me she's enjoying my hands pinching her pert nipples and my fervent nips across her shoulder.

It's an odd sensation, his hands moving over her and through me. Reason suggests I should feel them, but they pass through my chest without noticing.

"Do you want to fuck us both?" She pulls back from him just enough to give a whimpering nod. Working one hand down her belly, I plunge a finger into her hot little slit. "Hmm, I think you do. That cunt is so wet already." She moans as I stroke her clit until her hips begin to buck against me.

Mark rubs static small circles on her shoulders.

Sniveling sap. He doesn't know that my girl wants to be taken. Not to be pet like she's a neurotic barn cat with tentative light meanderings.

She's my feral vixen who will scream and claw.

"Wrap your legs around him while I fuck you." As her thigh shifts over his, it opens her to my hand and I push two fingers deep into her tight little pussy.

"That's my girl. Squeeze my fingers." Every time I pinch her nipple, she tightens her sheath around me.

Mark's belly sits firmly against hers as she pulls him to her, but my hand still moves freely through him to flick her hard clit until she squirms and pants.

When I shift down, my knees end up floating somewhere through his legs and my body is nearly fully submerged into the couch. But, all I feel is her. The pulsing wetness of her needy cunt beckons the tip of my cock and I thrust into her in one roll of my hips.

Her head tilts back onto the cushions and a moan quivers through her. One of her hands latches onto my thigh and I can feel her nails sink into the skin in a fiery rake.

Her pants pose no obstacle to me as I withdraw and agonizingly slowly push back into her gripping confines.

I want her to build a deep blaze within her. A grinding erosion that tears at her resolve until she is worn into a molten pool.

Mark grips her shoulders and hovers over her. "Do you want me to continue?"

What a fucking ragdoll.

Rut her like a rabid bull. That's what she likes.

Alice slips a nonsensical groan as I fill her tight pussy again.

The blank look on Mark's face pulls a laugh from me.

"Tell him what you want, love. He needs his hand held." I tilt her head so her ear is closer to my lips. She needs to hear me clearly. "Tell him to fuck your cunt now that I have you dripping wet." Her hands need to touch him, so I lift her arm to rub onto his side.

"Tell him." I follow my words with a nip to her earlobe.

"Mark," she breathes. "Take off your clothes."

I watch his eyes widen and he leans back to peel his shirt over his head baring his thin chest. It makes me feel better knowing I could have crushed him in another life.

The fire of her touch on my thigh centers me. "Now, it's your turn." I can't resist giving her a gentle kiss as I shift from under her.

My cock cools as I withdraw and she kicks her legs up to slide her pants down.

Cracking my knuckles into fists, I know if she finds this worthwhile, she may let me still cling to her vestiges.

"Do you have a condom?" She looks at Mark while unbuttoning her undergarment.

"What is that?" My hand traces a slow circle around one of her engorged nipples making her jump when I flick the tip.

"You'll see," she says quietly. She squeezes my thigh subtly before freeing the beauty of her breasts.

"Huh?" Mark is digging through his billfold and swaying slightly on his feet. That bottle of tequila they tapped into must be loading him up.

"I just said," Alice reaches up and runs her finger over his stomach, teasing the belt of his pants. "If you don't, I'll see if I have one."

"My little vixen, you are such a clever girl."

She gives a wiggle of her ass knowing she is rubbing against my raging cock pressing into her back.

Mark cries out triumphantly holding a small square above his head. Shoving his wallet into his pocket, he lowers his linen pants unceremoniously.

Brilliant white short knickers that hug his waist appear. The bulge he sports is less stunning.

Too bad she cannot see my grin.

With his thumbs in his waistband, Mark pauses and watches Alice undulating on the couch below him. His eyes close heavily and reopen slowly.

Foolish sot. Too plastered to function? I've never reached such a point.

"Tell him to hurry."

She giggles as she repeats my words. Albeit tipsy, I think she is far from as sodden as he is.

As if shaken from a stupor, Mark smiles and slides the blinding fabric down and tears the small square he still pinches between his fingers.

He rolls a sheath of some sorts over his peckish cock and reaches for Alice.

"Is that a condom?"

She giggles again. "Mmhmm."

I'm sidetracking now. My curiosity is piqued over his

covering. It doesn't even rankle me when he climbs over Alice and aligns at her entrance.

"Are you ready?" he asks.

For fuck's sake. I thrust my hips, forcing hers up as well to envelope his poised bitty cock.

With a whining groan, Mark sinks into her. His face is only inches from mine and I find myself pulling away from his reddening features.

"Turn him over. Stick your plump ass up so I can take what's mine." Moving to her side, I'm met with the full view of him covering her.

"What?" she murmurs.

Fighting the growl that struggles to escape, I wind my hand beneath her thigh and begin leveraging her out from under him until she straddles him on the couch.

"Good girl." I give her round cheek a sharp snap of my hand and she jolts and squeals. "Now, ride his little cock."

Mark's eyes loll backwards into his head as it bobs against the cushions. One hand sits on her knee, but otherwise, he's a floundering fish of helpfulness.

My girl wouldn't even get off if left to him. Selfish prick.

Pushing her down between her shoulders, her delectable ass rises to the heavens.

She has me drooling with how scrumptious she looks. I let a pool of saliva trail down onto my hand to wet my fingers.

"Are you still ready for me?" Glistening still from how wet she got while I fucked her, I drag her juices upwards to the tight star of her ass. With a bruising grasp up her hip, I push a finger into her while Mark still pathetically twitches below.

She looses a small scream, but doesn't pull away.

Instead, she pushes back against the pressure of my hand and starts riding my finger.

"You like that, don't you?"

She rises onto her arms and turns back towards me.

"Yes! I didn't know it could feel that good." When she bites her lip with the red flush of lust across her neck, I nearly come against her leg.

My palm stings on her other hip, leaving matching red handprints. "That's for denying me." She whimpers and twitches as I rub the anger from my mark. "I know what is best for you. Remember that." Her head tosses back, the dark tendrils sweeping across her pale skin.

I slide another finger in while watching Mark's tepid cock try to keep a rhythm. Her hips jerk again, but not as hard.

A deep moan forms in her chest as I roll my hand into her. She takes what I give her and begs for more.

I want to split her in two. My prick is so engorged it hurts.

As tempting as it is to plunge back into her tight cunt, I can't fathom sharing that space with Mark and his softening cock.

I think the bastard is falling asleep.

Pulling my fingers from her hot body, I drop another pool of saliva into my palm to polish the mushroomed head of my cock.

"Come to me." Grappling her hair in my fist, I yank her to her knees. "I want you to feel me, how badly I want you." Her hand reaches behind to stroke me in a burning path before she cups my stones and rolls them with her fingers.

Spasms hit my loins and I leak enough it drips from the end of my cock. "You're going to like this. You'll scream my name. Now, just relax your little ass and let me fuck what's mine."

Mark seems to have rousted himself and begins to piston his hips with fervor below her.

The vibrations from his movements ease her hesitancy as I line myself up. With a slow and steady series of small pushes, I gain entrance into her ass.

My ass.

My arm wraps around her and snugs her against my chest while her head rolls back to lay on my shoulder.

Each stroke sinks deeper as her moans grow louder.

She's a vice trembling around me. The scalding furrows of her nails embed themselves into my thighs as she clings to me, tugging at me to go deeper, faster.

The need to grab her, to consume her becomes overwhelming. My fingers wrap around her neck, and I crush her against my own until our breaths become one.

"Say my name." My thighs slap against hers, every withdrawal feeling as if I'll leave my cock behind. Her body is fighting to lodge me deeper with every contraction of her muscles.

Another moan crests from her swollen lips and spills under my jaw.

"I'll only let you breathe if you scream my name." I'm clamping firmly around the delicate lines of her throat, and she begins to buck her body against mine. Spasms of pressure squeeze my length and I fear I may lose control at any moment.

Allowing her to gasp, she purges her cloistered air from her lungs.

"Hen—ry!"

Mark's eyes flutter open when his own body tenses below her. His abs twitch as he joins her in release.

"You're." I ram into her twice more, the spurting of my cum burning its way from my very soul. "Mine." I finish in a ragged sigh.

"Yours." Her soft word tickles into my ear before she collapses onto his chest.

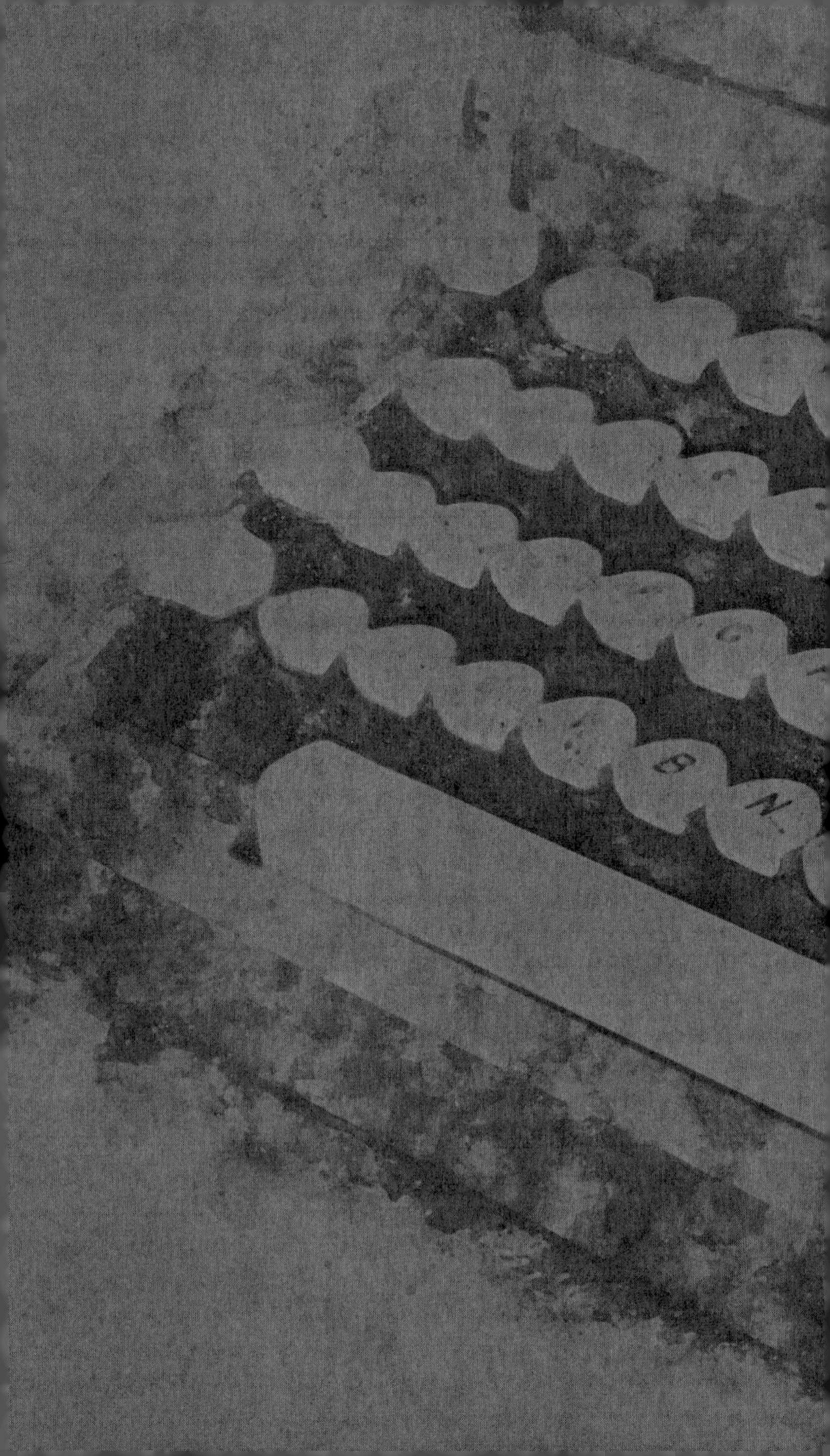

Chapter 18

Alice

Spent. Stretched. Fucked.

I'm a complete overcooked noodle and Henry is reveling in it.

Meanwhile, Mark begins snoring in my ear. I knew I shouldn't have poured him that last round.

"Did you like that, my little minx? Having two cocks filling you?" His softening dick is pressing against my thigh and I can feel him dripping down my leg.

But, his hands feel so good running up and down my back. Their strong grip working loose every muscle.

"Mmhmm." That's it. It's everything I have to make that little noise.

His hands curl beneath me and he picks me up off Mark's splayed form. As he cradles me to his chest, my eyes close reflexively and I burrow against the heat of his embrace.

"Alice." The deep vibration of his voice is a soft lullaby in my current state of absolute relaxation.

"Alice, I wish a small favor." Now he has my curiosity.

Flickering a glance is a mistake. I'm floating in the middle of the room in a ball.

This can't be real.

Squeezing my lids shut again, I just want to ignore the crazy for a little bit and enjoy how good he feels right now.

"What's the favor?" He never asks for anything, so this is new.

"Put my ring on his hand. Please."

"What? No. It's mine." My fist tightens around my thumb. *Henry is mine.*

"I need to test a theory." He lowers me gently to my feet next to the couch. Gazing down, I see Mark has his head thrown back in chainsaw mode and one leg's hanging off the end.

"I don't understand." I don't want to lose my ring. The Henry I imagine may not be real, but the ring is. And pretending that he's real to me is so much easier with the weight of it on my hand.

"Just, try." There is a pleading sound to his question that I'm not familiar with either.

Well, if it's so important, I guess it won't hurt. Mark is out for the count. I'll just take the ring back once Henry is satisfied.

Even though I'm naked as a jaybird, I feel bare and exposed when I slide the heavy signet from my thumb.

It fits over his pinky that is dangling just off the cushion.

"Okay." I reach back seeking the comfort of Henry. "Nothing happened. Can I take the ring back now?"

Mark's eyes fly open and look wildly around the room before they land on me. His features soften into a large smile as he sits up.

It isn't the same smile he's given me all night. This one is a little lopsided. More with the left than the right.

His hand snakes out and grabs mine, bringing my fingers tenderly to his lips.

"Alice. I've waited an eternity for you to see me." He turns my palm over and kisses it in small nibbles.

"Mark. Um, how are you feeling?" I'm so fucking confused.

A rumble comes from his chest as he stands. His hands reach out to my shoulders and he pulls me closer.

"My little vixen. I was hoping this would work." His fingers cup my cheek and thread into my hair.

My stomach twists and I swear I'm going to puke. The level of derangement I must have for this to be happening is unreal.

"Henry?" It can't be. Not even I could hallucinate this well.

"Now, I can take care of you how I've longed too. At least, for a little while."

Before I know it, I'm scooped up and nestled against his chest, just as I was a few moments ago.

It feels different, but he holds me the same.

"Henry, how is this possible?" My voice cracks. I can't quite get enough air and my vision blurs.

"Alice. Relax. Take a deep breath." He pauses, but I can't stop trying to inhale faster.

"Do I need to choke your pretty little neck again?" His voice drops as he carries me into the bedroom and sits on the edge of the bed with me on his lap.

Holy fuck. It is him.

My hands find his jaw as I stare into his eyes.

Mark's blue eyes are so full of warmth when they gaze back it brings tears to mine. They make hot paths down my cheeks. My chest hurts with so much emotion as the reality sets in.

"Henry? Really? How?" My mind is flying at a million miles an hour. Can he really be here? All this time I believed he was a figment. How badly I wished he was real.

"I have a confession. I discovered the ability the first night you took those snake oil pills to sleep. In your slumber, a light burned from my ring and when I touched it, I was able to borrow you."

Realization dawns. "You're the one who ate the strawberries?" Manic laughter rips out of me. "Oh, my god, I thought I was sleep eating! Wait. You 'borrowed' me? That's fucked up." I may feel a little pouty, but it doesn't stop me from staring at him.

How can he look like Mark, but still look so *different?*

His lopsided grin grows and he sweeps a hair back from my forehead. "Let's just say, I know your cunt better than anyone else ever could. Inside and out."

It is him. Grabbing his neck, I pull him down so I can taste his lips. He devours my mouth, his tongue pressing into me and sweeping my teeth.

As only he does.

A contented moan escapes me and I wiggle on his naked lap.

Disappointment tinges it as he pulls away. "No. I'm not going to fuck you with his little cock. But—" He stands again with me still in his arms and carries me into the bathroom. "—I've dreamed of being able to lather your body and bring you a drink. Please let me lavish you with the attention I cannot normally do." He drops a long gentle kiss to my forehead as he lowers me to the bathmat. "Start the water. It still perplexes me. I shall return imminently."

The cold shiver that overtakes me in his absence is soon replaced by the steam filling the small room.

Mark, er, Henry, returns with a triumphant grin carrying a glass of wine and a package of grapes.

"We're out of strawberries. I should have rationed the staples in hopes of tonight." He balances them on the edge of the tub and steps in behind me. "Blazes! The fires run hot that heats this bath!" He laughs and wraps his arms around me. "I should have known my little minx likes it fiery."

His teeth nip the back of my neck as his fingers pinch my nipples beneath the sultry rivulets streaming over us.

My head is in a vortex. All of my doubts come crashing down as his fingers lather my hair with shampoo. My tears mingle with the bubbles running down my face.

He's real.

He's mine.

When he turns me to rinse my hair, I watch his face as he focuses on pushing the soap from my head. The way he looks at me. Like I'm the most precious thing in the world. As if he's trying to memorize every inch of me. It brings a knot into my throat and I can't help but choke out a sob.

"No, no call to fuss," he admonishes. Dropping another light kiss to my temple, he gathers a handful of grapes and feeds them to me one at a time. The cold crisp bites make my jaw tingle and I can't help but smile at the look of adoration he gives me as he presses each one against my lips.

"What about Mark? Is he still in there?" He said he borrowed me, but I don't remember it.

"He's there. If he awakens, I'll get yarded out." A mischievous smile teases up the left side of his lips. "Remember yesterday when you awoke on the floor near your bed because Daisy was barking? She pulled you from your dreams and I was booted free to watch you fall to the floor."

"Huh? That was your fault? I'm not sure if I'm supposed to be pissed at you now." I want to touch him, so I lean my ear against his chest to listen to Mark's heart beating.

"Henry?"

His chest vibrates his response.

"You're real." It isn't a question anymore. "I don't want Mark. Is that strange?" When I tilt my head back to look at him, his lips press to mine.

"That's because we are bound. A force greater than us drew the tether tight. We are meant to be." His face nestles into the crook of my neck as he hugs me close.

He makes my heart and my lady bits all melty. I never knew I could feel this way about someone. Possessive. Complete. Yet, owned. I trust him to do anything he wants to me. And, every time I do, he makes me feel so damn good.

The water cools and he takes his time drying me off with one of my oversized terry cloth towels. "This did not feel the way I expected." He rolls it between his hands before he looks up, a lecherous smile on his lips.

"Can you do a little show?"

Did he seriously just wag his eyebrows?

"Put on your finest undergarments so I can peel them off you. I want to make each one rub on your needy pussy until the friction rubs it raw." The sting of his palm on my ass makes me squeal and jump to my dresser.

"Why do you want it raw?" I don't care. There's a little part that is giddy to play dress-up for him.

"So after I'm done borrowing Little Mark, you'll remember for days what it felt like to have me tearing your clothes off. And I'll lick the burn until it's healed."

His mouth.

Shit.

I swear I'm so wet it's running down my thighs. Maybe I should drag that towel over here to keep from making a puddle on the floor.

I give him the best striptease I've ever done until my panty drawer is empty and most of my good ones lay in tatters.

Dim light of the sunrise begins sneaking into the windows.

"Alice." His lips are tight and he clenches his jaw. "I'm going to dress him back into his clothes. So, when he awakens, make him leave." His hands frame my face as he pulls me close. "I've never been as happy as when you've been able to set your gaze on me. Even wearing the mask of another, it has been the finest night I have ever had."

"Why does this feel like goodbye?" Unbidden tears tickle down my face and salt the corner of my mouth.

The lopsided grin returns. "Far from goodbye. I'm destined to haunt you for eternity." He dresses into Mark's clothes and stretches out on the couch. "Don't forget to take the ring." He holds his hand up and closes his eyes.

It's warm when I pull it off Mark's hand and slide it back to its rightful place on my thumb.

His features go slack like he's in a deep slumber and his hand slumps to his side.

Maybe he'll be cold. I pull the afghan down over his legs and something squishes beneath my foot.

Gross. The used condom smears some of its contents on the floor.

Ugh. Pinching the very end of it, I rush to the garbage can like cooties will crawl up my arm the longer I hold it.

Henry's deep laughter comes from behind me as I feel

him brush my back. "The look on your face was of the vilest disgust. You surely don't make that expression when you swallow my seed."

He's right. "What can I say, I'm a walking conundrum." I can't fight my goofy smile as I head to the bedroom. It sits differently knowing he's real.

"Alice, cover what's mine," he growls. His voice is deeper than when he spoke through Mark.

I like it better.

"With what, you've torn up all of my panties." I do my best to look pouty, but dig out my least stained sweatpants and slide them on with a baggy tee shirt.

"You should wear your thickest coat in the hopes he forgets what your beautiful body looks like bare."

"Here in a few minutes, he'll be so turned off by my snores and drool that you won't have to worry." I'm completely exhausted. The earlier calisthenics combined with an all-nighter playing show and tell has me wiped.

The heat of his breath whispers through my hair as he snuggles against me. "I love your snores and drool."

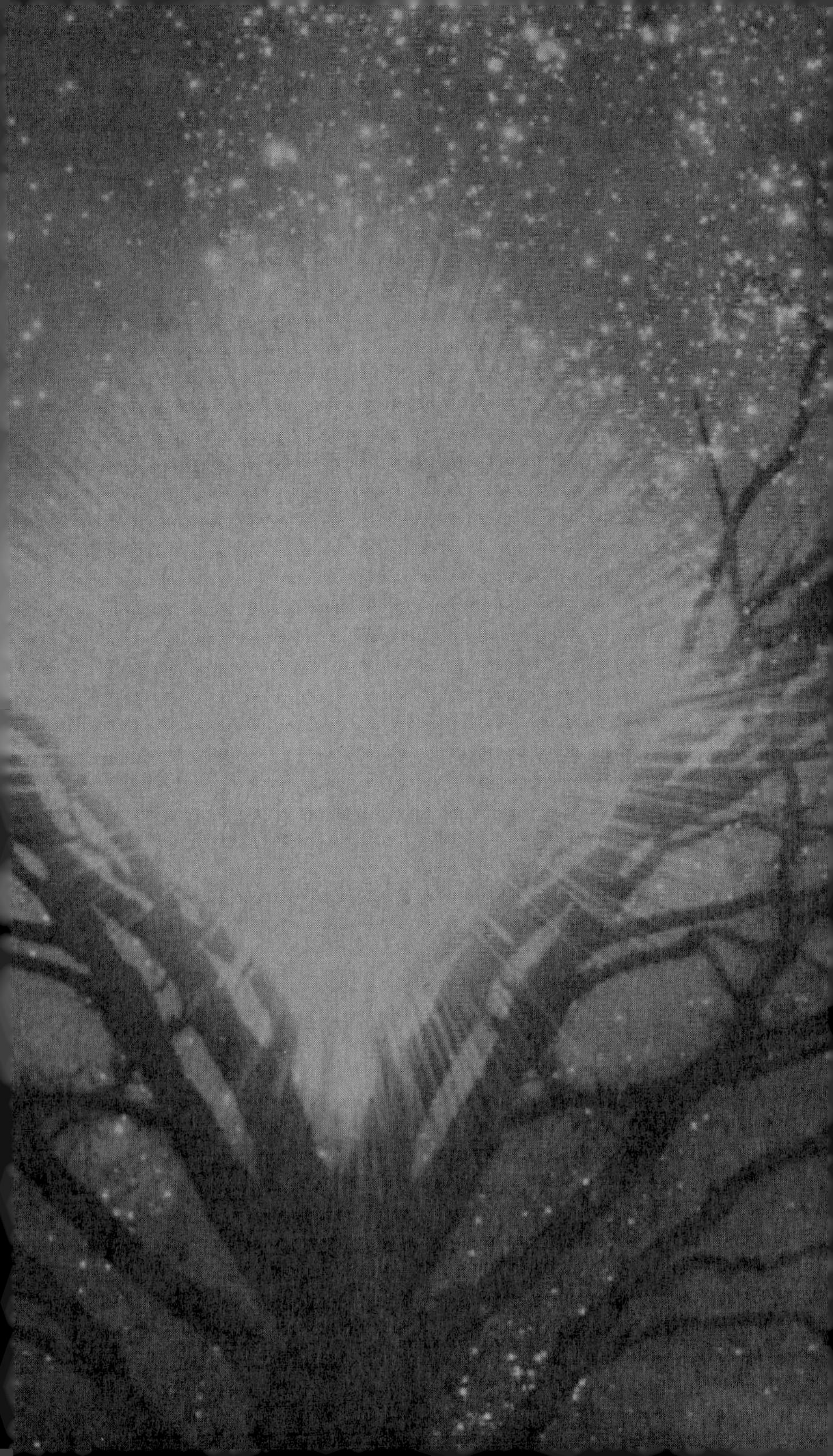

Chapter 19

Henry

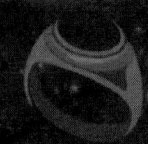

It's nearly afternoon when Mark awakens with a groan and rubs his head.

I bet it hurts. He drank enough to pickle himself. Doesn't strike me as the sort who does it often.

His bleary eyes take in the room and I feel a bit sorry for the lad. I don't miss those days. The pounding head or the rolling guts.

Daisy looks from me to him as he groans again.

He rolls over enough to reach his jacket lying on the floor and digs out one of those small rectangles. With a flick of his thumb, the screen lights up and he squints at it with one eye closed.

"Dang It."

This gent is funny. Even here with nothing but the dog, he acts as if a child may lurk around the corner.

Gaining his footing is a lesson in theatrics. Wobbly and weaving, he moves to the kitchen and uses his hand to get water from the spigot.

I have to commend him for being the finest color of beige.

It does rile me when he goes to her bedroom door.

Daisy notices. I'd say it puts her on notice as well. She jumps up and barks as he approaches.

"Good girl."

She keeps him at bay long enough for my sleepy vixen to awaken.

"Hi, Mark. Did you sleep okay?" It's adorable how she rubs her eyes. I'm besotted with her. Everything she does is alluring, including the snoring.

"I, I think so. I'm sorry, I don't remember much. That bottle went quickly." His laugh seems uncomfortable as he runs his hand roughly over his face. "I apologize if I made an ass of myself."

"Oh, no. You were fine." A tint of pink pushes up her cheeks. "You really don't remember?"

His hand works at the back of his neck as he shakes his head. "No. Maybe it will come back to me. Gosh, I feel really bad."

When he leans against the wall, my knuckles crack when my fingers curl.

"I had a nice time at dinner. Maybe, we could try that again? And we'll leave the bottle of tequila alone?"

The bastard just put on his charming smile.

I wore it better.

If only there were a way to wipe that look off his face.

"Maybe?" Her brows prickle above her nose.

"Can I call you later?" His hand reaches for her arm, and I tug it away.

"Tell him no." She's mine. I only shared to keep up the charade until she learned the truth.

"I don't know. It was a nice dinner, though. Thank you." Her paltry grimace of a smile should be enough to take the hint.

His face flickers a frown, but the smile returns. "I'll text you and see about next week."

A growl escapes my lips. I grab her about the waist and pick her up to drag her back into her room.

She gives a small yelp, but it is quickly eclipsed by the earsplitting scream from Mark.

Her floating in midair and being thrown backward onto her bed may not be a regular occurrence for him.

Alice is still bouncing her landing when the walls shake from the slamming of the front door.

Her giggles drown the sounds of his vehicle spinning its wheels in the gravel. "Henry! That was both hysterical and crazy! You scared the shit out of him! I bet there's a trail all the way down my porch!" Her face turns red and tears squeeze from her eyes as she rolls around with great belly laughs.

"I guess now someone else has officially seen you. I'm not crazy." The smile fades as she sprawls her limbs to stare at the ceiling. "Then, what is in my head?

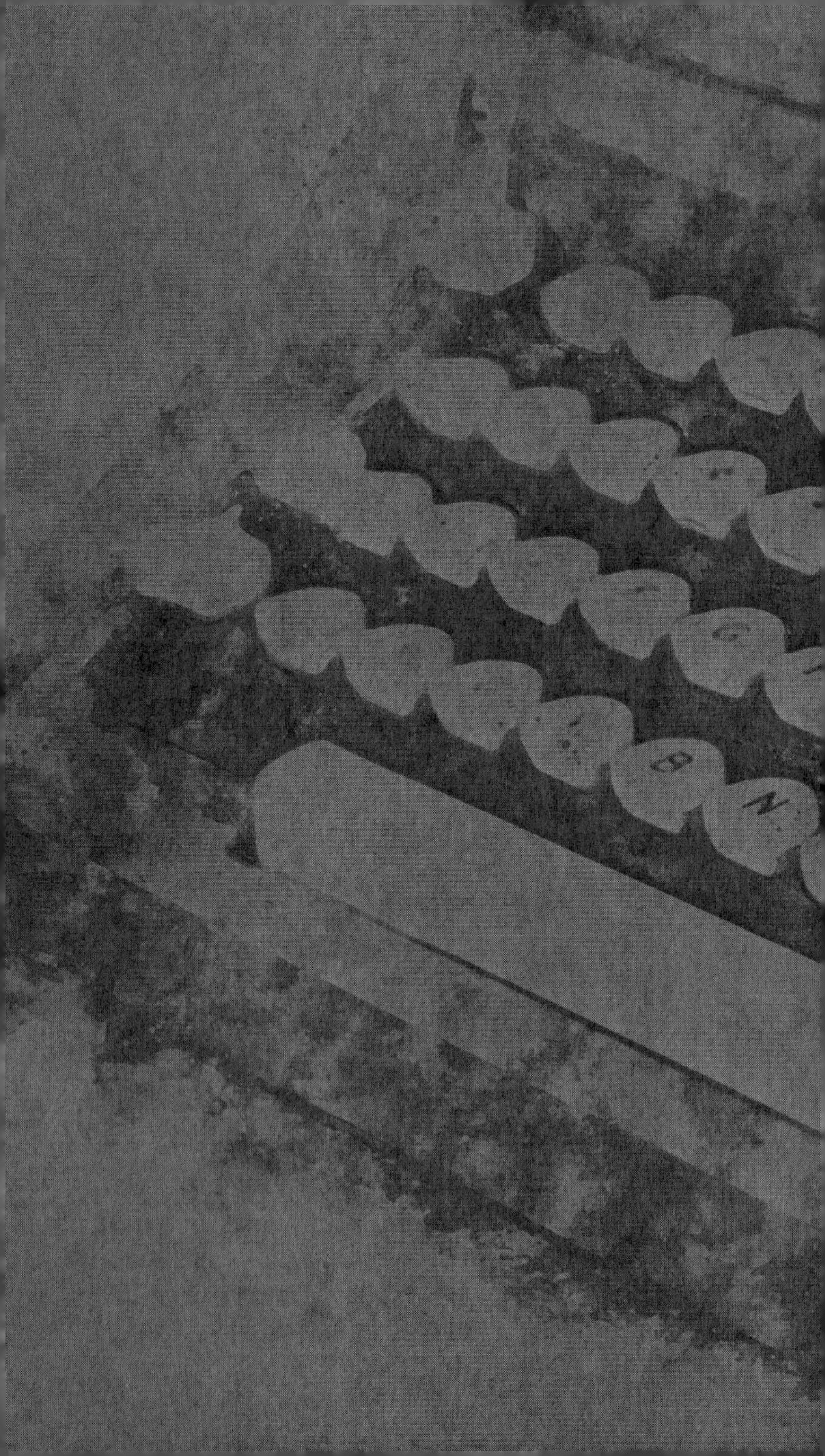

Chapter 20

Alice

The oncologist who Dr. Myers recommended is an uptight asshole. But, he seems thorough.

One-on-one visits with him are minimal, thank goodness. The first day he made me sign record release forms for every cough, hiccup and fart I've ever had. Then, he sends me on some kind of torture schedule of the next three weeks of lab tests, spinal taps and an MRI.

Henry even managed to behave himself that time.

We finally watch Tombstone, and he laughs throughout it. Once he learned that it wasn't real, he took great pride in picking apart all of the small historic inaccuracies.

My ghost, the movie critic.

Who knew my life would consist of evenings of watching bad spaghetti westerns while he has me howling with his sarcastic takedowns.

Poor Clint Eastwood. May he never know how horrible those movies were.

It has inspired me to start writing a smutty western period piece. I've generally shied away from them in the past, but I have my very own historian handy to verify details for me.

"Henry? Did you write in my book last night?" I'm still not very comfortable with him "borrowing" my body. He does make it up to me though. Who knew my big burly scoundrel would sweep a floor? I bet it makes it easier knowing he can play with my tits anytime he wants, too.

Some limits had to be set on desserts when I discovered I had gained five pounds. And my body still needs sleep, so I showed him how to use the timer in the kitchen.

"Perhaps? It needed more fucking." He doesn't try to hide the chuckle behind his words.

"You wrote 'I fuck her cunt. I fuck her breasts. I fuck her mouth. It was good.' I'm not sure if I'll be able to keep those exact words. Is it okay if I, hmm, dress them up a little?"

His hands slide up my shoulders and cup my neck. "You can write it any way you please. It was just me letting you know my checklist for today."

My skin heats under his hands. The things he does to my body...my mother would turn over in her grave if she knew.

Fuck. I hope she isn't a ghost sitting in the corner watching me write book porn and screwing Henry.

No. I'm not even considering that Freudian rabbit hole.

"Daisy, why are there paw prints all over the floor?" Did I forget to wipe her feet *again?*

She raises her head and tilts it while the very tip of her tongue sticks out.

"There are days I rue the fact I cannot be of help." Henry's touch drifts away after his words.

He gets so pissy when he is reminded he's dead. And he usually disappears when he does.

Better than having him show his anger. There are some edges to him even transparency can't smooth out.

When I put my keyboard on my desk, I notice it's later than I thought.

Dammit.

"Your muddy prints will have to wait." I need just one more coffee for the road. Dr. Asshole has me scheduled for three on the dot to go over my test results.

My stomach is in knots as I close the door behind me. Nerves run so tightly through me that it makes my skin itch and my ears ring.

Buzz. I don't hear bells, I hear a drone that transforms into a swarm of mosquitos around my head, and they're sucking me dry before I can even make it to my car.

Where the fuck did they all come from?

Sitting in my Subaru, inhaling the dying new car scent, my hands sting from smacking so many of them. It's a hot April, and I have just a light tee shirt on.

Easy prey.

I don't remember them ever being this bad before. Missouri is humid, but not exactly a breeding ground of this magnitude.

What could have caused—

The tree. There's still a giant ass hole in my yard, and the recent rains have filled it up.

"Henry, your hole is nasty. It's time to fill it." I'm laughing so hard I snort.

Maybe he heard me?

Hiring a landscaper or handyman to come out quickly moves to the top of my list. That tree needs to go and there is no way I'm chopping it up. But, there would be enough wood there to last me nearly all winter.

With my fingers thrumming on the steering wheel and my legs twitching, I make it to the doctor's office in record time.

The ball of nervous energy only gets worse as I pace around the small waiting room. Surely, they wouldn't keep me waiting if it was serious? Doesn't he realize I'm seconds away from a full-blown panic attack? My chest is already tight and there just isn't enough oxygen in here.

"Relax, love." Henry's touch on my back is warm and comforting.

Thank fuck he's here.

"Where'd you run off to?" I'm well-versed in pretending to be on the phone in public now. Wireless earbuds are the best prop ever when you don't want people thinking you're talking to yourself. When they flash me a weird look, I can glare back and violently point at my ear. I almost always get their hands flying up and they back away apologizing.

"I needed a walkabout. But, when you mentioned filling my hole, I thought it best to remain at arm's length for a little while longer."

Did I just snort again?

"Miss Brooks? The doctor will see you now." I swear the girl looks like she's barely old enough to drive, but she gives a very practiced smile as she points down the hall.

"Thank you." Dr. Richardson's office is the third on the right. My fate lies behind a boring brown door.

After I rap my knuckles softly against the hollow wood, his gruff voice beckons me in.

He's a bit wild looking. White hair frames his head in an angry cloud and he always looks like he's scowling at me through his thick glasses.

"Miss Brooks. Your lab results look normal." He starts

right in before I even can sit in the world's most uncomfortable wooden seat. Add a couple of straps and an electrode, it'd make a handy electric chair.

"There is an anomaly with your MRI." His gaze doesn't rise from the papers on his desk.

My fingers dig into the arms of the chair. As the silence drags on, I'm tempted to stand up and scream.

"Relax," Henry's deep voice croons next to my ear. His warm palm covers mine and I struggle to slow my breathing.

"Your initial sign-in paperwork makes no mention of a previous injury. But, hospital records have a head injury when you were—" He shuffles a page. "—six."

Does he have to squint at me like I've just been found guilty of murder?

"I, um, I don't remember a head injury. Oh. I do, now. I fell off a piano bench and got a couple of stitches. I do remember I got to stay in a hospital room for a little while and eat ice cream."

His eyebrows draw so close together they look like they form a small animal on his forehead. "That is not what is indicated here. You were unconscious for four days and had to have a stint." His fingers interlace and his frown deepens. "What you have is extensive scar tissue."

"Okay." My voice is squeaky. This guy is intense.

"Congratulations. You are otherwise fairly healthy. Your cholesterol is a little high. Follow up with your general practitioner for that. I suggest you continue with Dr. Myers to address your other, um, issues." He closes the folder containing my paperwork and puts it unceremoniously into a drawer at the bottom of his desk.

"Um. Thank you, Doctor."

He grunts, but doesn't look up at me.

"Fuck him. Time to celebrate." Henry tugs on my elbow and hurries me out the door. "I want you to do another striptease for me. I'll rub your clit so hard, it will be like the burns your panties gave you weeks ago."

He growls as he talks.

God, I love it when he does that.

"I long to tear them off with my teeth again. To feel their silken pull when I snug them tight and split your beautiful cunt in two." He lets out a long exhale as I walk down the hall.

"Why the sigh?" It isn't normal for him to do that. Yell and cuss, yes. But, a pitiful sound? Not like my ghost at all.

"I sometimes wonder if perhaps you should ask Little Mark to return?"

"I am *not* fucking him again!" Shit. I said that too loud. The clerk at the desk gives me a sour look.

So, I glower back and point at my earbud.

Her eyebrows shoot up and she makes a point of looking down at her hands.

That's right. Private conversation.

"You can hornswoggle him with your feminine wiles and give him more tequila. I just want to touch the world with you in it. It has nothing to do with his mousey pecker."

"I don't think Mark wants to talk to me. When I texted him about the balance left from the payment, he never replied. I just got a check in the mail." I'll never forget the look on his face when Henry picked me up in front of him.

The puddle outside the door was evidence enough of his abject fear.

"Well, I still plan on fucking you sideways until you collapse on my cock." His fingers slip between my ass crack as I'm walking to my car.

I try really hard not to jump too noticeably.

"I love that plan. Let me call someone to fix your hole in the yard, and then I'm all yours."

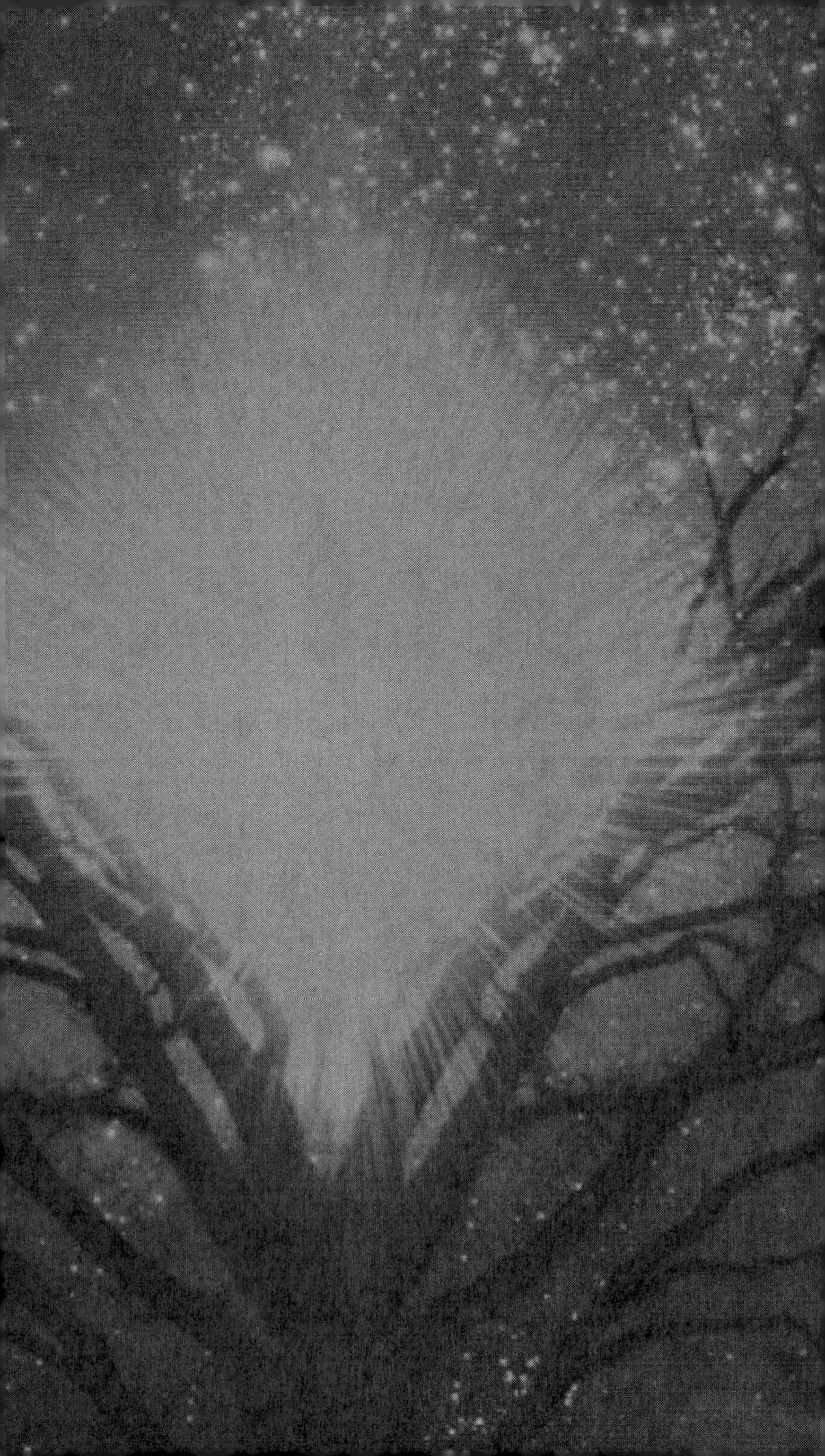

All of these men have eyed her. To be visible would be all I would wish for at this moment. So, I can stand near her, wrap my arm around her, and show them she is *mine*.

Instead, I must pace in the shadows while she discusses plans with the man in charge. A big lout of a fellow who eerily reminds me of a man I once knew. The bane and the death of me: Jonathan.

Built like a tree trunk himself and topped with thick hair of copper, I can see why Alice smiles when she talks to him.

I wonder if she's envisioning how big his cock is.

The way he adjusts himself when she isn't looking, he could rival me. And the lecherous comments he makes to his workers about what he would do to her when he has the chance stirs an ire in me that nearly sends me to the void.

I'd beat him to death with it for thinking of her so.

But, then another idea begins to brew.

This undying rage at betrayal shifts to this new man. The ache in my gut for revenge against the enemy who no longer exists. Unrequited fury still simmers below my imperceptible skin.

I didn't think it still mattered, but seeing him now, this newer version, has thrown me often into the void to scream out my frustrations.

"Does he have to remove his shirt to carry branches?"

She winces at my grip on her arm and casts a questioning expression in my direction.

"It's hot out, Henry. Like, eighty, at least. I'm surprised they aren't all stripped down naked. I would be if the mosquitos weren't so bad." Her tone is teasing, but I wonder upon her words.

I may not be enough for her. Perhaps she covets a man to gaze upon, a man to take her out and parade her as she deserves.

"You're watching him closely." I can see the flush in her cheeks, the pant in her breathing. "I bet your cunt is soaking wet watching him."

"Jealous? Don't be. There's a lot more to being happy than a nice chest. He's just eye candy." She turns and walks back to her desk. Inspiration must have hit for her to move so brusquely.

The thought of her desire for another man being poured onto a page rankles me. That she would dwell on thoughts of him, converting her lust into permanence that she would share with the world.

To drive others to seek the romance she creates without focus on their own.

Like Nora.

She didn't know what she had when she sought Jonathan's embrace. I never took her as my own. I was always subjecting myself to her whims to grovel for what soft touches she offered.

I should have known. It was because her needs were being sated by another.

A rolling surge of bile taints my throat.

"I have an idea." Her fingers pause their typing to listen to my proposal. "Perchance we could kill two birds with one stone. Help me to borrow him for a bit."

It will be fitting, using the body of a man who used me.

No, it isn't *him*, but the resemblance is uncanny. Down to the gravel in his voice and the way he knocks his hair back from his eyes.

Damnation. The pause in her reply could only mean she's considering it.

"How exactly will that work? He's a big guy. I don't have that much tequila." She laughs and resumes typing.

"Your snake oil pills have you nearly dead some nights. Perhaps a drink with a couple of those tossed in may work? They don't affect my abilities to move your limbs when you imbibe." It took me several minutes of scrubbing one evening to remove the dried spittle from her cheek, she was sleeping so deeply.

"Henry. I'm not going to drug someone."

"Just once. Let me pull your chair out at a restaurant and wash your body again. To clink a glass with you and sit adjacent in your carriage." Fuck, I just want her to look *at* me again.

The more I admit to her, the greater the genuine longing. I desperately want to be a part of every aspect of her life. It should be me out there shoveling sod in that hole or chopping that tree. Showing her with my sweat and calluses that I will work for anything she desires.

Ah, she pauses her lustful story and turns to me. Hands held wide, she raises from her chair and beckons me near.

Nestling against my chest, her warm hands run up and down my back.

"There isn't anything I want from you that you can't provide. I love that you're mine and mine alone and I don't have to worry about other women looking at you. Or luring you away." Her face turns up with her eyes closed.

I know she wants me to ravage her. My frustration is thinly veiled.

"Do you not understand that these are the thoughts I have as well? Yet they don't see me by your side! They see just you. And I see how they look at you when your back is turned. It is a fool's errand for me to believe I can be anything more than your cock on demand. How long before I become your cuck as well?" My fingers dig into the soft flesh of her arms, but she does not flinch.

Tears brighten the emeralds of her eyes over her clenching jaw as she stares through me. "Neither of us chose this, Henry. I'm happy with you. I love what we have. It doesn't have to be more!"

My arms wrap her to me and I squeeze her against my chest until she struggles to breathe. "I love you, Alice. I want to be more. For you."

The morning light frames her against the window in a halo of pale gold as she watches the men unpacking to begin their final day of work. She sips her coffee with the same full lips that just last night worshiped my body.

I don't feel as inadequate today. Her throes of passion were a testament to my capabilities. My hands are gentle today when they run over the bruises on her arms caused by my grip of envy.

"Okay." The word leaves a foggy circle on the glass.

"What?"

She's been silent before now.

"Okay. I'll help you borrow him. *But*, only once. You need to promise that you'll be happy with me as we are, after. I don't want to make a habit of taking what isn't mine."

My stomach flip-flops. I'm not sure how I feel about this now. All the men I've killed or ruined, I've never felt a pang of guilt.

But, she's willing to do something she doesn't agree with, for me.

"Fuck, you're so perfect. If you had lived during my time, we would have ruled the town."

Her body leans against me and shakes with laughter. "I always joked, if I had lived back then, I would have run a brothel."

"Hmm, but you'd only be my whore." My lips find the soft skin under her ear and nip it gently as my hands cross over her stomach to hold her. We both watch the men in the yard moving and stacking the cut wood and raking the debris into a pile. "Have you thought of what to do?"

"Yea. I have some work I need done in the bathroom, so I was going to see if he'd be willing to do that as an extra job after the yard is done. There won't be as many people here." The coffee in her cup wavers as her hand shakes.

"Alice, if you don't—"

Her hand covers mine.

"I'm sure. I want to see you again. It's surreal. But, I really want to. And it's not exactly like I can put up an online ad looking for a host body." She shivers. "Fuck. I could. But, you do *not* want to see who would respond to that shit."

"Besides." She refocuses on the men already sweating in the morning heat. "You'll look hot as fuck in that body."

"Mmm, is my minx getting wet at the thought? You told me that in this modern age we are not to view people as objects."

"Henry, I can't view you at all, but I think about your object all the time." She reaches her villainous hand behind her and rubs my thickening cock.

I hear her gasp and then the crash of her cup shattering on the floor as I throw her over my shoulder and carry her back to bed.

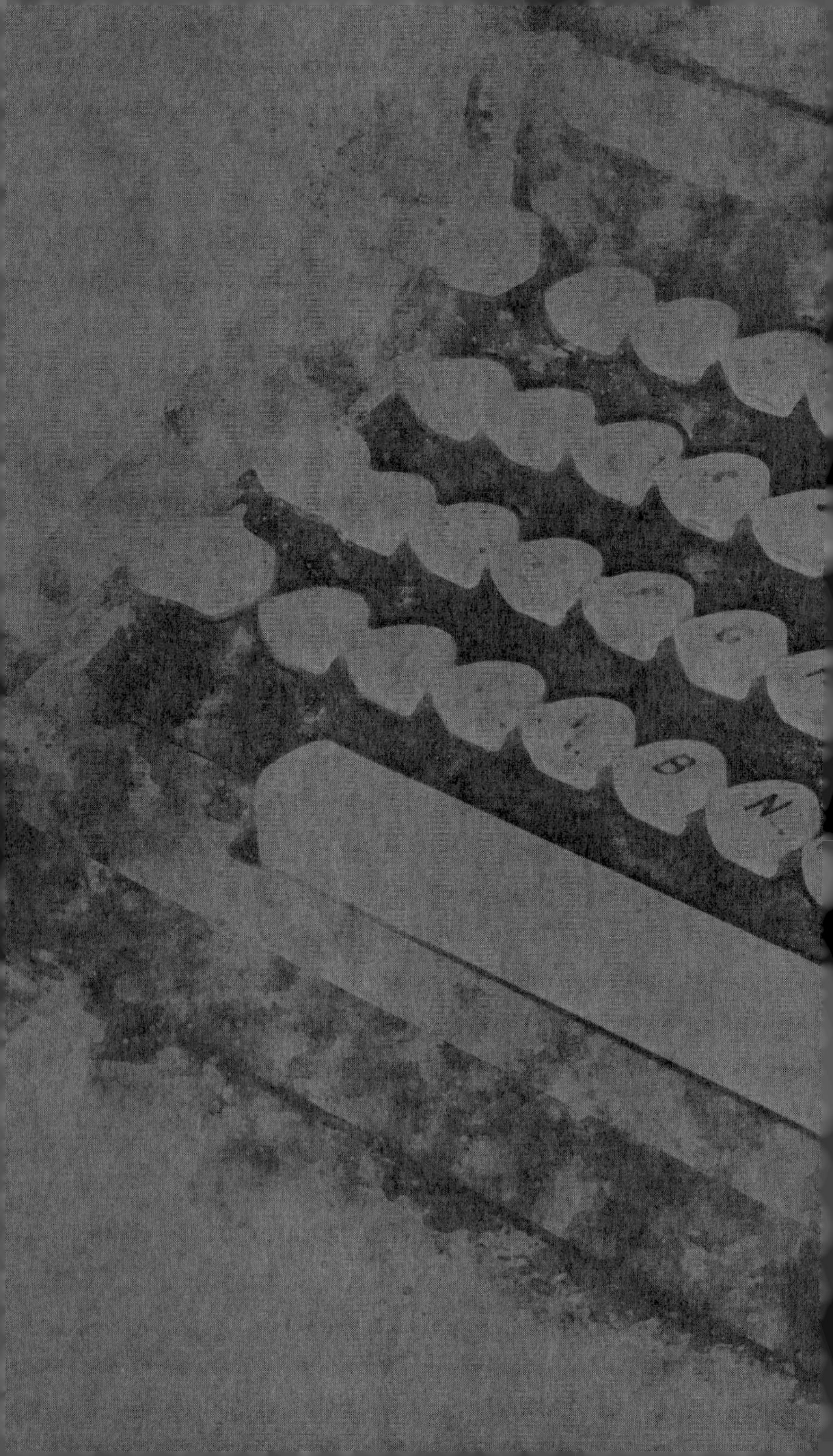
B
N

Chapter 22

Alice

"JJ?" I step gingerly down the front porch stairs. My legs are still slightly wobbly from my recent round of orgasms.

"Yes, ma'am." He looks kind of like what I envision Henry to look like. Big, broad shoulders, narrow waist. His beard is trimmed, but long enough to cover his skin. It makes me wonder if it would feel the same between my thighs when it's Henry's tongue powering it.

"I have a question. You said you do all kinds of handyman work? Does that include bathroom remodels?" I know it does. I double checked their company website.

"I can do those. Do you have something specific in mind?" He stands up and wipes his hands on a rag he pulls from his back pocket. His eyes are brazen as they rake my body, sending both heat and ice through me.

Damn. He is fine. And, without a shirt, I can see every muscle ripple as he twists the cloth.

"Um, yes." His nipples are eye level and very distracting. "I need the flooring replaced and I'd like different tile in the shower. Is there a way to get a quote?"

His left pec twitches as he reaches for his shirt.

I'm acting like a chaste cat lady. Not like someone who got laid exactly ten minutes ago.

"You bet. I'd love the chance to hang out more. Let's take a look." He barks a quick order to one of his nearby helpers then follows me toward the house.

I can feel his eyes on my ass as I go back up the porch.

"The bathroom is this door. It seems like the seal is leaking around the tub. I had a guy check it for mold a few weeks ago, but I want to make sure it doesn't get worse."

"Caulk," he grunts through a smile.

"What the fuck does that mean?" Henry's grip is tight on my wrist.

"I'm sorry?" I'll feign ignorance for Henry's sake.

"The seal is called caulk or caulking. The more the better." His laugh is deep and genuine. "Let me take a few measurements, and I'll be able to run some numbers by you in a few minutes. Did you have an idea if you wanted to replace the floor with linoleum or tile?"

"Caulk is a seal? I hate this man." Henry grumbles, but his grip remains firm.

"Tile would be amazing, but maybe a quote for each? I haven't had a good social media day for a little while." I don't want to say it's because I've been so busy having sex I could give two shits about sitting at my computer.

JJ raises his eyebrows. "What, are you some cam girl?" He flashes his even smile as his eyes slide up and down me.

"Um, no. I write books, so I promote them online." This guy is coming on strong, so it shouldn't be hard to convince him.

"Ah. Well, not as exciting, but pretty nice." His eyes hood as watches me.

"Thank you. Would you like a glass of tea or coffee? I

have some of both." I've got to butter him up so he'll accept the next one. The *special* one.

"Sure, a cup of coffee would be great. Milk if you have it?"

"Good choice. Thank you for checking this out." He smells like wood, chainsaw oil and sweat when I brush by.

"I'm quite willing to check anything out." His voice is deep and suggestive.

This might be fun.

Like trying out a new dildo with no commitment to buy.

Fuck. What is wrong with me? A few weeks with a ghost and I'm willing to commit a felony. Maybe I should be seeing Dr. Myers again. I blew her off after finding out there wasn't anything serious going on with my brain.

Yet, I find myself trying to estimate his body weight to compare it to mine so I can make sure the dosage is right.

I just want him to sleep, not be comatose.

He's leaning into the shower in a way that his ass is sticking out. With his low slung jeans, I can see the dimples in the small of his back.

It's a very nice view.

"Here's your coffee."

"Thanks, I'm just about finished here. You'll have quite a few options to choose from. Your layout will be easy to customize." He straightens and turns to me. "I can have whatever you want laid in here in no time." His arm lands against the wall near my shoulder, caging me near him.

I feel tiny wedged against the door with him standing so close. The warmth of his body sends tingles through mine.

"Okay, let me know when you're done." In my hurry to

back away, I run into the door jam and nearly knock myself out.

Henry's hand stabilizes me when I stumble.

"Thank you," I breathe as I head back to the kitchen.

"I'll always be here for you." His grip is gentle as he cups my elbow.

It makes my chest hurt how much I care for him. I wish more than anything he were here, in flesh and blood. It's a cruel twist of fate to have only part of the man I've grown to love.

"So, here are some tentative budget options." JJ slides a clipboard across the island counter to me. He has it broken down into three columns.

"Whichever one you pick, I'll send you an email with color and tile choices so we can get them ordered."

"That sounds great! How long does that usually take?" Now that I've decided, I'm itching to see Henry looking back at me through JJ's deep brown eyes.

"If you choose stuff that's in stock at the hardware store, I should be able to get started next week. If there aren't any issues with the subflooring, you'll only be blessed with my company for a few days." He picks up the coffee and takes a tentative sip.

I'm pretty sure he just winked at me. This might be easier than I thought.

"This is really good, thank you." He takes another drink.

I know it is. It's one thing I splurge on.

Can't wait for you to try the next cup.

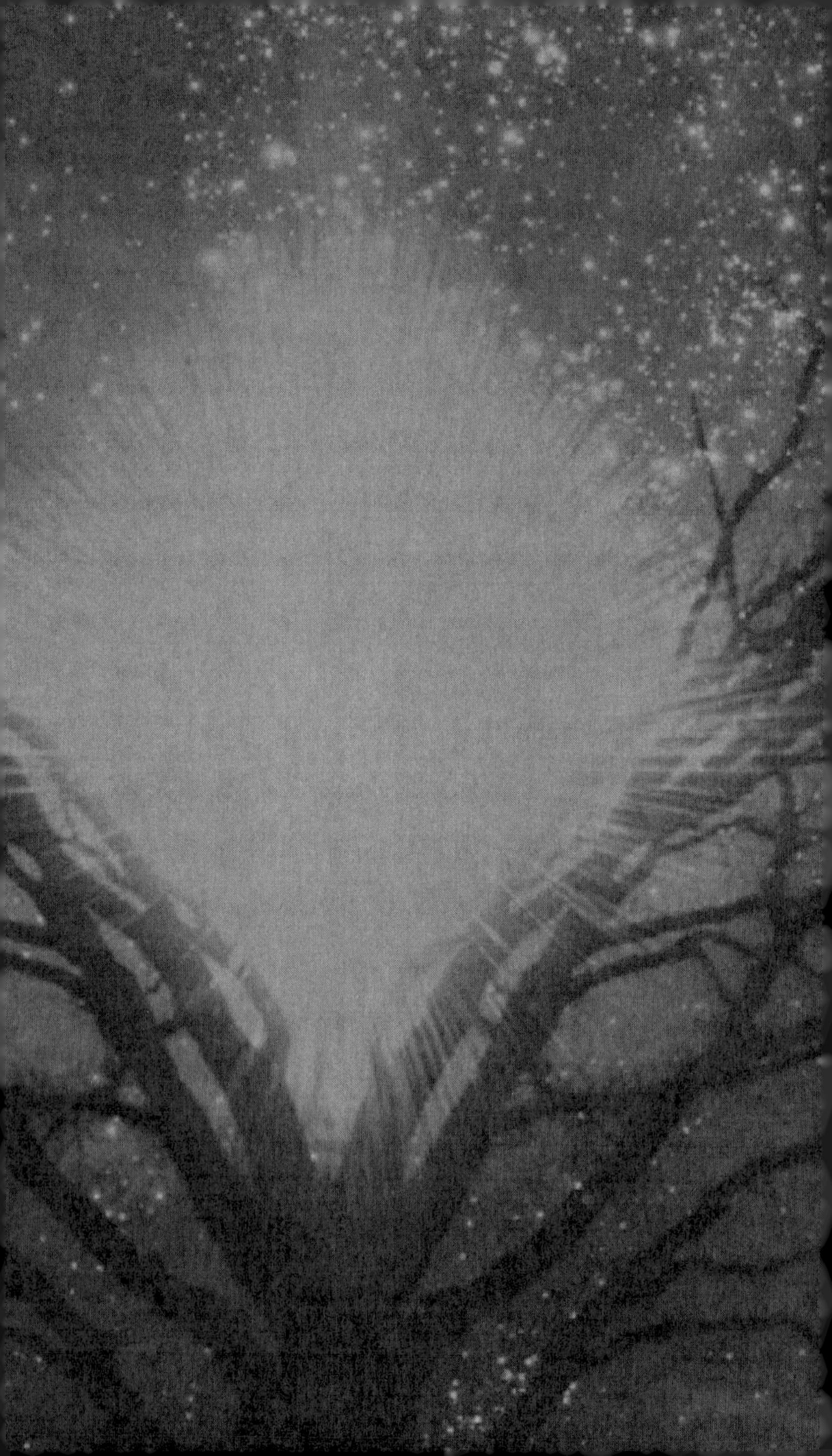

It's the tenth day. The anticipation is going to kill me, as if I wasn't already dead.

He shows up on time, just as he says he will.

Alice is pacing when he pulls into the driveway.

"We don't need to do this. I shouldn't have put this on you." We are standing once again in the morning light in the window with her leaning against my chest. "I can be happy with what I have."

Perhaps I am a little jealous.

What if she covets his body more than mine? Could I bear the idea of her being happy with him in my stead?

When she rolls her head back, it fits perfectly beneath my chin.

"I've gone back and forth over it all week. I'm looking forward to being able to see you again. Even if it's just once more."

The knock makes us both jump. Daisy barks in circles near the door, but minds enough to back away as Alice opens it.

"Good morning, JJ."

He stands with a tool bag and supplies. I hate how put together he looks. I'm jealous of his mere existence. That he can be alive and the focus of her attention.

Knowing she will soon be gazing at me helps to temper the fire in my gut.

"Hi. I brought some stuff so I can start on the demo today." He brushes past her and heads into the bathroom. "The shower will be out of commission for a couple of days until the grout sets, but you'll still be able to use the toilet."

"That's great news. I was worried about that part." She gives him a nervous smile that only I can see. He tosses another grin over his shoulder, then begins to set up.

When he turns away, the smile drops and a hungry look takes over. He would only need a small push and she wouldn't need me to occupy his body to be ravaged by him.

After several trips from his vehicle to his new work zone, he begins to remove the existing covers of tile and flooring. Large garbage bags leave along the same path.

He is a busy man.

"I wonder if he's getting thirsty." Alice is so quiet as she stands in the kitchen. She prepared the pills into a fine powder last evening.

The coffeepot makes a final gurgling sound almost on cue as the fresh pot finishes brewing.

With that sexy set of her jaw, she heads to the bathroom.

"JJ, I just made a fresh pot of coffee. Would you like a cup?" I can barely notice the tremor in her voice.

We would have made a wicked team in my time.

"That would be very nice. Thank you." He doesn't turn to her as he peels strips from the floor.

She makes my cock achingly hard. I can't resist rubbing it along her hip as she tips the powder into his cup.

"You're such a good girl, doing this for me. I'm going to torture you with your little purple toy later. Make your scream your penance while you watch me fuck you." I've wanted to hold it in my hand and do with it what I wish. I've had her use it while I've been buried in her ass. But, to control it will be divine.

Having her eyes on me while I do it, the thought makes my stones tingle and my belly tighten.

The clink of her spoon stirring his coffee is the only sound until she lets out a long sigh and carries it to the bathroom.

"Here you go." She sets it on the edge of the sink and goes to her desk.

Her skin is pallid and her hands have a tremor when she picks up her keyboard.

I'm drawn to her silence. My lips find the top of her head. "Waiting for the moment is the hardest part. We had a dugger in our crew who would shit his knickers before every job."

Noises continue from the bathroom. The pounding of his chisel slows. It isn't long before he emerges with another loaded bag of debris and leaves through the front door.

"I'll watch him." One last gentle rub of her neck before I drift away. Cutting through the bathroom wall, I see the empty cup sitting precariously near the edge of the sink.

Drifting outside, he's sitting behind the steering wheel of his truck with the door still open and a giant yawn cracking his maw.

It doesn't take long for the effects to take hold.

His thumb flips across the screen of the rectangle of his phone and he leans across the seat, letting his legs dangle over the edge.

"Alice, he's asleep."

She startles at my thought as if I've woken her from a reverie.

My mischievous minx raises her lips in a vexing smile. "Good."

The rolling river of excitement tingles through my limbs as we draw near. Loud snores echo from the confines of his cab.

"JJ?" Her voice is timid at first as she taps his heavy leather boot. Strength grows in her words when she forcefully pushes his limp leg.

Her furtive glance is pointless. There's no one for miles. It's adorable how careful she is being. I daren't tell her of the times I went in, guns firing red hot, to sort out a catastrophe of my own making.

A string within my chest pangs when she removes her ring. The minute split in my tether to her tugs toward him as she slides it on his smallest finger.

Gold and fiery orange, the light burns from my ring up his arm and across his chest before I reach out to touch it.

Trying to shut my eyes to the nauseating lights that swirl around me in a tightening pattern, I open them to my arm flung over my face.

Two hard objects jab into my back as I lay across the stiff seat. Rough fabric burns against my elbows as I push myself up.

Alice watches me, her dark hair moving in the soft breeze. Her emerald eyes, wide and unblinking, slowly tighten in scrutiny.

"I'm here, my vixen." I offer my charming smile, an emulation of Little Mark.

Her features relax into a large grin as I slide from the truck and pull her tightly against my chest. "Thank you. To see your gaze light upon me once more is worth an eternity of damnation."

Cool fingers dance over my jaw.

"Henry, I love your smile. I can tell it's you right away."

With a heavy kick of my foot, the truck door slams shut behind me as I scoop her up into my arms. After carrying her up the steps to the house, I set her gently down and open the door with a grand flourish.

"Your abode, m'lady." To do this most mundane of tasks feels better than a bank heist. The euphoria is a heady drug as I pull her chair out for her to sit, then bring her a cup of fresh coffee.

To spoil my queen is all I wish to do today. I'd move a mountain if I had the time.

Her giggles and blushes make my cock tighten in these denim jeans. Palming it, I'm pleased to discover it isn't much different than mine in size.

"Are you checking him out?" Her look is lascivious as she watches my hand move over my hard length, still confined by the heavy zipper.

"We both will be soon if you keep licking your dirty lips that way." My thumb finds her eager mouth and pushes it open. "I can barely wait to see you looking up at me with my cock in your mouth. I want your eyes open." Fire sizzles through me when her teeth grab me and she sucks on my hand as if it would spurt into her with effort.

Squeezing my leaking cock, I arrest my hand from my temptress and pull her to her feet so I can taste her sweet tongue.

The flavor is even better with flesh and blood taste buds. Watching my hands move over her body, the feel of her clothes against my skin, it is nearly overwhelming. I have longed for this day.

"Come, let us feast while the day is still early and the drugs are the strongest. I want to sample food while staring into your eyes." My fingers knot into her shirt as I pull her forward for one more kiss.

"I can't wait for you to ride in the car for real." Her smile is giddy as she tugs my hand. "I know of a little cafe that we can go to. They have amazing chicken-fried steak."

She's patient as she helps me get into the adjoining seat in her vehicle. It's smaller than it seemed when I could just waver through the seats and not care if my feet dangled through to the street below.

The restraint belt sits tightly and I argue briefly with her regarding its use.

"Henry, you promised to take care of JJ. We wouldn't want him getting hurt."

"This already hurts, love. It binds across my waist and is scurring the fuck out of my chest." Perhaps I'm overly sensitive to these new sensations. But, it's perturbing in its distraction.

"And you don't even have boobs. It could be worse." She laughs at me, the wench. I can't help but grin in response. The rubbing annoyance lessens when she seats herself adjacent and runs her hand along my thigh.

Much better.

The ride into town is reminiscent of a high speed getaway. She takes the long way so I can enjoy the twists and turns of the country road. I'd forgotten the pull of gravity, the sway and the bumps that shudder through me.

And at every chance, I see her eyes on me, and I revel in it.

The heat of the sun surprises me when we step out of her car onto the street. It had been cool on the ride.

That is a modern marvel I wish I could have had in the

past. The luxury of a cool repose on a hot day. Now, I don't feel temperature unless I'm pressed against Alice's burning body.

A rush of pride fills my chest as I hold the glass door open for her. Another blanket of temperate air washes over us.

"Let's sit in the back." Her eyes dart as if she's expecting a nefarious lout to jump from the shadows.

But, as I am now, I'd be able to fend them off. Pummel them to the dust.

Thoughts of gratifying violence expands my shoulders and straightens my back. I can protect her in this form.

If only there was some way to make this permanent.

The wooden chair creaks under my weight. I'd forgotten the ramifications of size. JJ is similar in height and girth to me in all aspects.

A rugged life makes a man built to bear it.

My hands splay across the worn wooden table as I lean forward. "You look ravishing." My lip pulls up in a lopsided smile. Even in another body, I can't overcome the scarring of my old one.

Her face lights up and her eyes well with tears. "This is a wonderful moment."

A frail brunette woman arrives with a notepad and two glasses of water. "Good morning. Our special today is two eggs, bacon, hashbrowns and toast."

"I'd like the chicken-fried steak." I throw Alice a wink. "Eggs, toast and an ale."

She hides her face behind her menu as she laughs.

The waitress raises her eyebrows. "An ale? We have coffee." Her lips thin as she stares at me.

Fuck. I've been pining for a good ale. "Coffee." My jaw clenches as I lower my eyes to Alice.

She is struggling to fight a smile.

"I'll have the same. But, coffee is just fine for me. Thank you."

As the waitress stiffly leaves, Alice reaches her hand to me. "No one drinks alcohol in the morning. I'll stop and pick you some up on the way home."

My legs reach for her and pen hers within them. The stiff fabric of these pants pinch my cock and stones uncomfortably.

"I'm looking forward to that. I'll drink it from your navel and mix your honey flavor in."

The pink flush I crave works its way up her neck as she shifts in her seat.

"Mmhmm. Henry, I can't wait. To see you over me." She nibbles on her bottom lip so decadently. It's a dessert I'll indulge in soon.

Two large plates of heavenly smelling food arrive. "Soon, my minx."

Blending flavors rush through me. I've not been brave enough to master her kitchen, though she has left me samples in the past to savor.

But, this hearty meal, it sates a need I'd long forgotten. "It's nice to have company while I glutton myself. I grow weary of us sharing vittles in turns."

One of her dark eyebrows raise as she takes a bite of runny eggs. I'm smitten with watching her throat move as she swallows.

"JJ! Good to see you man." A clap of a broad hand lands on my shoulder heavily.

Fuck.

Short and broad, a heavyset man with a pimpled bispeckled face breathes raggedly near my side.

"I'm busy." Rude? Perhaps. He can fuck off.

"Yeah. I see that. How's Brenda?" I can smell his sweat leaking from his fevered pits. He's goading me.

"Who is Brenda?"

Alice's eyes are popping from her face as she tries to subtly shake her head at me. Her full lips press tightly.

I know she's attempting to discourage me, but my grave has already been made. My time here is limited, I don't wish to spend it with this cockwomble.

"Your wife, dude. Whatever. If you're doing this shit again, I'll see ya." His sausage fingers slip from my arm. I feel as if I need to wipe away the oily residue he has soured our mood with.

"Henry," she whispers. "I think we should go. This was a mistake."

I'm scowling so hard it makes my forehead ache. "No. There is nothing wrong with two people sharing a meal in a public place. My hopes would be that JJ tars and feathers that jackhole when he sees him next." Stuffing the last few bits into my mouth, it's a hard knot to swallow down the bile in my throat.

"I didn't know he was married." She pushes her food around on her plate, eyes downcast and tearful.

"Alice, he isn't doing anything. He isn't here. It's just me, love." My hand covers hers and she glances up.

"Let's just go." She digs within her satchel and tosses some money on the table. Pushing past me, she leads the way back to her car.

This time, she doesn't argue over the restraint belt. There are no side trips or stops, either.

"Next time," she mutters, "no leaving the house."

Her words take me by such surprise I cannot stop the deep laughter that erupts from my chest. "Next time?" My hand seeks the warmth of her thighs and I give one a firm squeeze, then settle against the cushions of the seat.

"You look hot as fuck, I won't lie. And knowing it's the man I love inside...It's hard to not want this." Her arm snakes out and her palm runs over the bulge in my jeans. "I can't wait to see you over me."

"Horny girl. I was pondering how we could do this more often. If only there was some way to make this permanent." Her fingers stroke embers over my stiffening cock. Damn these tight jeans strangling me back. "I must free myself. I want you to see what you're touching." Relief floods me when I unzip the torturous pants and free JJ's large length.

"Holy shit." We both stare in awe at the impressive member standing in my lap.

"When your jaw drops like that, it makes me want to shove this down your throat." Her fingers wrap around me and she moves them up and down, stroking fire with each movement.

The tires crunch over the gravel as we pull into the driveway next to JJ's truck. She stops abruptly and I nearly fall forward without the restraint belt.

"See?" she admonishes. "I told you to buckle up."

"I'm not a child to be chastised. But, I will take you over my knee like the naughty girl you are."

She squeals and giggles as I chase her up the path toward the stairs.

Oh, she's a tease. Turning and running across the yard with her red cheeks and begging grin. As she rounds the corner, she turns her head and waggles her brows before disappearing past the house.

"I'm going to catch you!" I cry as I give chase. My feet pound over the soft ground where the roots of the oak once stood. Gulping a great lungful of air, I turn the corner in time to catch a glimpse of her jacket as she darts behind one of the hickory trees.

"My little temptress? I shall sniff you out and eat you whole." I let a growl slip into my words.

"Hen-ry!" Her yell is tinged with laughter and I see her make another change in direction.

I'm gaining on her, even while holding my unzipped pants up with one hand as I run.

My hand reaches out and slips across the smooth fabric of her coat before she jumps to the right and dodges behind another tree.

Momentum carries me forward a few steps, so she lengthens her lead before I can turn and pursue.

Hot air sears into my lungs and the humidity dampens my hair to my face. Pushing the red locks from my eyes, I can't see her any longer.

Stalking her through the woods makes it difficult to walk. My cock is aching against my stomach and leaking onto my hand that holds the breach of the pants. Clenching my fist to keep them from falling to my ankles, I strain to hear her.

She's hiding. The woods are quiet.

Rustling in the grass draws my attention to a flash of brown, slinking low between two pines.

What the fuck?

Sidestepping around a gnarled trunk, I see it again.

"Daisy! What are you doing? Help me find Alice. She's been a very bad girl."

The heeler wags her tail and sniffs the air away from me. Turning with intent, she takes two large leaps and dives behind a tree.

Giggles erupt as I burst around into the hollow where Alice is crouched. Daisy is licking her face.

"You traitor! You showed him right where to go! I'm revoking your doggy door privileges." Her eyes light when she sees me. "You found me." That devil of a tongue pokes from her lips and catches between her teeth.

"I will always find you. I love you." Pulling her into my arms, my lips find hers and I crush her to me.

Our tongues rage in battle as I push her against the slick bark of the tree.

A flicker of Daisy scampering twixt the trees flashes before I lose myself in the feel of Alice.

My hands dig through her hair as her nails scrape my back. She pulls from our heated kiss and stares into my eyes.

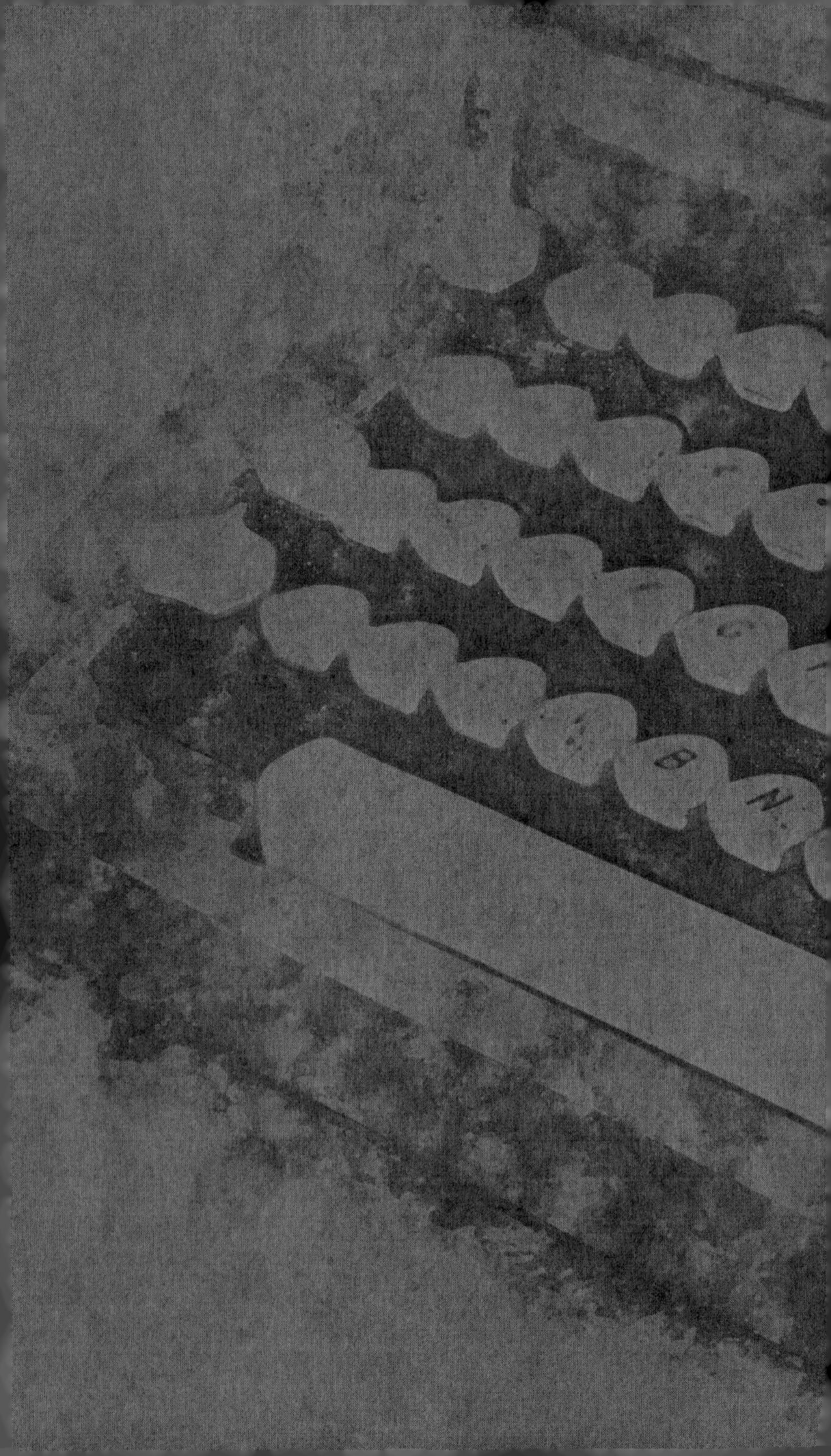
B
N

Chapter 24

Alice

"I love you, too. Getting to see you is worth the fear and the worry." I see Henry past the mask he wears. The warmth of love in his eyes. His tender touch.

My chest hurts with how much I feel.

He's right, we are bound. In a deeper way than I ever knew could exist. Stronger than time or even this plane of existence.

His firm lips find mine as his large hands caress my cheeks.

I want to keep my eyes open and stare at him, into him. To watch his body move against mine. Hot tears leak from me and roll down his fingers.

"My sultry vixen, what plagues you to cry?" His burning tongue moves down my neck and I feel his teeth nip his way to my shoulder. Each bite sends a lance of fire through me.

The calluses on his hand rub coarsely against my belly as he slides his hand up my shirt.

"I wish this wouldn't end. It's the only thing that could

make you more perfect for me." Threading my fingers through the thick copper hair, I hold on as his hot mouth finds one of my nipples beneath my shirt.

"This clothing is an annoyance I don't generally have. Take them off." His growl makes my pussy clench.

His jeans have gathered around his ankles with his giant cock between us. He helps me pull my jacket, then shirt off.

When I unhook my bra, I dangle it over his hard on and grin. "Bet it's been a while since you've been used as a clothes rack."

"That dirty mouth. I want you to suck this rack while you continue to strip." He knots his fingers in my hair and pulls me down until my cheek is bouncing off of his dripping cock. "That's it. I'll flog you with it first. Pull off those panties." His hips twist and he grasps himself with his free hand, then bounces the purple head against my mouth and nose.

It's hard to pull off my underwear when all I want to do is play with myself to relieve some of this pressure growing in my belly. They're soaked when I step out of them.

I try, I really do, to catch the head of his dick in my lips as he smacks it over my lips. I even stick my tongue out like a landing pad, but it just makes him groan.

Once I'm naked, I fall to my knees and absorb the image of him standing over me.

He's gorgeous. Copper hair and beard, framed by the sun. He peels his shirt off to give me the full effect. Hard pecs over tight abs that narrow like a neon sign down to a red tuft of hair that frames the monster he's thumping against my face.

And all with my Henry inside.

It pulls a moan from my throat at how badly I want him.

"That's a good girl, looking up at me and begging for my cock. For that, I'll let you have a little taste." He rubs the engorged tip up my tongue and I suck it in as hard as I can.

A shuddering groan has him leaning on the tree behind me for support. Hearing him nearly makes me come and I drop one hand from his thigh to find myself already dripping wet for him.

"You can't wait, can you? Your greedy little cunt is just crying for attention." When I whine my agreement around his thick dick in my throat, his hips jerk and he seats himself deeper. He's so far in I can't breathe.

My eyes water as his hand holds my hair tightly and he fucks my mouth. Harder he thrusts, until I feel as if I'm suffocating.

With my chest tightening, I can feel my lungs spasming, trying to pull in a breath. Tears run down my cheeks and then he withdraws, covering my gasping mouth with his.

Oxygen rushes through me and the pressure in my belly explodes as I climax.

Fuck, he always knows right where to stop so I come the hardest.

"Did my girl get off choking on my cock?" He spreads out my jacket and his shirt and pushes me back onto the soft grass beneath the tree.

Guiltily, I grin. "I can't help it. Seeing how much you were enjoying yourself was all it took."

Kneeling between my legs, his body covers mine until we are nose to nose. Seeing him cage me in already has a new fire building in me.

"I'm torn—" His voice is hoarse. "—I want to taste your delicious pussy, but I want to stare you in the eyes."

I can feel how hard he is against my thigh, but his lips are gentle and slow down my chin.

It's strange running my hands over his smooth back. I'm so used to feeling the scars he carries, this unblemished skin feels foreign.

"I love everything you do to me, Henry." My chest aches at how deeply I feel for him.

"You've never looked me in the eyes while I've been inside you." He rolls his hips so the tip of his dick rests against my entrance.

His elbows confine my ribs while he cradles me in his strong hands. Our eyes lock. With a single motion, he sinks himself into me, filling me.

It's so fucking hard not to throw my head back in ecstasy at how good he feels.

He doesn't move.

Neither do I.

Our quivering bodies cling to this moment until both of our hearts are racing. The walls of my pussy clench him tighter and that seems to be the trigger to make him begin to move. A long slow pull, and then he thrusts again.

"Fuck, Alice. I love you."

My heels dig into his thighs. I want him deeper, faster, harder. But I want this moment to last forever, too.

Tugging at my knee with his hand, he pulls it higher as he plunges deeper.

I can't help it. My head throws back and my eyes close as waves of tightening ripples of please roll through me.

"Eyes on me." His hand moves from my knee to my neck and he grips beneath my jaw. "Watch me as you come."

His movements hasten. I can feel the mushroomed head of his cock kneading in and out, stroking me higher and higher.

"Yes! Faster!" I try to urge him, digging my nails into his ass cheeks.

A broad lopsided smile spreads over his lips as he squeezes my neck, cutting my air to a fraction. My body tightens into a devastating orgasm. I'm bucking my hips and writhing beneath him. He ducks his head and his weight settles heavily over me for a breath.

His hand tightens as he raises his head. An even grimace has replaced the smile.

"What the fuck?" he murmurs. Leaning back, his other hand encircles the first, and they both squeeze.

I can't breathe.

He isn't pumping into me.

"What did you do to me? Did you fucking drug me?" Something in my neck pops as I claw at his hands. I'm silently pleading with him to release me.

Anger and hatred stare back.

"Alice! Fight!" I hear Henry's voice, but it isn't coming from the man above me.

My mouth gapes in silence. I try to buck my hips, but he's braced me tightly.

I can't reach his face to scratch at his eyes.

"Fucking whore. I can't get caught like this again." He squeezes tighter.

It feels like my neck is being crushed.

Weakly, I try to pull his fingers loose. But, my vision is starting to blur.

The trees close in over us and the day turns to night.

Another set of hands tries to pull on my arm, to free me from the grasp of the man above.

Futilely, my leg kicks at his calf.

But, still the hands crush me.

My arms are weak. I can't pick them up.

A soft warmth spreads through them as my chest stops heaving.

I hear a voice calling my name.

Numbness blankets my body.

Darkness covers my eyes.

THE END

Beware the rings of broken souls,
Who carry a lifetime of toils and woes.
Their love may be fierce,
And your heart they may pierce,
But, in the end it will be for you the bell tolls.

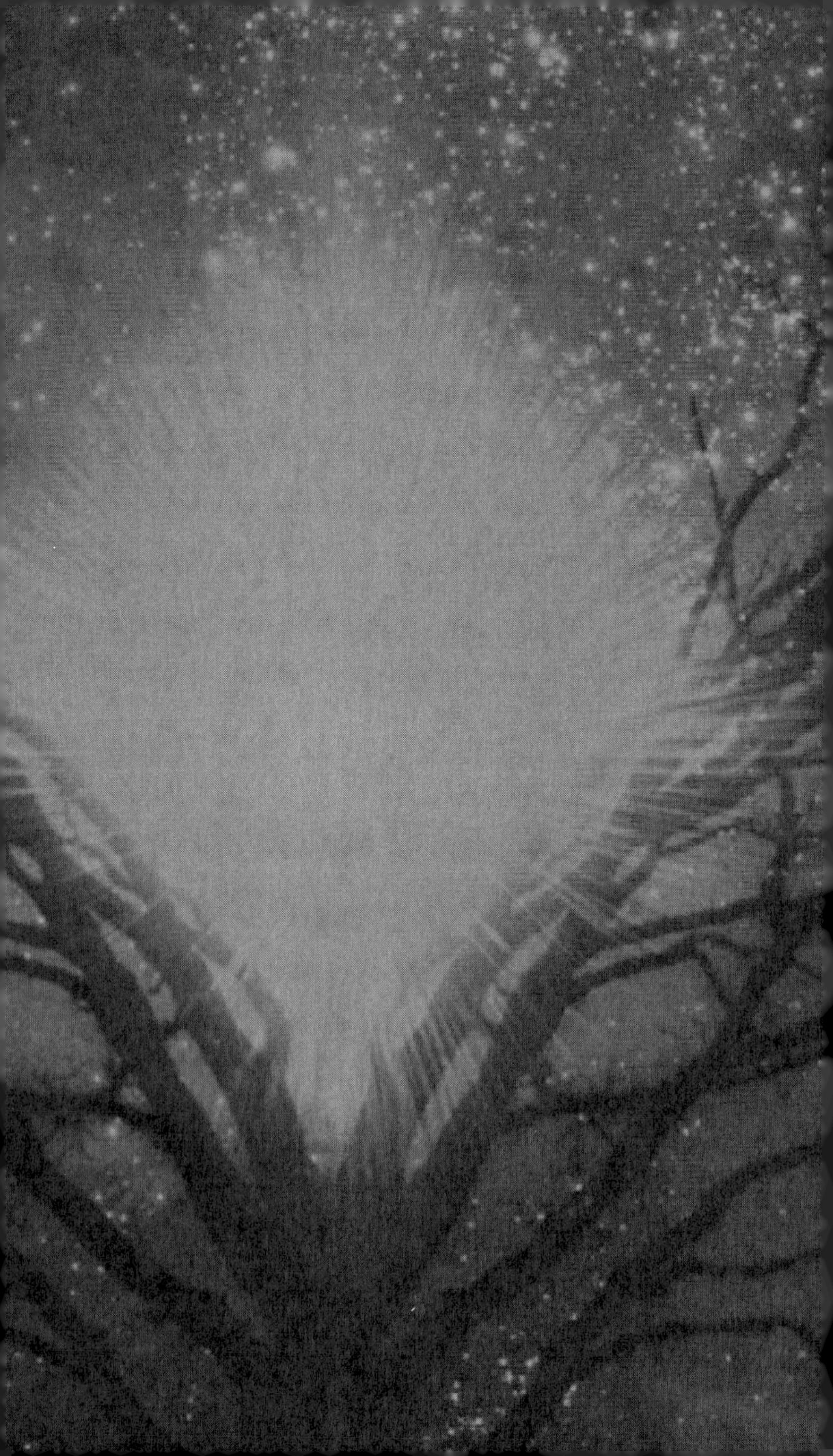

Epilogue I

Henry

With violence, I am thrown from his body to tumble into the void.

It takes me a moment to shake off the throes of passion and realize I'm no longer buried in Alice's tight cunt.

A pang of jealousy surges through me to see him still buried between her thighs while she bucks beneath him.

But, then the truth of her thrashing becomes obvious. Her eyes bulge, her face turns red and nearly blue. Her fingers flail trying to scratch his face.

Rage erupts through me and I charge.

My fists go through him. I've tried to push, pull, bite, kick, but like the useless cuck I am, I can only wisp as if the air.

I tried to pull her away, but as the life slipped from her body, so did my hold on her.

Screaming her name, my fingers fade through hers until I am reduced to kneeling by her side as her eyes unfocus and her wrist falls limply to the ground.

My beautiful love. The bond I have relied on has shattered. I only feel the pull of my ring still affixed to the monster before me.

His features still twist in anger when he unclenches his fists from her delicate and broken throat.

"Fucking bitch." He spits into the ground near her mottled face. "The fuck." He stands, naked, and stares down at her.

The red fades from her cheeks until she looks almost peaceful. Her eyes are fixed and glossy with a lock of her dark hair covering her mouth.

Damned if I can tuck it behind her ear now. My fingers move through her as if she isn't there.

I'm not here. Barely held by my ring, the world is blurry and gray.

Or it may be from the tears running heavily to mar my vision.

Agony seizes my chest in ripping heaves. I can't feel her.

I'm shredded.

Alone.

She rolls closer to me, and I feel a burst of hope, until I see JJ tugging his shirt from beneath her and shrugging it over his shoulders.

The ring pulls me as he walks away.

He's abandoned her. Strewn into the grass like a discarded doll.

Sobs wrack me in harrowing gasps and I find myself coiling into a ball like a child. My hand rests with hers, within hers.

"Alice, love, please come back to me." My forehead nearly touches hers as the knot in my throat chokes out my words.

A grating sound cuts through my grief. JJ stands over us

and he sinks a shovel through my midsection into the earth below.

Hoisting a clod of soil, he tosses it to the side and buries his spade for another bite.

The hollow silence is only punctuated by the sounds of his efforts.

One churning load of dirt after another slowly eats a hole large enough for her body.

I can't even move. I let him pierce through me over and over, wishing I could feel it. Begging for it to tear me in half so I can no longer suffer the cruel misery of finding my love and losing her.

The lolling of her head startles me from my anguish as he rolls her into his improvised grave.

Like garbage stuffed into a pit, he folds her limbs to make her fit.

With each flick of dirt, her face disappears a little more. Soon I'm left sitting next to the depression of soft earth with nothing to show of her life except a writhing worm dislodged by his digging.

Chaos, hatred, despair. They all conflict within me as I sit, a vapid pile of emptiness next to the bare spot in the grass.

This was my idea. To beg her to use him. My own selfish needs encouraged her to push herself beyond her boundaries.

To stroke my selfish ego.

This must have been the greater plan. Luring me with a sense of completion, happiness even. And letting my own wicked desires ruin it.

My just reward.

I will lament my actions for eternity.

Light slowly shifts to grays and I feel the pull of the ring grow tenuous.

I know he is leaving. His work here is done.

A low whine distracts me. Daisy slinks forward and lays upon the turned ground. Her small body trembles and she coils into a ball atop the clods of soil.

"I'm sorry." My voice is broken and weak.

Her ears perk and she gives a tiny wag of her tail before nestling her nose back between her feet.

Fuck.

Trees fade into a haze, as does Daisy. My tenuous tether draws thin with distance.

I finally relent and let it pull me. He must still be wearing my ring for the line to remain taut.

Or, perhaps, it is Alice at the other end?

A glimmer of hope hurries my flight as I allow myself to follow the thin lead.

Through a wall of brick and mortar, I'm thrust into a bright room of loud images on a screen and a woman in a kitchen screaming profanities over a burning pot.

JJ sits in an overstuffed chair. A litany of empty bottles tumble at his side.

His face is haggard and pale. Spittle flies from his mouth as he screams at his woman to leave him alone.

The bastard still has dirt under his fingernails from burying my love.

A rat-looking dog barks in circles at my feet.

Of course they can see me.

Here this man sits. Living the life I covet.

A wife. A home.

And him, a murderer. He stole from me my one source of happiness.

Curse of the Mourning Ring

My knuckles crack as my fists tighten. Envy and rage burn white hot within me.

Keep wearing my ring, you fuck. Keep drinking your cheap scour-gut beer.

You'll be asleep soon enough.

The incessant noise of their bickering has finally waned. She has stomped to the recesses of the house and he lies in repose on his chair.

Deep cavernous snores rattle the empty bottles that sit atop his lap. Rat-dog gave up barking at me hours ago and is hidden somewhere with the woman.

The light gold glow from my ring has spread to his chest, beckoning me with its iridescence.

My plan unfolds.

Swirling multi-colored lights overtake my vision when I touch him. The familiarity of his body hastens the use of his limbs.

Careful to not create unnecessary noise, I remove each bottle singularly and place them on the floor beside me.

I want to crash one against the table and use the jagged edge to filet his skin. Simmering fury at being in the flesh of the man who stole my heart from me boils within my chest.

Bile forms at the disgust and I heave the innards of his stomach onto the floor.

Louse. Mongrel. Disgrace.

My father's words echo his disappointment in my head. He told me I'd never find happiness. I'd never find someone to accept the creature I became.

I've proven him wrong, but now, I embrace the fearsome reputation I fostered.

Death.

With slow and deliberate movements, I move to the storage room beyond the kitchen and retrieve what I had discovered in my earlier investigation.

A heavy braided rope loops over my shoulder. And the kitchen chair is light in my hand as I push my way through the back door into the dark yard.

Lit with only a mediocre light, it's enough to illuminate the heavy oak that spreads its boughs over their cluttered lawn.

Fitting.

The fibers of the course lanyard dig through my palms when I toss the end over a large branch. Memories of other trees assail me, their leaves shaking with the weight of the thrashing men I've decorated their limbs with.

This one will be special.

Hatred and betrayal manifest in the man whose skin I wear. The sins of the past are coming back to bear on his judgment.

Standing on the precarious wooden chair, I make sure that the length is right before slipping my head into the loop.

Sagging into the tight pull around my neck, with one final kick, I fling the step far from reach.

Dangling, the air is trapped within my lungs. Pain sears through me and my hands claw as I hold them down. The body itself is striving to survive.

My legs kick out in a feeble attempt at relief from the pressure in my chest.

When my vision begins to darken, I slide the ring from my finger.

Ripped again from his body into the void, I dig through the mists to fight my way back to him.

My tie to the ring is shallow, but exists like a small beacon to lead me.

Panic laces his eyes as they bulge venous and red from his cheeks. Red welts and scratches blemish his neck where his fingers dig at the rope tightened against his jaw.

Grim satisfaction settles in me as the light fades from his eyes.

Not unlike those of my love just a few short hours ago.

The world mists and grays around me.

A new tug at my chest.

It seems my time on this plane is done.

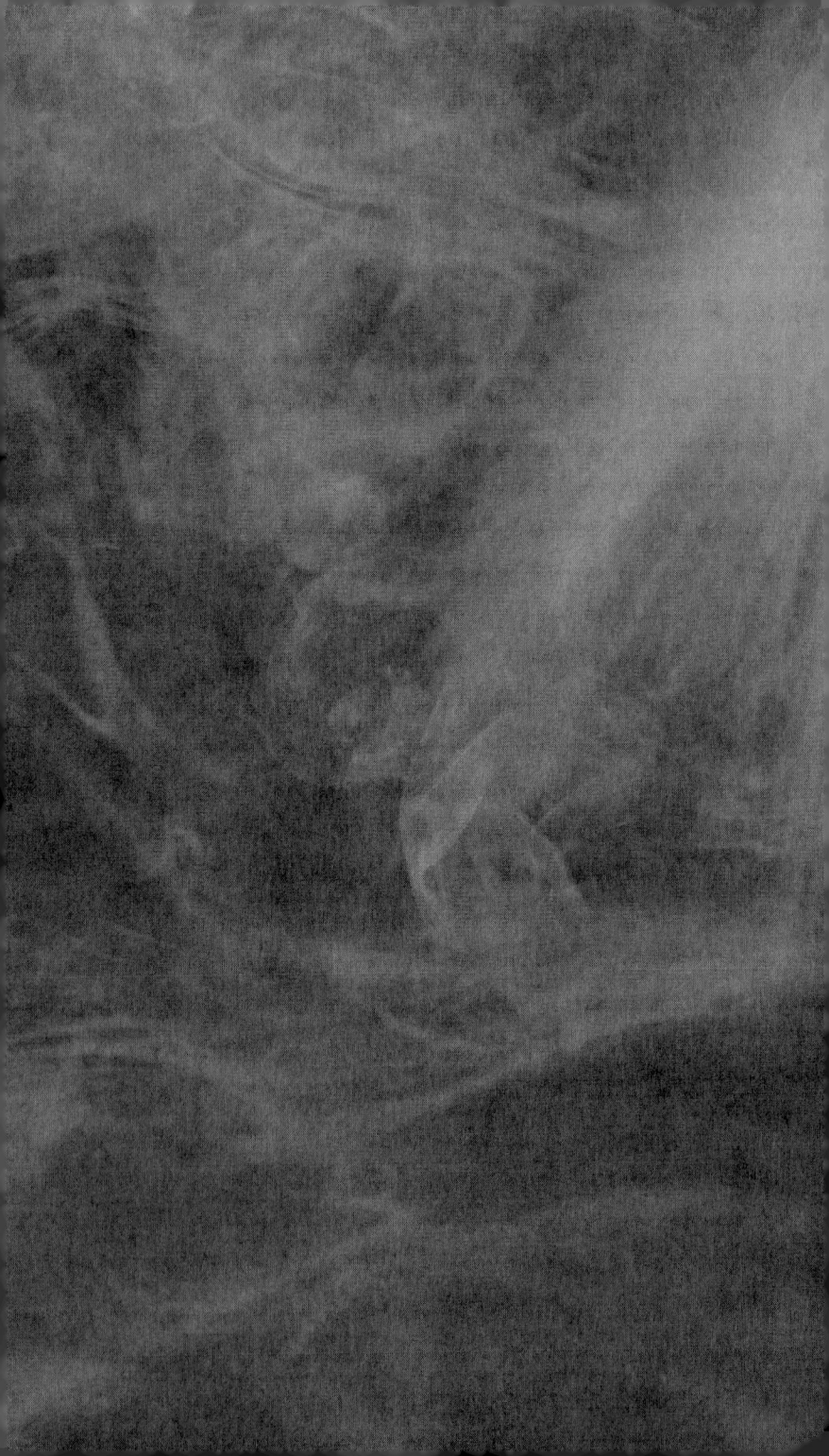

Epilogue II

Alice

Where am I?

It's like I'm in a heavy fog, but I can't feel up or down. My feet float and there isn't any light or direction.

How did I get here?

I don't remember where I came from.

I'm just here.

In nothing.

It's peaceful. Serene. Silent.

Like I've been longing for silence. For a quiet where I can hear my own heartbeats.

But, I can't.

A tug in my chest pulls me. It's small, tenuous, but consistent. A slow fade into edges, a room I don't recognize.

But, I do see a familiar shape.

Red ears roll on a carpet, a long red tongue lolls as Daisy wiggles on a brightly covered carpet.

A child? Five? Maybe six? Lying on the floor next to her.

How long have I been floating?

I find myself drifting back into the void, a smile tugging my lips.

Trying to move, I kick my legs and swim my arms. There's no resistance. Something is missing. I wave my arms before my face, trying to recollect something. My palms turn as I inspect them. Opening and closing my fingers, something stirs within me.

It reminds me of movements I made recently.

Scratching, clawing, flailing.

Fuck.

I remember.

His copper hair backlit by the sun as he squeezed my neck.

Pain. Retribution for my choices.

Fear.

And, Henry. His was the last voice I heard. Calling me to fight.

My heart aches. Selfish longing for him sent me here.The consequences of my love for a man whose soul belonged here. A man I've never seen but would give anything for.

Even my life.

Maybe that means he is here?

"Henry!" I can't hear my voice, but it doesn't stop my scream.

"Henry! Please! I need you!"

There's a tight pang in my chest as it feels as if something has lashed around me and is tugging me. My arms and legs float behind me as I move through the dark vacuum.

Every time I call his name, the tie feels stronger. As if it's coaxing me to call again. It offers something of substance for me to lean into.

A thrumming on the cord around me vibrates through my body.

"Henry!" I scream until my stomach hurts and my toes curl.

He has to be here. Somewhere.

It could be seconds, it could be hours that I float. Time seems to fade as each moment seems intense, yet dull.

A pinpoint of light forms and slowly grows into a tall shape.

Arms, legs and a head grow defined as the glow gets closer. The shine from its outline firms into clothing and skin.

It's a giant of a man with a dark mop of hair and a ruddy bearded face. Dark caramel eyes soften into a teary half-smile as he reaches for me.

"My minx. Alice, I've found you." The heavy leather of his coat shifts to a light cotton shirt, billowing in the airless dark around us. I can see the outline of his broad chest and tapered waist that narrows into tight trousers that hug his thick legs. A true bear of a man. My man.

"Henry?" The same lopsided grin I have seen on other faces now shines over me.

"Yes, love. I was terrified I'd lost you." He wraps his arms around me and cradles me to his chest. The intimate rumble of his groan echoes through me and I can smell him. The familiar smell of gunpowder and whiskey washes over me. It's really him.

"Let me see you, please." I need to. The man I've dreamt about and slept with. I should feel guilty for loving him so fiercely and never having laid an eye on him. But, despite the scars on his face, he's the most handsome man I've ever seen. Or maybe it's because of his scars. They give him a dangerous edge that I know means he would fight for me. A firm nose and full lips, his hair falls over his eye and tucks behind his ears in soft waves. "You're gorgeous, Henry. All those lies you told me about how horrible you looked." My hands trace the bearded jaw as I've done a thousand times.

I can feel my lips pull up into a smile as I gaze at him.

The man I love.

"I'm sorry you have joined me on this side. But, I'll forever be grateful I found you. I've lost the tie to my damned ring, but it did its job." His broad hands frame my face and he touches his forehead to mine. "I love you, Alice. We are more than bound. Do you know what the oath was that brought me to you?"

My nose rubs his and my hands entwine behind his neck. "I imagine it was like mine. I wished on your ring, Henry. I wished for you to love me fiercely."

His hands move down my back and he pulls me tightly against him. I mold myself to him as I have so easily before.

"I swore I would find someone who would love me for eternity." His lips touch mine and electricity buzzes through my body. Our hands move in a frantic pace over each other trying to touch every inch at once.

"Who knew we'd find it like this?" I don't feel sad at my loss. In fact, I feel happier than I ever have.

I have him, whole and in my arms.

"I'll cherish you for eternity." His words whisper across my skin before his teeth nip at my soft neck.

"Henry?"

"Hmm?" His mouth is full, working at a frantic pace along my jaw. I can feel him hardening against me.

"Can you see that glow?"

He raises his head and the light grows. A soft golden heat erupts from both of our chests. His eyebrows shoot up to his forehead.

"What is it?" I've never seen anything so beautiful.

"It is the same light that would beckon me before I was pulled within another."

He's right. It does have a pull. I feel as if my fingers are being drawn to touch him. An ache in my stomach is screaming at me to reach out.

"What should we do? I want to touch you so badly."

"As do I, love. I don't know what will happen." His lips touch my forehead as my eyes remain transfixed on the fiery glow.

"Maybe we should touch it at the same time?" The need to reach out to him is nearly overwhelming. My fingers trace down his shoulders and dig into his skin as I fight the urge.

He cups one of my hands in his and his other wavers over my breast. "Ready?" The caramel of his eyes brightens and we drop our hands onto each other's chest.

A swirling vortex of light overtakes me, yet I feel his hand holding mine.

About the Author

www.macobb.com

Find me on goodreads!

instagram.com/m.a.cobb_author

amazon.com/stores/M.A.-Cobb/author/B0BMXXHB71

Also by M.A. Cobb

The Sunburst Trilogy:

Burst of Fate

Living far from the city, Avery worried only about her garden and farmer's markets. She never expected love to appear on her doorstep. But after rescuing the tall red-headed stranger from a horrible crash, they both discover the world is much darker than they originally thought. Will Avery and Morgan find hope in this new, powerless world?

https://mybook.to/yUGx

Burst of Shadows

Trapped beneath the city of Seattle when an irreversible darkness falls, Carly and James discover more than just light at the end of the tunnel. As they flee the impending collapse of society, chaos and danger are around every turn. Finally escaping the confines of the suffocating streets, they find that their temporary sanctuary in a small town has its own set of perils. Will their love survive the threat in the shadows that pursue them?

https://mybook.to/WZvfY

Coming soon:

Burst of Retribution

A year after the world goes black, Maddy decides to leave the safety of her new home to check on the family she left behind. But when she finds her childhood home empty, she discovers that the darkness in her past is merely the beginning of something more dire. Struggling to fight the memories, she's forced to choose to rescue her family, or fall victim to the darkness again. Captured by a man whose intentions are unknown, will she be able to escape to find the justice she deserves?

The Dire Reaction

As a veterinarian, Dr. Danielle Michelson was excited to be involved with a new genetic therapy designed to help fight a common pet ailment. She even knew the perfect canine to enroll in the treatment, one belonging to the tall blond cowboy, Sam Downing. Little did she know, while things were heating up between them, the world itself was transforming. The cure turned into a curse, and created an army of monsters that thrive on pure chaos and destruction. The worst of them all, was someone they both knew.

Now, they must find allies to fight back against the onslaught of carnal evil that threatens to overtake them.

Will Dani and Sam survive the monstrous terror that is overrunning their city? Or will the hordes of ravenous creatures consume everything, and everyone, in their path?

https://mybook.to/FoQnj

Coming Soon:

The Dire Legacy

After the virus ravaged the earth, it left a wake of men and terrifying monsters, vying for power.

But, sometimes, the monsters were not the ones with fur. Sometimes, they look like you and I.

Michael fled the only home he knew before his truth was revealed. Was he a monster like his father? Or did the world around him change so much he no longer fit in?

When he meets Hope, everything he thought he knew shifts. She redefines this new world, and reveals the true evil that still walks among us.

https://mybook.to/oK6Jm2E

Manufactured by Amazon.ca
Acheson, AB